FARMING THE
DARKNESS

FARMING THE DARKNESS

Agricultural Loci in
Classic Speculative Fiction

Edited by Chad Arment

COACHWHIP PUBLICATIONS
GREENVILLE, OHIO

Farming the Darkness: Agricultural Loci in Classic Speculative Fiction
© 2025 Coachwhip Publications

Front cover: 'Moonlight' by George Inness

CoachwhipBooks.com

ISBN 1-61646-620-0
ISBN-13 978-1-61646-620-6

CONTENTS

THE FIELD OF TERROR

Friedrich de la Motte Fouqué

(1850)

I

During the latter part of the war, which terminated with the peace of Westphalia, there assembled at the foot of the Riesenberg, in a beautiful part of the country of Silesia, a number of persons who were the relations, and had lately succeeded to the property, of an opulent deceased farmer. This man had died without children, and had left several farms and fields scattered about that fertile country; and his heirs were now met together to divide the inheritance.

For this purpose they assembled in the principal inn of one of the villages; and they found no difficulty among themselves as to the allotment of every part of the estate except one particular piece of ground, which was known by the name of the "Haunted Field," or "Field of Terror," on account of the wonderful stories which were told concerning it. The field was entirely overgrown with wild flowers, and an abundance of rank and luxuriant shrubs, which, while they bore ample testimony to the vigour and fertility of the soil, were equally indicative of the neglect and desolation to which it was abandoned. For a long series of years no ploughshare had penetrated its surface, and no seed had been cast upon its furrows; or if at intervals the attempt was made, the cattle had been invariably seized with frenzy, had wildly broken from the yoke, and the ploughman and his men had rushed from the spot in fright and alarm, affirming that it was haunted by the most terrific phantoms, who followed the labourer in his occupation with the most fearful familiarity, looking over his shoulder with such hideous aspects, that no one could venture to continue his work.

The question now arose, to whom this field should be allotted. As is the common course in the world, every one felt that this spot, which would be useless and of no value in his own case, might yet be extremely applicable, and even advantageous, to his neighbor; and thus the contest for its right appropriation continued till a late hour of the evening. At length one of the party proposed a remedy, which, though not directly benefiting any one present, seemed to promise a settlement of the dispute.

"By a codicil in the will," said he, "we are enjoined to shew some mark of kindness to a poor relation of the testator, who lives hard by in the village. It is true, the girl is very distantly related to us; and there can be no doubt that, portionless as she is, she will yet procure a good husband, for she is virtuous and frugal, and goes by the name of the pretty Sabine. Suppose we give up this 'Field of Terror' to her; we shall in this way discharge the injunctions of our lamented relative; and, to say the truth, it may yet prove a rich dowry for her, provided she can find a husband who will venture to cultivate it."

The others immediately consented to this proposal, and one of the relatives was despatched to communicate the intelligence of their bounty.

In the mean time, as the twilight drew on, somebody tapped at Sabine's cottage-window; and to her question of "Who's there?" a reply was given which had the instant effect of withdrawing the rustic bolt of her little window. It was a voice long and anxiously expected,—the voice of her brave Frederick; who, born poor as herself, had some years before set out for the wars, in the hope of gaining some little subsistence to enable him to marry his beloved Sabine, whose heart, filled with the purest affection, was entirely devoted to him.

It was a delightful picture to see Sabine leaning out of her wired lattice, with tears of joy starting in her beautiful eyes, as the erect and youthful soldier gazed upon her in modest silent bliss, and extended towards her his faithful hand.

"Ah, Frederick!" she said, in a low and bashful voice, "God be praised, thou art returned safe; this has been my constant prayer morn and evening. And tell me, Frederick, have you made your fortune in the campaign?"

"Fortunes are not so soon won," said Frederick, shaking his head, and smiling; "and prizes do not fall to every one. However, I am better off than when I went away; and if you have but a courageous heart, I think we may marry, and get through the world pretty well."

"Kind-hearted Frederick," ejaculated Sabine, "to take a poor orphan for better and worse!"

"Come," said Frederick, "give me but one friendly yes, and promise to be mine, and we shall be happy in each other, and thrive, and live like princes."

"And have you got your discharge, and are you really no longer a soldier?"

Frederick, looking into his knapsack, that held his treasures, brought out a silver medal, which he reached to Sabine, and as she received it, the light of the little lamp in her chamber fell on the piece. There was a burst drum figured in an old-fashioned manner, and over it were written the words, "God be praised, the war is ended!"

"Perhaps," added Frederick, helping her to decipher the medal, "it is not yet peace, but it is thought we shall have no more fighting at present, and our colonel has therefore discharged his men."

At this intelligence Sabine held out her hand as a pledge of her affection to her lover, and invited him to come into her little dwelling, where he seated himself by her side, and related how he had won his gold and silver in honourable battle, and in the open field, from a foreign officer of rank whom he had made prisoner; having obtained the money as his ransom.

Sabine, as she turned her wheel, listened with deep attention to her lover's recital, bestowing, from time to time, a smile of fond approbation upon his conduct, and inwardly rejoicing that no reproach could hereafter be thrown upon their slender means, thus honourably acquired.

Their conversation was now interrupted by the appearance of the person who came to communicate the message entrusted to him. Sabine, with maidenly blushes, presented her intended husband to the stranger; and the latter replied, "This is well—I have arrived very opportunely; for if your betrothed has not brought back a fortune from the wars, the gift which I am directed to present to you in the name of your relations will be a welcome addition; indeed, it was the will of the testator that you should be remembered in a handsome way."

Frederick was too much offended at the boasting manner in which this communication was made, to testify any joy on the occasion. But the humble Sabine, ignorant of the mode in which her relatives had evinced their generosity, received the communication as an interposition of Providence, with her head modestly bent down, while a smile of heartfelt grateful joy shone on her countenance. But as soon as she heard that the Field of Terror was assigned to her as her portion and in liquidation of her just claims, the sordid behaviour of her relations pressed on her heart with a painful sickening coldness, and she felt it impossible to refrain from shedding tears of disappointed hope.

Her relation, with a smile of half-suppressed contempt, expressed his regret that she should have allowed herself to expect more than her friends had thought right to allot her.

"And indeed," he observed, "this is a much larger proportion of the inheritance than you could fairly hope to receive as a matter of right."

With this speech he was about to retire, when Frederick interrupted him; and with that deliberate coolness which attends a mind conscious of its own superiority, he said, "Sir, I perceive that you and your fellows have been pleased to convert the benevolent intentions of the deceased into a mere piece of mockery, and that it is your joint determination to withhold every shilling of his property from my bride. But we will nevertheless accept your offer, in full confidence that, under the guidance of God, this haunted field, in the hands of an honest and active soldier, will be a more productive bargain than a set of covetous, envious relations intend it to be."

The messenger, who felt rather uneasy at the tone and manner assumed by the young soldier, did not hazard a reply; and with an altered countenance hurried out of the cottage, and made the best of his way back.

Frederick now kissed away the tears from Sabine's cheeks, and hastened to the priest to fix an early day for their marriage.

II

After the lapse of a few weeks, Frederick and Sabine were married, and entered upon their slender house-keeping. The gold and silver pieces he had brought from the wars, the young soldier chiefly expended in the purchase of a fine yoke of oxen; part was invested in seed and in the necessary implements of husbandry, and the articles of household furniture; the rest was reserved for daily expenditure, to be dealt out in the most frugal manner, till the harvest of the succeeding year should replenish their stores. But as Frederick took his departure, with his cattle and plough, for the field of labour, he looked back and smiled to his good Sabine, saying, that he was now going to invest his gold, which another year would restore to him two-fold. Sabine could only follow him with her anxious looks, and wish, in her heart, that he were once safely returned from the dreaded "Field of Terror."

And home, truly, he came, and that long before the vesper-bell had sounded: but far from being so cheerful, as, in the native confidence of his heart, he had promised himself in the morning, when he went forth singing to his work. He dragged laboriously after him the fragments of his shattered plough; before him paced, with difficulty, one of his oxen sorely maimed, and marks of blood were seen on his own head and shoulder. But still his soldier-spirit did not fail him, and he bore up under his misfortunes with a courageous and even merry heart, consoling, at the same time, the grief of the weeping Sabine. "Come," said he, smilingly, "get your pickling-tubs in order; for this goblin who reigns in the 'Field of Terror' has provided us with an abundance of beef. The beast I brought home with me has so injured himself in his frenzy, that he will not be fit for any farther work; and as for the other, he ran off into the mountains, and there I saw him plunge from a steep rock into the torrent below, where I fancy he now lies, and from whence, I dare say, he will never again make his appearance."

"Oh, these relations! these wicked relations!" sobbed the disconsolate Sabine.

"My hurt is of no consequence," said Frederick; "it was but the oxen that crushed me between them when they ran mad, and I endeavored to stop them; but it matters not grieving, and in the morning I will start afresh."

Sabine was now so terrified at what had happened, that she used every means in her power to dissuade her husband from any farther attempt at cultivating the unlucky field; but he only replied, by saying, "that so long as he could move an arm or a leg, the field should have no rest. Land which we cannot plough, we must delve; and I am no timid beast of labor, but a good and steady soldier, over whom a goblin can have no power."

He now slaughtered the wounded ox, and cut it up: and on the next morning, while Sabine was busied in preparing it for pickle, Frederick pursued his road to the haunted field with his pickaxe and spade, with almost as good a heart as on the day before, when he set out with his fine yoke of oxen and his handsome new plough.

This time he returned rather late in the evening, somewhat pale and exhausted, but in high spirits, and ready to tranquillize his anxious wife.

"This is rather hard work," said he, laughing; "for there comes a sort of goblin-fellow, who stands first on this side, then on that, sometimes in one form, sometimes in another, and mocks me with his foolish talk and tricks; but he seems to feel no small surprise that I give so little heed to his pranks; and from this I begin to take fresh courage. Besides, why should an honest man, who goes straight forward, and minds his work, care for such beings?"

The same kind of thing continued for many days together. The brave Frederick pursued, without interruption, his daily tour of digging, sowing, and destroying the weeds and useless plants which had overspread the field. It is true the slow process of the spade enabled him to cultivate only a small portion of the whole ground, but this served to make him all the more zealous and industrious in his labours: and he was at length rewarded by seeing a crop spring up, which promised, and eventually produced, a sufficient, if not an abundant harvest. Even the toil of reaping, and transporting it from the field to the barn, was thrown entirely upon his own shoulders; for the labourers in the vicinity would not have engaged, for any consideration, to spend a day upon the dreaded "Field of Terror;" and he would, on no account, permit Sabine to lend her assistance.

A child was born, and in three years two more; and so things went on without any remarkable occurrence. By hard striving and industry Frederick compelled the Haunted Field to yield him one crop after another: and thus, like an honest man, redeemed his word to Sabine, that he would find sufficient to support her.

It happened one evening in autumn, as the shades of night began to draw on, and Frederick was still busied with his spade, that a tall robust man, of unusual size of limb, black and sooty as a charcoal-burner, and holding a huge furnace-iron in his hand, appeared suddenly before him, and said, "Are there no cattle to be had in this part of the country, that you thus labour away with your two hands? One would suppose, by the extent of your landmarks, that you were a wealthy farmer."

Frederick was perfectly aware of who it was that addressed him, and treated him in the same cool way with which he usually received the goblin in the field. He held his tongue, endeavored to withdraw his attention from the figure before him to his work, and to labor on with redoubled ardor. But his swarthy visitor, instead of disappearing, as is the usual practice of these goblins, to present himself again in a more frightful and hideous form, remained where he stood, and in a friendly tone continued, "My good fellow, you are doing both yourself and me injustice by this conduct of yours. Give me now an honest and candid answer, and perhaps I may be able to find a remedy for your misfortunes."

"Well, then," rejoined Frederick, "in God's name be it so. If you are but cajoling me with these friendly words, the fault be at your door, and not at mine."

With this he began to relate the whole story of his adventures since he had taken possession of the field. He gave an undisguised recital of his first distress, a faithful representation of his just and honest indignation against the goblin who haunted his property, and detailed the difficulty he found, under such continual interruption and provocation, in supporting his family by the mere application of his hoe and spade.

The stranger gave an attentive ear to the narrative, seemed lost in thought for a few minutes, and then broke forth in the following address:

"It would seem, friend, that you know who I am; and I look upon it as a proof of your frank and manly disposition, that you have made no concealment, but that you have spoken out boldly of the displeasure you entertain towards me. To say the truth, you have certainly had sufficient cause; but in thus putting your courage to the test, I will make a proposal which will, I hope, indemnify you for a good deal of what is past. You must know, then, that I have had my fill of wild and fantastic tricks through wood, and field and mountain, and I begin to fancy I should like to attach myself to some quiet family, that I may live for some half a year or so a peaceful orderly life. What do you say to taking me for six months as your servant?"

"It is not right of people of your sort," said Frederick, "thus to pass your jokes upon an honest man, who reposes confidence in you."

"No, no!" replied the other, "there is no joke in it; I tell you it is my serious intention. You will find in me a sturdy, active servant; and as long as I live with you, not a single spirit or goblin will venture to shew himself on the 'Field of Terror,' so that you may admit whole herds of cattle to browse upon it."

"I should like the thing well enough," rejoined Frederick, "if I were but sure that you would keep your word, and, moreover, that I were doing right in dealing with you at all."

"That must be your own affair," said the stranger; "but I have never broken my word since these Riesenberg mountains have stood: and a mere creature of evil and malice I certainly am not. A little merry, and wild, and tricky sometimes, I own—but that is all!"

"Why, then," said Frederick, "I believe that you are the celebrated Rubezahl."

"Harkee!" cried the stranger, interrupting him, with a frown, "if that be your opinion, I would also have you to know, that the mighty spirit of the mountains will not permit that name, and that he chooses to call himself the Monarch of the Hills."

"That would be an odd sort of a servant whom I must call the Monarch of the Hills," said Frederick, in a tone of raillery.

"You may call me Waldmann, then," rejoined his companion.

Frederick looked awhile towards the ground, pondering upon the course he should adopt, and at length exclaimed, "Well, so be it!   I think I can hardly do amiss in accepting your services. I nave often seen irrational animals drilled into domestic use—carrying parcels, turning spits, and other household duties—why not a goblin?"

His new servant burst into a hearty laugh at this observation, and said, "I must acknowledge such an estimate was never made of any of my kind before. But that I heed not—'tis my humor, and so 'tis a bargain, my honored master!"

Frederick, however, made it a condition that his new servant should on no account whatever discover to Sabine or the children that he had lived in the Haunted Field, or in the old caverns of the Riesenberg, nor at any time play any goblin tricks about the house or farm. Waldmann pledged his word to all this; so the matter was concluded, and home they both went together in a very friendly mood.

III

Sabine was not a little surprised at this addition to their household, and could scarcely look upon the swarthy gigantic servant without fear. The children were at first so much alarmed that they would not. venture out of doors when he was at work in the garden or in the yard; but his quiet, and good-natured, and friendly behaviour soon reconciled all the household to his presence; and if he now and then had a frolicksome fit, and chased the dog and the fowls, they thought it only sportiveness and good humour, and a single look from the master was at any time sufficient to bring him within proper bounds.

In full reliance upon the promises of the Mountain-lord, Frederick applied the slender savings of many years to the purchase of oxen; and with his newly mended plough drove to the field in the highest glee. Sabine looked after him with an anxious sorrowful countenance, and with an equally anxious mind awaited his return in the evening, fearing a renewal of the same disasters and the same disappointed hopes, or that his personal injuries this time might be more dangerous and alarming than before. But with the sound of the vesper-bell Frederick came home singing through the village, driving his sleek, well-fed oxen before him, kissed his wife and children in the fulness of his joy, and shook his servant cordially by the hand.

Waldmann now frequently went to the field alone, while his master remained behind engaged about the yard or garden. A considerable portion of the Field of Terror was cleared and cultivated; and to the great astonishment of the village neighbours, and the equal discontent and envy of Sabine's selfish relations, every thing assumed an air of prosperity and comfort. It is true, Frederick, when alone, often reflected that all this might be but of short duration; "and I know not how I shall manage with the harvest," he exclaimed, "for Waldmann's time will then be out, and the goblin of the field may choose to appear with redoubled power." But he considered that the gathering-in of the crop was a labour which of itself gave additional vigour to the workman's arm and heart; and it was possible that Waldmann, for old acquaintance-sake, might keep the land free from such guests—as in fact, at times of cheerful relaxation, he almost seemed to intimate.

In the course of time the needful labours of the field were completed. Winter arrived, and Frederick daily drove to the forest for a stock of fuel and wood. On one of these days it so chanced that Sabine was entreated to visit a poor widow in the village, who lay dangerously ill, and whom, as far as their increasing means admitted, Frederick and his wife had been accustomed to relieve. She was at a loss how to dispose of the children during her absence; but Waldmann offered his services, with whose stories the children were always delighted, and with whom they were ever pleased to remain; and she proceeded on her charitable errand without further hesitation.

About an hour after her departure, Frederick returned from the forest; and having disposed of his wagon in the outhouse, and put up his cattle in the stall, he proceeded towards the house to revive his numbed and frozen limbs by the blaze of a cheerful fire. On approaching the door, a cry of painful distress from his children met his ear. He rushed into the house, and on entering the room found the children creeping behind the stove, and crying aloud for help, while Waldmann was wildly jumping about the room with shouts of violent laughter, making the most hideous faces, and with a crown of sparks and rays of flame playing about his head.

"What is all this?" said Frederick, in a tone of indignant anger; and the fiery decorations of Waldmann's head disappeared, his fantastic merriment instantly ceased, and, standing in a humble posture, he began to excuse himself by saying that he was only trying to amuse the children. But the children ran towards their father, crying and complaining that Waldmann had first of all told them a number of most horrific stories, and that then he had assumed a variety of frightful disguises, sometimes appearing with the head of a ram, sometimes with that of a dog.

"Enough! enough!" exclaimed Frederick. "Away, sirrah! you and I no longer remain under the same roof."

With this he seized Waldmann by the arm, and pushed him violently out of the house, desiring the children to remain quietly in the room, and to dismiss their fears, as their father was now come, and they were quite safe.

Waldmann suffered all this without uttering a word of expostulation; but as soon as he found himself alone with Frederick in the open court, he said, with a smiling countenance:

"Hear, master; suppose we hush this matter up, and make a fresh bargain. I know I have done a very foolish thing; but, I assure you, it shall never happen again. Somehow or other my old humour came upon me, and I forgot myself for the time."

"For that very reason, because you can forget yourself," rejoined Frederick, "we part. You might terrify my children into a paroxysm of madness; and, as I have said, our contract is at an end."

"My half-year has not expired," said Waldmann, in a dogged tone; "I will go back into the house."

"Not a step further, at your peril: you shall not again touch my threshold!" cried Frederick. "You have broken the agreement by your accursed goblin-pranks, and all that I can do is to pay you your full wages. Here, take it and be off with you."

"My full wages?" said the Mountain-spirit, with a contemptuous sneer; "have you never seen my stores of gold in the caverns of yonder hills?"

"I do this more on my own account than yours," said Frederick; "no man shall call me his debtor." And with that he forced the money into Waldmann's pocket.

"And what is to be done with the Field of Terror?" inquired Waldmann, in a grave but almost angry tone.

"Whatever God wills," rejoined Frederick. "Twenty fields of terror are of no importance to me in comparison with the safety of a single hair of my poor children's heads. Take yourself away, or I shall serve you in a way you may not like, or soon forget."

"Softly!" cried the Mountain-spirit, "softly, my friend. When such as I condescend to assume a human form, we choose one of rather stern materials. You might chance to come by the worst in this fray, and then, God be merciful unto you!"

"That He has ever been," said Frederick, "and has also given me a good strength of arm, as thou shalt find. Back to your mountains, you odious being! I warn you for the last time."

Excited by this reproach to a pitch of violent fury, Waldman sprung upon Frederick, and an obstinate fight ensued. They struggled about the yard for a considerable time, each using every means in his power to overthrow his adversary, without victory declaring itself on either side; till at length Frederick, by his superior skill in wrestling, managed to bring his opponent to the earth, and having placed his knee upon the chest of his fallen foe, began to beat him most lustily, exclaiming, "I will teach you to attack your master, my precious Lord of the Hills!"

The Lord of the Hills, however, laughed so heartily at this address, that Frederick, conceiving his manly efforts to be the subject of derision, only laid on with redoubled vigour, till at length the former exclaimed, "Mercy! enough! Hold! I am not laughing at you, I am laughing at myself, and I humbly beg your pardon!"

"That is another affair," said Frederick, as he rose up and assisted his conquered adversary to regain his legs.

"I have now learnt what human life is, from the very foundation upwards," said the latter, still continuing his noisy laughter; "I doubt if any of my kindred have ever pursued the study so profoundly. But harkee, my good friend, you must admit that I carried on the war in an honourable way; for, as you will see yourself, I might with ease have called in half a dozen mountain-spirits to my assistance, though, amidst all this laughter, I know not how I should have set about it."

Frederick, with a serious air, now looked at the still laughing Rubezahl, and said, "You will, I suppose, entertain a grudge against me; and this will not only be repaid me at the Field of Terror, but in many an evil chance elsewhere. Still I cannot repent of what I have done. I have only exercised my just authority in protecting my children; and were the thing to do over again, I should treat you just in the same way."

"No, no!" said Rubezahl, laughingly, "don't make yourself uneasy. I have had quite enough for once. Cultivate the Field of Terror from year to year, at your own will and pleasure; and I here promise you that no fearful phantom shall be seen upon it from this day forwards, as long as the Riesenberg stands. And so farewell, my honest, strong-handed master!"

With this he gave a friendly nod, and disappeared; nor was he ever more seen by Frederick. But he kept his word to the full, and even more. An unheard-of degree of prosperity attended all the labours of his former master, and Frederick soon became the richest farmer in the village. And when his children were permitted to play in the Field of Terror—a spot which both they and Sabine now visited without the smallest fear—they would relate in the evening how Waldmann had appeared to them and told them humorous tales, and how they found choice confectionaries, or beautiful carved toys, or golden ducats, in their pockets on their return home.

O'REILLY'S IMPROVEMENTS

Frances Brown

(1850)

The diocese of Killmore is best known to history as the bishopric of the pious and philanthropic Bedel, whose efforts to obliterate the hereditary enmity between Celt and Saxon were so successful in his day, till, as he declared, the iniquitous administration of Lord Strafford broke his heart. The lands of the see are situated in one of the most fertile and cultivated districts of the county Cavan, in Southern Ulster, and it is named from a small village standing in the midst of a pleasant English-like landscape, studded with handsome, though antiquated, villas, and possessing little to interest the passing stranger, except a rather rustic cathedral, in which the good bishop is said to have preached in their native tongue to the Irish.

In that old country church, before (to use the peasant's phrase) "Buoneparte had ris the rents an' ruined Irelan intirely," there worshipped for many a year—all unconscious, and, it must be added, unimitative, of Bedel's history—a respectably-dressed, stout-figured, ruddy-faced bachelor, with more than half gray hair, and a soberly, self-important manner, who was known to his neighbors as Mr. Lacy Hamilton. The Mr., indeed, was not always annexed; for, though reckoned rich as a miracle, Lacy was descended from a line of save-alls, a character, by the way, generally inspiring the reverse of popular respect in

Ireland. They had lived, and gathered, and died, in the same old and rudely-built farm-house, every generation adding to their possessions, not only by their own savings, but sundry bequests from unmarried relatives, till, on the death of his father, a considerable property in land, and some thousands in the Ulster bank, which rumor, of course, doubled, reverted to Lacy.

It was the concern of his mother's widowed days to increase this heritage, and guard her son from unprofitable matrimony. In the last endeavor she succeeded wonderfully, with the help of another property, which Lacy had not received from his ancestors—namely, an extraordinary amount of vulgar pride, partly in himself and partly in his riches. When, at length, in his thirty-fifth year, death closed the eyes, and set at rest the hands, of that busy and watchful dame, it was exhibited in a singular fashion. Lacy levelled the old farm-house to the ground, and erected at some distance a new, square, and rather imposing mansion, the large rooms of which he furnished in an expensive but imperfect manner, promulgated the plan of a lawn in front, a garden in the rear, with farm-yard and offices to match; but there his energies suddenly relaxed; and for twenty years the great house stood alone on a bare rising ground, with docks and nettles growing thick about its walls and wretchedly incongruous offices in the rear.

Travellers from the sister isles, who occasionally passed it on coach or car, were apt to remark that nothing similar could be seen out of the green land; but Lacy's neighbors had familiar solutions for the problem. They knew that he had hopefully waited for his mother's departure in order to make his money available in securing a place among the surrounding gentry, into some family of whom he had determined to marry, and leave the peasant ranks forever behind him. But being an instance of that powerless ambition which has the will but not the way to rise,

Mr. Lacy's manners and education belonged so completely to the class in which he was born, that the poorest of the superior cast could not be induced to associate with him, and their general contempt and ridicule rewarded all his endeavors after gentility. From that adverse field Mr. Lacy had retired to live in solitary pride at his new-built mansion, which he made many an ineffectual attempt to have called Hamilton House, and rarely left except for the church, the market, or his surrounding farm-fields. Debarred the gentry's society, he would put up with nothing less; and the neighboring farmers recalled many a tale of his family's money-griping and hard-working ways, by way of comment on Mr. Hamilton's brief replies and haughty salutations. Similar doings of his own were gradually added to the list; for it seemed that unsuccessful outlay of his money had taught him more abundantly the value of what remained; and the elderly woman who constituted his entire in-door establishment, as well as the laborers of his farm, could testify to his profiting by that lesson. Lacy had also tenants able to corroborate their evidence. Besides the hundred acres himself cultivated, he was the proprietor of sundry small farms, which, being bishop's land, were held by leases renewable forever; but he and his predecessors, in common with most small Irish proprietors, preferred letting them only to tenants-at-will. One of these, which lay nearest Hamilton's own domain, and far exceeded it in cultivation, had been called O'Reilly's farm long before he or his family became its landlords. Carrol O'Reilly, its occupant at the period of our story, averred that some of his people had lived and labored on it since the County Cavan was called O'Reilly's country, concerning which golden age of his name the man had many a strange tradition.

Such matters were, however, but the entertainment of leisure hours, and few and far between did they come to

Carrol. He was a more strong than ordinary specimen of
the native Ulster peasant. Tall, active, and somewhat dig-
nified in appearance, despite a life of labor, and the hum-
blest education, Carrol had the ready wit and tireless energy, with a clearer judgment and a larger portion of worldly
wisdom than generally fall to the share of his countrymen.
Moreover, Carrol was regarded by his neighbors as emphatically a just man, whose motto was to owe no man
anything. He was even charitable, according to his means;
but the man had a regard for his own rights, of which his
priest had more than once complained, as rather beyond
his management, and a temper whose enduring fierceness
warned off provocation.

Carrol's estate consisted of ten acres—reputed the
worst land in the parish, under the management of many
a preceding O'Reilly. Their last lease had expired when
it came into the jurisdiction of Lacy's father, and Carrol
commenced life on his own account with such an addition
to the rent as the practice of those times allowed. Carrol
had toiled upon it in all weathers since then; he had
labored in other men's fields, and expended the proceeds
on his own; his brothers had lent their assistance, his sons
had taken early lessons of industry there, and marvellous
was the change produced by their united exertions. Fences
rose where such had never been before; drains were made
of which nobody had dreamed; and O'Reilly's farm had at
length fields whose fertility the neighboring gentry strove
to emulate in vain. Carrol was bordering on fifty-five,
and had been twice married, the statement of which fact
he was wont to conclude after a singularly pious fashion,
with, "The Lord's will be done." His first helpmate had
been the mother of a large family; they were early wedded,
and, it was said, lived happily till the eldest of the eight
children was almost grown, when the typhus fever entered
his cottage one summer, and took the mother from them.

Carrol's grief lasted longer than that of the widowed in general, but if he didn't find comfort in the ten acres, they afforded him the next best thing, namely, occupation. Out of them he settled his eldest son on a neighboring farm, with what he called "a little girl of fortin'," made the second a priest, fitted out two for emigration to America; married a couple of daughters respectably in their father's station, and placed the two younger at good service in Castle Crosby.

Being alone in his cottage after these varied achievements, Carrol one day brought it home a second mistress, in the shape of Alley Flannigan, the bonnet-maker of Killmore. Alley was an orphan cousin of the parish priest, to whose advice Carrol particularly attributed the match; though his reverence averred it was the first time he had ever known counsel to take effect on him. The strength of her kindred were, a stepmother who had remarried, and some half dozen of brothers and sisters, with large families of their own.

Alley had learned her trade in Cavan, and maintained herself by it, in a manner. All the parish knew her to be honest, careful, and desirous of well doing, but that was the bound of Alley's abilities; for energy, invention, or foresight, she had none. A poor and lonely life had the widow led, with her bonnet-blocks, to a certain age, at which she looked still neat and comely, though it was believed that Alley never had an offer except from a recruiting-sergeant who was quartered in the town about ten years previous. Alley was young then, and did not like a seat on the baggage-cart, or thought the sergeant, who was a gay, dashing young fellow, insincere; but ever after her neighbors were unanimous in the opinion that Alley rued the non-entertainment of that proposal. None of them were therefore surprised, when Carrol paid his addresses, at his almost immediate acceptance. The pair stepped quietly one evening to the house of Father Flannigan, who made them one with the celerity of a practised hand; and Alley was found next morning making things neat about the cottage.

The Irish peasantry entertain strong prejudices against second marriages, and Carrol's children were no exception to that rule. They showed little liking for their stepmother, inoffensive as she was, which Carrol said was but natural; adding, that "He nivir intinded to put any man in the place ov the woman that wis in heavin; but seein' that the house wis lonely, and Alley dissolute, he thought it well to purvide a comforter for his ould days and lave her the farm improvemints whin he wint to meet his blissed Norah."

That farm was a spot in which poor Carrol took no little pride; its fields with the hedge-rows, and the fruit trees he had planted among them, lay so pleasant round the neat white cottage, whose rose-wreathed windows and pretty curtains within rivalled the rustic homes of England. All was the fruit of his own labor; but Carrol had yet to learn that more admiring eyes than his were upon it.

That quiet wedding was scarcely a month over when the solitude of Mr. Lacy's large house was also enlivened by the arrival of a young man, who bore a diminutive resemblance to himself, and was called his nephew. Master Charles Hamilton had been brought up at Swanlinhar; he was a low-set, impudent-looking fellow, whose aim was to be a country beau, and whose habits and manners were such as might be expected from one reared among the lowest of the peasantry, but taught to value himself on some advantageous connexion. Old gossips accounted for all by recollecting that, subsequent to the death of Mr. Lacy's mother, a maid whom she had specially kept for fine spinning had privately retired from her household, under rather equivocal circumstances, to the above-named locality in her native Connaught; and that ever after Mr. Lacy had obscure but frequently recurring business to transact in that quarter.

"Troth, his nose tells the whole story on the ould sinner," said Alley, as she and her husband made the circuit of their own fields, by way of walk, in a July evening, when, as Carrol remarked, there was little to do but see the corn growing, and Mr. Lacy stood earnestly talking to his nephew at the mairing ditch, or boundary of his own farm.

"What can he be pointin' here for, Alley?" interrupted Carrol. "Come away, woman—they'll think we are listenin';" and the spirited peasant turned homewards; but there was a story between Lacy and his nephew that evening which the latter's nose did not reveal to the O'Reillys.

As the harvest drew on, the looks of both were more frequently directed to Carrol's fields, as if estimating their worth and fertility; and at length, as the husband and wife were shearing together at the earliest of their corn, Master Charlie, who had grown familiar of late, opened his mind in the following manner:—

"It's a wonder to me, Mr. O'Rilly, that you slave yirself wid so much lan', an' all yir childer away. Man, the farm's far too big for ye; but if ye wud like an easy change, I'm sure my uncle could give ye a nice bit of three acres down in the stoney craft," and he pointed to the opposite extreme of Hamilton's property.

"Masther Charlie," said Carrol, looking sharply up at him, "I hive no objections, in case I'm well paid for my improvements; there's many a year's sweat an' sore bones of mine in thim. Yer uncle has always got his rint honestly from me; and I hope he'll understan' that I know the rights of a tinint."

"Yer only a tinint at will, Mr. O'Rilly, a'm thinkin'," said Master Charlie.

"That's what we're all in this worl', me young man," responded Carrol. "Bit justice is unmutirable, as me son, the preisht, says; an' thim that takes my farm, widout payin'

for the labor it cost me, 'ill get their reward, either here
or hereafter." With which warning words Carrol seized his
hook, and Master Charlie sneaked home to tell the tale.

The conversation that ensued between the O'Reillys
was low and earnest, varied by outbursts of indignation
from Carrol, as the Hamiltons' designs on his farm re-
curred to him in all their iniquity, till it was suddenly
interrupted by a challenge from the next field, given by
Jamie Sullivan, a neighbor's son, whose cherished wish had
long been to rival Carrol's well known abilities in shearing; and he now inquired if "Mr. O'Rilly wud hive the
condiscintion to try him for a stook." Carrol never refused a challenge of that kind; and a contest immediately
commenced, which called the attention of many a reaper,
thronged as the fields around them were in that sultry
August day, to the rival shearers.

The stipulated twelve sheaves were soon cut down, but,
to the discomfiture of the challenger, Carrol maintained
his wonted superiority. Jamie, however, was not to be foiled
easily; he insisted that his loss of victory was by reason of
a cramp in his fingers, "bad cess till it," and loudly demanded another trial. Stook after stook was thus reaped,
Carrol always winning, and Jamie renewing the combat
with perseverance worthy of a prouder cause. The style
in which he would take the conceit out of Carrol on the
harvest ridge had been his boast throughout the preceding
seasons; and his neighbors were proportionably amused,
not only by his repeated defeats, but the various apologies
he found for them. Now it was his hook; then the cramp;
and again the sun shining on the corn. Some took part
with him, some with Carrol; but all encouraged Jamie to
persevere, fun having, as usual in Ireland, taken the place
of every other consideration. Hooks and sheaves were left
in the surrounding fields—man, woman, and child, within

hearing, having gathered to the scene of contest. It happened to border on the highway, and, amid the shouts of applause and laughter which accompanied Jamie's efforts, no one took note of a passing traveller, who stood leaning his arms on the fence, and gazing earnestly at Alley, as that undisturbed spirit sat, hook in hand, on the new-cut ridge, enjoying her share of the sport.

"Throth, ye may give up, Jamie, wid a clean conscience," said Carrol, finishing his last stook, and wiping his brow, which had not been dry for hours past. "There's the sun settin', shame a stook I'll shear more;" and the old man, now covered with dust and perspiration, threw himself on the ridge beside Alley.

"Well," said Jamie, resignedly, "since you won't give me another chance. Bad luck till this hook ov mine, I'll break it in flinders when I go home."

"Buy one that'll shear ov itself, Jamie," responded Mrs. O'Reilly; and her remark was followed by a general laugh, in which the traveller joined. He was a man of Carrol's fashion, but some fifteen years younger, with a face that had seen foreign climates, certain military reminiscences about his dress, and that air of somewhat reckless gayety and freedom characteristic of the Irish soldier. A closer inspection might also have discovered that half the fingers of his left hand were wanting, that he walked with a partial lameness from an injury in the right knee, and had a sly, cunning look, which the world's ways might have taught him, about the eyes.

"A pleasant evening, sir," said Carrol, addressing the stranger.

"Very fine, Mister O'Reilly," answered he in the tone of one determined to create a sensation; "and it's my surprise that you havn't failed one sheaf in the shearing since I had the pleasure of seeing you last."

"Dad, then it's long ago," responded Carrol; "for the thransackshin has escaped my memory."

"I'm sorry for it," said the stranger, growing suddenly subdued; "but time makes great changes. Maybe you, nor nobody else here, can recollect Sergeant Allison?"

"Murther!" said Carrol, springing to his feet and seizing the traveller's both hands, "it's you that's welcome back. Oh! werr-anthrue, are two ov yer fingers clane aff? Don't a min' when ye wur courtin' Alley, now Mrs. O'Reilly here? an' troth she was a great fool not to take you!"

Carrol's welcome, even to its last clause, was confirmed by the bystanders, including Alley herself, who added by way of softener, that "ther' wis a fate in them things," an' she must go home to get on the supper.

"No doubt of it," said Carrol, in response to both her observations; and Sergeant Allison entered the field by general invitation, and proceeded to satisfy his old friends' curiosity, by explaining how he had been for years in India—how he lost his fingers and partly the use of his knee-joint in a battle with the troops of Hyder Ali, on which account having obtained a pension, he had returned to his native village, in an adjoining county; but his parents were dead, his brothers and sisters all married; and, finding himself, as he expressed it, a stranger in the place, he was on his way to see his old acquaintance in Killmore.

"It's late," said Carrol, when the sergeant had assisted him to bind and arrange the sheaves for the night. "Blessins on ye for helpin' me! shure I nivir was as tired. But won't ye take a bed at the house? Alley and me has it all to ourselves now."

The invitation was cheerfully accepted, and they spent a marvellous evening with the sergeant's exploits and adventures; but all that night Carrol tossed and groaned—in the morning he was unable to go to the harvest field as usual, and it was soon evident that the over-exertion which vanquished Jamie Sullivan in that burning day had brought on a rapid form of that disease known as pleurisy. Some half-score of rustic remedies, including sundry decoctions of herbs, and a charm from the wise woman of that district, were successively put in requisition; still Carrol grew worse, and the village doctor was at length sent for; but his appointed time was come, and in less than eight days' illness he went the way of all living, leaving most of his children, whom sorrow had reconciled to Alley, weeping with her round his bed, and a will in favor of her and his two unmarried daughters, witnessed by Father O'Flannigan and Sergeant Allison; the latter having, to O'Reilly's gratitude, remained to take charge of the harvest.

Poor Alley's grief, though sincere, was not excessive. "Shure he took me whin nobody else wud!" was her plain-spoken lamentation, to which consoling neighbors replied, "Troth, ye may say that, not to mention his lavin' ye share of the improvements."

Carrol's children did not dispute the will, which was, on the whole, equitable, as all had been previously provided for, excepting the younger girls, who expected their portions off the farm. How valuable it had been made by poor Carrol's exertions was well known; and the O'Reillys were in doubt whether to dispose of his improvements and tenant-right to the highest bidder, and divide the proceeds at once among the three legatees, or endeavor to retain them in the family, by uniting to manage the farm for the behoof of their sisters and stepmother. Sergeant Allison, whose counsel was now heard as a tried friend of the family, gave his opinion in favor of the latter measure, which certainly was the most profitable, and also reminded the O'Reillys that it was necessary to consult their landlord.

Mr. Lacy kept studiously aloof from his tenants in the season of trial. Neither he nor his nephew had graced the wake or funeral with their presence—an instance of neglect which caused no little scandal in the neighborhood, and provoked sundry comparisons of their respective progenitors by no means favorable to the Hamilton line. Besides, Alley had misgivings in her mind regarding Master Charlie's last conversation with her husband, which she communicated confidentially to her eldest stepson and the sergeant, they being the family's accredited deputies, under the joint command of her cousin, Father O'Flannagan, and the reverend Terence O'Reilly, who had left his distant parish on the first intelligence of Carrol's illness. By those chiefs of the house it was therefore arranged that the eldest son and the sergeant should wait on Mr. Hamilton, (that worthy proprietor being in the habit of exhibiting his Protestantism by a marked incivility to all Catholic priests whatever,) explain to him the wishes of the O'Reillys to retain the farm, and learn his opinion on the subject.

The kitchen and one or two minor apartments were the only inhabited portions of Mr. Lacy's house. There were tales in the neighborhood of velvet tapestry hanging from the ceiling, and costly furniture, covered with dust and mould, in its superior rooms, which had been kept fast locked ever since his notable disappointment in the matter of a ball, to which all the neighboring gentry had been invited, and every one sent apologies. That was now twenty years ago. Old family habits had more than reestablished their sway over Lacy's heart and home; and his household had sat down to breakfast in the kitchen as usual, the farm servants at one table in the centre, and, at a convenient corner—for the double purpose of seeing that they did not consume too much time at the meal, and of superintending his housekeeper in its distribution—he and his nephew sat at another, when Tim O'Reilly and the sergeant made their appearance.

"I hope we 'r not disturbin' yer honor? Much comfort may ye have in what's before ye!" said Tim, considering it his duty to open the pleadings. "Shure it's fine weather for the harvest—thanks be to Him that sint it!"

"It is, my good man; but what might your business be?" replied Hamilton, in angry surprise at being caught off his greatness by a Catholic tenant.

Tim had not anticipated that salute, and it roused the slumbering wrath of the O'Reillys within him, touching the disrespect shown to his father's wake. His answer was accordingly brief and careless, merely informing Hamilton of the family's desire to cultivate the farm among them, and promising the accustomed rent in the name of his stepmother.

"I intend taking that farm into my own hand," interrupted Mr. Lacy, "for my nephew here. Your father was very foolish to marry at his time of life, but I will allow the widow twenty pounds in case she goes out quietly at November."

Tim darted upon him a look of fire, and the sergeant burst out with, "Twenty pounds wouldn't pay for Carrol O'Reilly's labor on one field, as you well know, Mr. Hamilton. There are still two daughters, as well as his wife, to be provided for, and it is to be hoped you won't take the weight of wronging both the widow and the fatherless on your conscience."

"Come away," cried Tim. "The curse ov greed's on him! God rest my father in his grave! but it's hard to expect he wud stay in it, when the farm his strength was spint on is a takin' from his own."

With these mild words the deputation retired; but there was woe and wrath, not only among the O'Reillys, but throughout the whole parish, when the result of their

mission was known. The act was one of such penurious
yet glaring injustice that proprietors of every class united
in declaring against the paltry pittance assigned to poor
Alley and her step-daughters; while to the peasantry it appeared as it really was, a taking of the fruits of O'Reilly's
labor to bestow them on his nephew. Neither the remon-
strances of the one order, nor the indignation of the other,
had the least effect on Hamilton; besides his hereditary
love of money, there was in his character a vein of unrea-
soning obstinacy strengthened by many bachelor years. He
refused to add a single shilling to Alley's liberal jointure.
The widow was regularly noticed to quit at the ensuing
term, and Master Charlie publicly signified his intention
of cropping the farm next spring. Alley said that "nothing
could go wrong wid thim that had justice on their side;"
and while the O'Reillys raged and threatened, while Master Charlie provided himself with pistols, and his uncle
talked of a constabulary force to protect Hamilton House,
she continued to inhabit the cottage in composed propri-
ety, assisted in the management of the poultry and dairy
by an orphan girl she had taken by way of servant, and
consoled by the occasional visits of Sergeant Allison, who
had now taken up his residence in the neighborhood, and
acted as the widow's man-of-all-work.

So the winter passed. But this state of things was not
for duration; an ejectment was served on Alley at the
spring term, and some further attempts at negotiation,
which were made at the instance of the sergeant, being rejected by the Hamiltons, to the surprise of the whole parish, Master Charlie one morning entered the fields with
his uncle's plough and horses, and fairly commenced till-
age for himself. The chief wonder was, that the O'Reillys
should look so quietly on this premature invasion. The
sergeant, indeed, had been heard to mutter that he and the
old miser might get a fright, but all the rest of the kindred

kept silent and distant, and seemed determined to leave Alley to her fate.

Matters were in this posture when Killmore was edified by a rumor to the effect that a certain agent, who stood high on his distant relationship to a bishop, and remote connexion with an M.P., had lately made striking advances of civility to Mr. Lacy, on account of some five hundred which he washed to borrow. They had met once or twice at church and market, and, in token of further friendship, as well as to settle the preliminaries, Mr. Davis, it was said, after some difficulties with his lady, invited both uncle and nephew to dine at his house about six o'clock on a breezy March evening.

It was asserted by those best informed on the subject, that things were arranged rather advantageously for Mr. Davis towards eleven o'clock, when his courtesy was so far extended, perhaps owing to the necessity of the case, as to send his guests comfortably home in his own vehicle, kept in token of special gentility, and denominated in Ireland an inside car. It was driven by no less a personage than Jamie Sullivan, who, after having mourned over the death of Carrol, and especially the fact that he "had nivir got time to take the consate out on him," entered Mr. Davis' household as a kind of general servant, to leave, as he expressed it, more room for the other nine on his father's four acres.

"Faith, a'll drive yez in style," said Jamie, mounting the seat of power, as the last "good nights" were exchanged, and the host and his friends separated like loving brothers; and in style, according to his own appreciation, he did drive them, in spite of threats from the nephew and entreaties from the uncle, making them acquainted in the most practical fashion with every stone and rut in the road; and in those days they were not few. The distance between Mr. Davis' residence and Hamilton House was

not more than five miles English, and the way led past the
now newly-ploughed fields, and pretty cottage owned by
Carrol O'Reilly.

As they approached that part of the road Jamie's driving
became, if possible, more furious; but, unfortunately, he
managed the whip better than the reins, and utterly forgot
that there was a deep and dirty ditch separating Carrol's
farm from the highway, till one of the wheels went in, and
nothing but immediate pulling up saved the whole party.
"Leap out, for the vargin's sake!" shouted Jamie at the top
of his voice; but both uncle and nephew, being now thoroughly angry as well as intoxicated, thought it beneath
their dignity to stir, and both replied with a volley of wild
curses on his careless driving.

The moon had been bright, but was now covered with
a cloud, and as it passed away Jamie uttered another cry;
but it was his prayers poured forth in a mingled stream of
creed and ave, where he sat holding back the horse with
all his might from the ditch, and staring into the adjoining field. The Hamiltons instinctively followed that gaze.
The field had just been prepared for sowing. It was one on
which Carrol had expended great pains and taken much
pride; and now, in the broad moonlight, a man stood in
the garments of the grave, sowing broad-cast on its ridges.
The trio gazed for a few seconds, and the figure moved
towards them. But Jamie could endure no longer; and,
uttering a still louder cry to the Virgin for protection,
he jumped from box and reins, flying at full speed to his
father's house, as, with a cry that startled the country, the
inside car and the Hamiltons went down into that muddy
ditch. When, about an hour after, a sufficient number of
the neighbors could be collected by the terror-stricken
Jamie to search for them there, the car was found dirty and
broken, the poor horse still struggling in the harness, but
Mr. Lacy and his nephew had been received in a fearful

plight by the housekeeper, whom their knocks and cries awoke from her first sleep. Of course, the inside car was sent home next morning; and the Hamiltons never cared to enter into the particulars of that night; but several of the neighbors testified to having seen that ghostly sower, though Alley said, "Glory be to goodness, he never frightened her!" and Jamie Sullivan, when minutely recollecting his appearance, was wont to remark that "the other worl' had made a great change on Carrol, for he niver knowed him to walk wid a hop before."

As for Master Charlie, no earthly power could ever after persuade him to think of that farm, and his uncle sent word to the widow she might stay as long as she pleased, as he had changed his mind about the ejectment. Of that permission Mrs. O'Reilly fully availed herself. The sergeant sowed the farm for her, and the harvest-home was celebrated by a wedding, at which all the O'Reillys danced, including, it is said, the reverend Terence. Tradition also records that their step-father proved a worthy portioner of Carrol's girls, who, in process of time, got married in their native parish. But one thing was remarked about the sergeant's farming, namely, that the haunted field brought forth among its produce an incredible amount of the shrub known as gorse or whin; also, that when that circumstance was in any way forced on his attention, Allison looked as if he sincerely repented of something; and, many a year after, when witnessing his laborers' exertions to root out those tenacious invaders, Jamie Sullivan, who alone attempted to account for their introduction, observed, with a look of terror, "Oh, sargint, dear, the ould man left ye hard work wid the last of his improvements!"

THE HAUNTED HOUSE
George H. Coomer
(1867)

"Speaking of spirit bell-ringings and rappings," said grandmother, "I listened to something quite as startling years before spirits resolved themselves into an institution. Then every ghost was independent. Not one of them thought of coming at set times to read, write or attend lectures; but whenever one did appear, at such irregular hours as suited its convenience, it created a sensation. A spirit of this kind would not 'down' at the bidding of ever so many Macbeths.

"When I was eighteen, Mr. Marvin, one of our neighbors, owned a farm in 'Gray Owl Dell,' a couple of miles from his homestead. He generally had a tenant upon the place, but in the year to which I have reference, having found no one willing to pay so high a rent as he demanded, he had allowed the house to remain empty, his boys, his hired man or himself going over occasionally to attend to the farm.

"It requires no great knowledge of human nature to assure one that a house standing remote from all others, in a lonesome and shadowy dell, could not long remain untenanted by humanity without acquiring the reputation of being haunted. The feline is intimately associated with ideas of the supernatural, and cats, astonishing in size and number, began to be seen about the premises at Gray Owl

41

Dell. The birds of Minerva, too, that perched now and then on the decaying buildings, were suspected of wearing their feathers merely as cloaks of deception, while the witch-spirit looked mockingly out from their great, round eyes.

"Will Ashley, who had attended Margaret Rivers from singing-school to her home on the back road, affirmed that while returning across lots, for a shorter cut, he had seen an owl, as large as Mr. Marvin's brindle ox, sitting on the chimney-top of the old farmhouse. This bird was no doubt the incarnation of a witch-spirit; and however much Will's dilated eyes may have magnified its proportions, it was lucky for poor old Polly Ruggles, the scold of the neighborhood, and an abominable hag altogether, that Salem fashions had lost their predominance in New England. The uncomfortable dame might out-scold the north wind, but unlike those of her profession in earlier days, she stood no chance of being dragged at a rope's end across a river, or pressed between two planks till she should acknowledge her iniquity—after confession, the pressing to go on worse than ever. Sad encouragement to penitence!

"One way and another, the opinion became prevalent that something evil hovered about the place. Widow Stebbins, who hired the privilege of fastening her cow there, testified that the cream yielded by this domestic animal was upon a certain occasion bewitched. The pious widow churned long in vain. Then she prayed; then she churned again. But the familiar spirit had not been exorcised by her devotions—perhaps she had lacked faith. Finally, she heated a horse-shoe, till it glowed like the star Arcturus, and all flaming as it was, dropped it into the cream. 'Such a hissing and screaming,' said the good widow, 'you never heard; and the butter came at once.' No doubt some incautious witch was sadly burned—the hissing and screaming directly pointing to such a conclusion, especially with the excellent woman, who had never been in a blacksmith's shop.

"During the summer, however, we young people were in little dread of the supernatural, and as the old place had tempting raspberries and apples, we often visited it, yet kept at a good distance from the house. But when winter had set in, putting imagination in shadow, and the days appeared like dim windows between the long, dark nights, I think we took pleasure in the full indulgence of credulity. Who cares for a July ghost, or looks for a withered witch in a field of blooming corn? The Thane of Glamis met the 'weird sisters' upon a blasted heath; and the idea of evil spirits is ever associated with desolation and darkness.

"I well recollect the advent, about this time, of a mysterious animal that our townspeople called a tiger cat. We felt a kind of scared pleasure in believing it not wholly of earth; and, indeed, there was much in its nightly operations to warrant such an opinion. It seemed an enemy of nothing but dogs, and it became a usual occurrence for a farmer on going out in the morning to find his dog dead on the doorstep, yet without any discoverable wound.

"My cousins, Thomas and John Conway, lived then with their father, who was a neighbor of ours; and I remember hearing John call to his brother, one bitter cold morning, saying:

"'Tom, Tom! the tiger cat has killed Cupid!' meaning their little dog.

"Sometimes on frosty evenings, when 'the stars shot down wi' sklentin' light,' a belated traveller would be startled by a momentary glimpse of some undefined shape that rushed past him like a cannon ball, and he felt that he had seen the tiger cat. As one of our neighbors was returning at a late hour to his home, a weird, strange object shot between his feet and instantly disappeared. The frightened man ran with all his might, and no logic could have convinced him that old Dame Ruggles had not darted between his boot tops in the shape of a monstrous cat.

"A being half of this world and half of a world unknown, always appears more terrible to us than the wholly supernatural, in which is no mingling of earth. But about this so-called tiger cat, there was certainly something unaccountable. That such a being existed, I have not the least doubt; yet why it killed the dogs, or how it could effect its purpose and still leave no outward sign of injury, I cannot imagine.

"There was, and still is, at the entrance of the seaport village near which we lived, a stone bridge, upon which it became usual to find in the morning a number of dogs, all slain as by a pestilence, like the warriors of Sennacharib. One night, a Mr. Manchester resolved to watch at this place. He had taken unusual care in the preparation of his gun—had screwed in the lock a new flint that would make the sparks fly in showers. Moreover, he was a cool, resolute man, and one whose word was accepted by the villagers almost as readily as the evidence of their own senses.

"As the clock struck twelve, the tiger cat appeared, dragging along a small dog. He set his captive on end, gave it two or three taps of the paw, and the dog rolled over dead. There had apparently been no attempt at resistance. Mr. Manchester said that at this moment he considered the tiger cat his certain prize. Bringing up his gun with the alacrity of an old sportsman, as he was, he snapped it. To his surprise it missed fire. Twice more he essayed, yet not a spark left the flint. He lowered the weapon with a feeling of dread, examined the lock for a moment, and on looking up, discovered that the creature had vanished. Raising his piece, he snapped it once more, but this time from mere curiosity. The flint threw out a host of sparks and the gun was discharged as usual. I doubt not there are many old people, who, like myself, have heard Mr. Manchester relate the circumstance.

"What bond of sympathy, if any, existed between Dame Ruggles and the tiger cat, I cannot say; but that the old woman was really a witch seems very probable. It was averred that the rendezvous of the weird sisterhood was in Gray Owl Dell; and Michael Flynn, Mr. Marvin's hired man, (and, by the way, in that early time the only Irishman in the town), going one morning to attend to the sheep at the farm, said that he heard voices over his head, and distinguished among them that of Dame Ruggles. Michael, who always stood for the last word with friends and enemies, shouted out:

"'Come down here, Mishtress Ruggles, ye indacent owld scowld, and I'll warrum ye wid a taste o' me pitchforruk, ye hag!'

"Whereat there was a loud, jeering laugh, so near his head that Michael threw his pitchfork with vengeance, hoping to hit some of his invisible tantalizers; but he was surprised to see the implement sail around in the air, as if some witch had bridled it for a horse.

"'Yez have got me forruk, yer wild bastes!' cried Mike; 'but be the houly Vargin, come down here thin; it's all I axes of yez, and I'll tan yer owld hides till yez scrame agin!'

"At mention of the Virgin, the witch merriment subsided into total silence, and Michael's 'forruk' lay at his feet as quietly as if it had been ridden in air by these 'posters of the sea and land.' Such was Mike's story, but it had often been hinted that his love of truth was no match for his imagination.

"It was, however, asserted by one in whose veracity the whole neighborhood reposed implicit confidence, that he had seen the form of Dame Ruggles stretched at full length across the chimney of Gray Owl Dell farmhouse, while her spirit was far away on some iniquitous mission. This may have been the very shape which Will Ashley had once mistaken for an owl of unearthly aspect; or, reversing the case, the owl may in the last instance have been taken for the dame—so uncertain are things which we know nothing about.

"But whether witch or not, there was in the circumstances attending the death of Dame Ruggles, which occurred that winter, something unaccountable. During her brief illness the old woman had been more querulous than ever, and the attempt of any kind Samaritan to draw the least appearance of gratitude from her jagged mind, was like trying to 'grab' a handful of shingle nails out of a keg.

"As her dissolution approached, the watchers, who had heard that no one can see a witch die, were alert for the closing scene. The night was cold, the bed-clothes were supposed insufficient, the fire upon the hearth, kindle it as they would, refused to bum brightly, and they therefore lighted a furnace of charcoal in the centre of the room. Did they a moment relax their vigilance, they would find their patient stretched upon her back across this flaming furnace, as if she loved fire, and felt her present agony soothed by this foretaste of her future inheritance. How her clothing fared remains an open question to this day, but she herself snapped and crackled like burning whale-bone.

"'She must go soon,' said one of the watchers, when for the last time the old woman had been removed from the furnace to her bed. 'We shall certainly see her die.'

"At this moment a tumult of voices outside drew the watchers' attention. Cats wawled, owls hooted, and there were strange screams intermingled with malicious laughter—yet no living creature was visible. They were about turning to their patient, when, as they averred, a some-thing, having the appearance of a red hot ball, shot past them and out at the window. This window, though closed, showed no mark of the singular exit. On reaching the old dame's side, they perceived that her spirit had departed.

"Now," continued grandmother, "I always took this story with some allowance; but, that unaccountable things have been done by people called witches, I have not the least doubt. I am by no means sure that Dame Ruggles's familiar spirit did not stir up a great commotion in the elements on the night of her death.

"It happened that early in the evening, a party of us had set out in two double sleighs for a ten-mile ride, with a view to a merry collation at a country tavern—'hotel,' you call it now. Will Ashley was with us, but blue-eyed Margaret Rivers, whom he had attended home on the night that he saw the witch owl, was not of our number. Some trifling misunderstanding between the comely farmer lad and the maiden of his love, had grown to a downright quarrel. Margaret had 'wept the weary day,' not doubting that this silly quarrel was the one great calamity of her life, which should shadow all nights and days to come. The jingle of our sleigh bells was like the dirge of all her joys, and she sat down to find what consolation she could in the 'Children of the Abbey.' One must indeed be far gone who comes to that!

"Will Ashley, no less miserable, appeared as the escort of Anna Franklin, between whom and Margaret there existed a feud. Will had been at some pains to place him-self in a position, the misery of which can be appreciat-ed by every spiteful lover, who has not only flung away his peace but drawn to his side a perpetual reminder of his folly. Anna Franklin's ill-concealed regard was like the bitterness of wormwood to poor Will. He tried to be gay, while Anna did her best to amuse and fascinate; but not all the attractions of her wit and beauty

> "'Were worth one pearl-drop, bright and sheen,
>   From Margaret's eyes that fell.'

"Before our party broke up, a furious snow storm set in. This great storm, on the night that Dame Ruggles died, was long talked of in the neighborhood. As we proceeded homeward, our way was often blocked by drifts that had formed in the narrow sleigh track since we had passed at twilight The clouds swept almost down to earth, and great trees, that we could hardly see for the driving snow, creaked and groaned outright in the cold, roaring wind. We had to pass Gray Owl Dell, some of our party living a mile or two beyond. Just as we came opposite the witch-haunted farmhouse, Dick Lee, the daredevil of our party, who, while the rest of us were almost chilled to death, had all the way been singing snatches of frightful old ballads, pointed out a gigantic poplar, bare and black by the highway, and writhing in the storm: then he shouted dramatically:

> "'A murderer yonder was hung in chaynes,
>   The sunne and the winde had shrunke hys veynes;
>   I bit off a sinew; I clipped hys hayre,
>   I brought off his ragges that danced in the ayre.'

As the last word left his lips the tree came crashing down, completely blocking our way. It seemed a judgment upon our party for Dick's presumption in repeating a witch's song at such an awful hour.

"Further progress with the sleigh was impossible, neither could we walk to our homes in such a tempest. Mr. Marvin's sons were of our party, and suggested that we should find shelter in the house. One of them entered through a back window, and opened the door to the party. Abundant fuel was at hand, and we kindled a fire, while the horses were led to the stables. Our quarters were soon comfortable. Dry walnut sticks blazed, crackled and fell asunder in the middle, while smoking coals fell out upon the hearth. But as outward comfort increased, our inner consciousness awoke to a keener sense of our peculiar situation. 'When the mind's free, the body's delicate'—and *vice versa.*

"We discussed the singularity of our position, most of us with growing uneasiness, while two or three treated the affair humorously. Will Ashley became abstracted; gazing now into the fire, and anon starting and peering into the corners of the room, or looking at the doors as if he expected them to open. He was thinking of Margaret Rivers, and anticipating some ghostly visitation for his momentary perfidy. The unearthly owl he had seen on the chimney top of this same house, while yet the course of love run smoothly, was a bird of evil omen; the falling of the great tree which had stopped our way, boded sorrow to some one, and Will doubted not that he himself was the Baalim on whose account some unseen spirit had barred the road. Suddenly, we all started to our feet.

"'What was that?' asked Anna Franklin, looking terrified.

"'Did you not hear a bell?' said another. 'It certainly was a bell. Dear me! I am frightened to death!'

"'What is the matter?' cried Dick Lee. 'What did you all jump up for? I thought the old one himself was coming. Don't you know any better than to scare a fellow out of his senses?'

"'Tinkle, tinkle, tinkle,' went the bell again.

"'Who on earth can be ringing a dinner bell this time of night?' continued Dick. 'Well, I must give in; the old gentleman has really come for us; but he won't hurt me; he and I have had too many good times together. He will be calling the roll soon, so prepare. We must answer to our names, as I once heard the Irish aldermen at a meeting of the board, when I was in Cork in a ship: "Will Ashley?" "'Ere, sir!" "Dick Lee?" "'Ere, yer honor!" And so he will go through the company.'

"'O, for heaven's sake, do stop, Dick!' cried Mary Moore. 'How can you make light of such things? I am almost dead with fright!'

"For some moments the bell was silent, but terror was impressed on every countenance save that of Dick Lee, who appeared resolved to brave it out.

"'Come, Will Ashley,' said he, 'cheer up, I know what you are thinking of—you have had a little flare-up with those blue eyes down the road yonder. That's the reason Margaret is not with us. So you expect the devil to carry you off, as he ought to. Hark! I will sing you a ballad for the occasion.'

"His rich voice added greatly to the mournful power of the lines, as to our consternation he sung that dear old English ballad, which, however beautiful, is not precisely the thing that one loves to hear in a haunted house.

"'Twas at the silent, solemn hour
     When night and morning meet,
 In glided Margaret's grimly ghost,
     And stood at William's feet.'

"Ere the singing ended, the bell-ringing was again heard, together with other sounds, apparently approaching the cellar stairs. Dick looked startled, but resolutely continued his singing—the rest of us standing in silent terror.

> "'This is the dark and fearful hour,
>   When injured ghosts complain—'

('Tinkle, tinkle, tinkle'—'tramp, tramp, tramp'—louder and nearer—but Dick was stout-hearted, and went on:)

> "'When dreary graves give up their dead,
>   To haunt the faithless swain.'

"But at this moment, the cellar door swung wide open. Dick looked over his shoulder, uttered a yell and rushed headlong from the room. All save Will Ashley and myself followed him out into the storm. Will, who had been scarcely less terrified by the ballad than the unaccountable sounds, imagining that restitution for his faithlessness was now at hand, and perhaps asking his own heart, like the Moor, 'why should honor outlive honesty?—let it go all,' sank powerless upon the floor. Why I did not fly with the others, I cannot tell. Perhaps the reason exists in some law of metaphysics which I do not understand. My eyes were fixed in unspeakable amazement upon the spectacle that rose before me. Through the shadowy passage to the cellar, rose a black, frightful face, crowned with horns that curled all around the head. Back of this apparition were others, all with long, wistful faces, apparently half-human and half-brute, and with eyes like great pieces of brass. Utter silence prevailed in the room, save so far as broken by the raging storm without. There I stood, confronting I knew not what, and feeling as if in a trance. Presently Will Ashley spoke.

"'O, Mr. Devil,' said he, 'I did not mean it—I did not mean to quarrel with Margie! Let me off this once, and I will go right back and tell her how sorry I am!'

"'Em-ba-ah!' said the spectre, and came clattering right out on the kitchen floor, while a bell under his neck tinkled furiously. The other heads crowded fast after him, the cloven feet clattering as they leaped from the upper stair into the room. I looked at Will, and Will at me. There was a queer expression upon his face—a shadow of lingering terror blended with an exceedingly foolish look of mortification. Still the strange visitors increased in number, stamping and bleating, and apparently looking for something. to eat. Then Will laughed wildly like an insane man, exclaiming:

"'O, the fool that I have been! 'Tis Mr. Marvin's flock of sheep! I heard a day or two ago that they were lost, and somehow they must have got into the cellar!'

"I, too, had heard that three days before Mr. Marvin had missed his entire flock. The same day there happened a fall of snow, so that he could not track them. Our terror was now entirely gone, and Will, rendered by the reaction more courageous than ever before in his life, volunteered to go into the cellar and examine. I was surprised, for he seemed as bold as a lion; but this I suppose was consistent with so inconsistent a thing as human nature. I was a farmer's daughter and not afraid of sheep, so he left me with them while he went down with a blazing brand. At the back of the house he found that a portion of the cellar wall had fallen. Through the aperture thus opened, the old leader must somehow have stumbled, followed, of course, by the whole flock. The opening was soon hidden by the falling snow, and as no one visited the house, the sheep had been in danger of starvation. It was not difficult for them to ascend the short stairway, above which, as the upper part of the door was glass, they had seen our light A blow from horns or feet had caused the opening of the door.

"Our panic-stricken companions had pursued their flight no further than the barn, and after a time, discovering that we were missing, Dick Lee and one or two others

came back in search of us. When the matter had been explained to the whole party, the young men brought arm-
fuls of fodder, and succeeded in enticing the hungry sheep
from the house to the barn.

"Once more we all assembled around the fire; but my
companions had much to tell of a frightfully great cat that
they could see on a beam in the barn, though she sat in
pitch darkness. Perhaps they saw her more with the mind's
eye than the natural organs. Presently another came and
sat down beside her; then another and another and another: and there they remained in awful silence, with eyes
horribly bright, and faces expressive of malignity softened
by some great sorrow.

"At last, the central cat, the immense creature at first
seen, uttered a cry so long-drawn and hideously mournful that no mortal could describe it. It was echoed by all
her four companions; and in a moment the entire company of unearthly felines vanished in the blackness of
that witch-ridden darkness. This must have been about
the hour that Dame Ruggles died; and I have sometimes
wondered if the central animal of the group was not the
famous tiger cat, and if so, what relationship she bore to
the witch dame.

"I must say, though, that Dick Lee told me next day
that the reason the cats vanished was that he threw a piece
of board at the biggest one, knocking her heels over head,
and that they went out through a hole in the loft—but I
never knew whether to believe him or not. I have only to
add that Will Ashley and Margaret Rivers were married in
the spring."

THE HEREDITARY BARN

Noah Brooks

(1886)

The old Joslin farm is on the road from Fairport to
Penobscot, near the head of the Northern Bay. It is a rag-
ged and hilly piece of upland, yielding good grass, and
capable of great possibilities in the way of potatoes. But
the Joslins never did stick to farming as a sole means of
getting a living. The old-fashioned, gambrel-roofed house,
mossy as to roof, and dark red as to its front, overlooked
the Northern Bay; and it was a pretty dull time when at
least one coaster could not be seen, lazily creeping up to
Penobscot with the tide in her favor; or it may have been
a hay-sloop that dropped down, equally lazy, with the ebb.
And it was a part of the domestic economy of the farmers
of the bay, that a goodly share of the winter's provisions
should consist of codfish, caught on the Grand Banks by
some younger member of the family, or "traded for" by the
head of the house with some more adventurous neighbor.
The population of the region around the Dotian Shore and
the head of the Northern Bay is largely amphibious. Fishing, coasting, and kindred seamanlike pursuits fill up the
chinks of the dull life of the tillers of the soil.

It is not an inspiring landscape that the eyes of the
Joslins were used to look on from the door-stone of their
ancient homestead. From the little pinched-up flower garden, where marigolds, hollyhocks, love-lies-bleeding, and

China asters disputed the starved ground with balm, sweet
marjoram, and mother-wort, the land sloped steeply off to
the bluff overhanging the river. A tidy rail-fence skirted
the lower edge of the place, and the Penobscot road, yellow with golden rod and ox-eyed daisies in autumn, and
gullied with heavy rains in spring, crept along under the
fence, half-hidden from the house and dangerously near
the crumbling bluff of the river bank.

From the house, overlooking road and bluff, the eye
fell on a long and narrow bay, or estuary, from the broader
bay of Penobscot. The farther shore was well-wooded,
and the somber spruces and firs, never very cheerful, were
black and mournful indeed in winter. The waters of the
bay were never vexed by many keels, and the few farming
settlements on the farther side of the water were so hidden
by the woods that one might almost fancy it an untrodden
wilderness, if it were not for the glimpses given here and
there, of bits of ploughed land. Beyond the woods that
rose upwards from the shore, was the serrated range of the
Mount Desert hills, blue and cold in the eastern sky; and
further to the north, the honest face of Blue Hill, rugged
and seamy, reposed against the horizon. The picture might
have been transferred to canvas, and shown to a northern
traveler as a view of a Norwegian fiord, so dark and cold
and stern was it.

The red-fronted house looked unwinkingly on the scene
from two Lutheran windows in its roof, and an open woodshed, that terminated in a hen-house, stretched itself from
the house almost over to a big barn, black with age, but
substantial, and more suggestive of wealth and comfort
than even the old farmhouse itself. It was a well-shing-
led and glass-windowed barn, ample with its haymows and
stalls for cattle, and even affording refuge for colonies of
barn-swallows that built their mud-nests under its hospi-
table eaves. It had a homely look—that time-blackened

barn; but far up in the northern gable an eye-shaped aperture for the martens which nested among the rafters within, looked over the head of the bay with a fixed and sinister stare. Seen from the road, at the height of a summer noon, when all hands were in the fields, and the cat kept house on the sun-drenched window-sill, the place seemed forlorn and lonely. It might have been a lost farm—a farm dropped by accident by some giant peddler passing that way with a load of buildings and fences for sale.

Very gloomy and poverty-stricken did the Joslin place appear to old man Joslin, in the winter of 1807, when, an embargo having been declared by the United States government, a blight fell on every industry of the New England seaboard States. There was Elkanah Joslin's hay waiting to be sold and shipped; in the cellar were fifty bushels of good sound potatoes, that would rot before a customer could be found for them. And even the five shares which Elkanah owned in the "John and Eliza" were worthless as so much driftwood; and there was the schooner "eating her head off," as the farmer sourly expressed it, in Portland harbor, idle and useless as long as the embargo lasted. Smuggling from the Provinces was the only thriving industry in the time of the embargo; but Elkanah Joslin was an uncompromising church-member. He would sooner starve than break the law of the land.

"'Pears to me that there ain't no sort of use tryin' to make a cent, nowdays," said Elkanah, complainingly. He sat down heavily on the blue-painted settle that shut off the draught from the door, and drawing back from the fire his lumbering and leaden feet, gazed moodily at his loosely-locked hands, that rested between his knees. "'Tain't no use," he repeated.

Brisk Marm Joslin, having carefully boxed the ears of young Amzi, who was filching an apple from the wooden bowl she held in her lap, said, as she added one more to the

heap of peeled fruit, "Wal, Elkanah, you are the beatenest critter to git diskerriged in no time that I almost ever
saw. It's morally sartin that the dimbargo will be declared
off airly in the spring. We've got enough in the house to
last us through till the frost comes out o' the ground; hogs
to kill, a calf comin' in in March, and clothes fit to kerry
us through. Land sake, alive! what does the man want? the
hull airth?"

Old man Joslin made no reply, except in a long-drawn
sigh that seemed to come up laboriously from the very
depths of his homespun garments. He looked fixedly at
his worn and stubby finger-nails and toil-worn hands, and
his watery blue eyes filled with unaccustomed moisture as
he revolved in his mind the desolateness and the poverty
of his lot. It was true that he had enough to eat and drink
for himself and his; but it irked him to think he had prop-
erties lying idle, deteriorating with disuse, and liable to
perish utterly. Besides, Jotham, his eldest and his hope,
had come home from Boston with a hacking cough, and
the doctor said that it looked as if he might go into a de-
cline. Most of the Philbricks—Marm Joslin was a Philbrick
—had gone off in declines; so Elkanah sat and brooded
over his troubles until the short December day was ended,
and the twilight came quickly around the gambrel-roofed
house, investing its sombreness with a yet deeper melancholy, and leaving all the outer landscape vague and weird
in the ghostliness of the approaching winter night.

Old Elkanah rose stiffly, resting his horny hand on the
top of the settle, to help bring his rusty frame into a per-
pendicular. Saying, "Guess I'll tend to the critters," he
shambled out of the end door, and was lost in the shadows of the barn. Her bowl of apples pared, Marm Joslin
also rose, but with a quick alertness strikingly in contrast
with the movements of her husband, wiped her hands,
pulled out the tea-table with a prodigious clatter, and

began laying the cloth. But, pausing in her work for a moment, before she lighted the whale-oil lamp that stood on the mantelpiece, she went to the window, and watched the drooping form of Elkanah as he plodded towards the barn.

"Poor Elkanah," she sighed to herself; "he don't look like the spry young feller he was forty year ago." Then she paused, as if recalling the memory of the young Elkanah who had courted her in Prospect, before the British evacuated Fairport, and while the colonists were not certain whether they were to be citizens of a republic or subjects of a king.

"But he is the beatenest critter," she murmured impatiently. Then she lighted her lamp, set the bowls and pewter trenchers in due order on the board, hung the samp-kettle over the rising blaze, and briskly forwarded preparations for supper.

Meanwhile, old man Joslin slouched into the big barn, and hearing Jotham's hacking cough in the hay-mow, mildly said: "You'd better go into the house, Jotham; I expect your ma wants you, for she's nigh out of firewood. I'll tend to the stock, and when Cal'line gits back from school (and it's nigh time), you tell her she needn't bother about the milkin'. I'll tend to that."

Jotham, lean, long, and lank, slid down from the hay-mow, coughed his acquiescence in the plan laid out by his father, and went into the house, from whose keeping-room windows now streamed forth a ruddy light.

Elkanah watched the youth as he went across the dabbled snow. Then, leaning in the barn-door, he gazed with dry and glassy eyes upward to the wintry sky, across which masses of cloud were driven. He marked the pale white moon, riding as if frighted in the flying scud that hurried by. He looked with unconcern at the twinkling light of the sloop at anchor in the bay, and he thought to himself that she must have an icy berth over there under the lee of Orphan Island. Then, his face growing pale and ghastly as he turned from the dim and lonesome nightlight reflected from the snow, Elkanah felt his way along the familiar boarding of the barn, reached over and took from the cowstall a halter that hung there, mounted to the haymow, threw himself upon his knees as if in silent prayer, climbed painfully and with many a half-uttered groan to the beam that crossed the barn from eaves to eaves, made fast one end of the rope around that timber, slipped the noose over his head, fitted it carefully around his neck, and, with firm-set lip, swung himself off into space.

The news that Elkanah Joslin had hanged himself in his barn traveled around the head of the bay in the most leisurely manner. The discovery of Elkanah was not made by the family until some hours had passed. When Caroline came home from her distant school-teaching, she had taken the milking pails and had gone directly to the barn. Not seeing or hearing her father, she stood in the barn-floor, and cried "Oh, I say, Pa!" but there was no response; and it did not occur to the mind of this healthy and honest young woman that there was anything fearsome or weird in the utter stillness and darkness of the place. Only the champing of the cows at their feed and the occasional grunt of the swine that were housed beneath the barn, disturbed the silence of the hour. So, tucking up her skirts, and singing a fragment of a camp-meeting hymn, like any modern farmer's girl, she went to work milking the three cows, one after the other.

Her mother, however, when Caroline returned with her brimming pails to the house, was more uneasy. Turning it over in her mind, she calculated that Pa had gone down the road a piece, to mend the fence where one of Robinson's cattle—Robinson's cattle were always straying up from their place—had broken through and had got at the fodder. She wondered what possessed him to go out on such an errand so late at night. He had had all day for that job. And she postponed taking up the supper, until Amzi, who was the youngest, and enjoyed his privileges as the spoiled child, made so great ado that she was fain to "dish up."

It was unusual for the head of the house to be absent from the evening meal. Jotham sighed as he looked at his father's empty chair. Caroline chatted about her day's experience in school. Amzi noisily absorbed mush-and-milk and fried mush deluged with New Orleans molasses, enjoying himself very much. The mother looked anxiously out of the window from where she sat, expecting to see the bent form of her husband trudge by on his way to the end door. But he never came. It was late in the night when Caroline went flying down the road to Captain Robinson's, with her white lips too tremulous to tell the doleful tidings to the frightened old man, who came and looked out at her as she pounded her small fists against the windowpanes of his bed-room. He was speedily joined by Mrs. Robinson, also just awakened from her early sleep. Thence the news was carried up to Watson's by Will Robinson, the Captain's burly son. And Sally Watson, before she ran down to comfort her bereaved friend Caroline, fled, trembling with cold and fear, still further up the road to the Sellers' place, woke up the family, and besought Jim Sellers to go with her down to the Joslins. It was commonly reported in the neighborhood that Jim was keeping company with Sally Watson.

And so it came to pass that by two o'clock in the morning a small, but excited group of neighbors was assembled in the keeping-room of the Joslin place, each new recruit coming in with silent and cautious tread, as if afraid of waking the dead man, who lay in the best room on the other side of the front entry. The tea things were taken

up and put away by the first woman who came in. The
family, in their terrified search for Elkanah, had let the
supper-table stand untouched, after they rose to look for
the missing man.

In those primitive days there was very little ceremony
observed in the disposal of the dead. Before a week had
passed, the snow was blowing dryly over the hillock of
icy clods that marked the spot where the mortal part of
the owner of the farm had been laid, just outside of the
tillable land, where, with New England thrift, the family
burying ground had been fenced off. The suicide was a
nine days' wonder in the settlement; yet Elkanah was not
readily forgotten, for, after that night, the few incidents
in the uneventful history of the community were dated
from the time "when Elkanah Joslin hung himself."

Ten years afterwards, that is to say, in 1817, after "the
last war" was over, and peace had returned to the distracted country, the sluggish surface of life around the head
of the Northern Bay was once more stirred to its depths
by the story that sped from lip to lip. Jotham Joslin had
hanged himself from the very identical beam from which
his father swung ten years before. Yet it was not altogether surprising that Jotham, hopeless of life, brooding
over his father's tragic end, and struggling hard to keep
up his drooping spirits, should have finally succumbed
to the depressing influence of the big barn in which he
spent so much of his time. There was much sympathetic
comment on Jotham's provocations. Some murmured that
it was mighty queer that two professors should have thus
flown in the face of Providence. For Jotham was a consistent church-member, as his father had been. Others said
that the son was certain sure to go in the way his father
went. "Sorter runs in the fam'ly," the aged captain down
the road remarked.

Very soon the people began to say that the Joslin barn was haunted. Not that anybody had ever seen or heard anything supernatural about that time-stained building. It was an honest looking and commonplace barn. It even had two glass windows in it, which in those times and in those parts was an uncommon architectural vanity in a barn. But the neighborhood, with common consent, decided that it ought to be haunted, if any building ever should have been. And passers-by began to notice that the diamond-shaped opening in the gable next the road had a peculiarly wicked and sinister expression. "Looks like an evil eye," was what one of the Penobscot men said. And the remark was popularly approved.

It was in 1825 that Amzi Joslin, after having gone down to Ellsworth on a prolonged spree, returned home one hot August night, and without entering the house, softly let himself into the barn by the back entrance, and hanged himself from the now historic timber that crossed the edge of the hay-mow. Amzi had buried his mother and his sister in the stony plot where his father and Jotham reposed under the gloomy and scanty turf. He was lonely, and his complaining wife and sickly baby did not lighten the morbidness of his life. He had taken to drink, as many another poor fool does, hoping that in this he might drown his sorrows, none of which was very weighty or very unique.

"It's a sickly, pindling little critter," said the neighbors, of Amzi's only baby—Amzi junior. "'Twont live to grow up. It's likely that it'll be the last of the Joslins in these parts."

But the infant Amzi lived to disappoint the croaking prophets by coming to manhood, a hale, blithesome, and strapping young fellow. There was no trace of morbidness in the youthful Amzi's disposition. And when he married, and his buxom wife—an importation from Deer Isle—bore

him a quiver-full of happy, hearty children, the old folks
who had predicted the dying out of the Joslins slunk away
to their appropriate burying-grounds, leaving the Joslins
in contented possession of the homestead.

Nevertheless, the barn, with its tragic recollections
clinging around it, stood, a perpetual reminder of the
fateful ending of the career of three of the Joslins. Amzi
often stood and looked at the fatal beam with a curious
feeling of inquiry in his heart. If he had not been of a
cheerful and sunny disposition, he would have dwelt with
misgivings on the possibility of his, at last, coming to end
his days on that timber. The thought sometimes flashed
through his mind, but was quickly put away. Younger
members of the family, to whom the gossips of the region
had dutifully told the tale of the haunted barn, snatched
a fearful joy in peering upwards to the tragical beam in
the darkness of the winter night, imagining that they saw
a ghostly ancestor hanging there. But the young Joslins,
as a rule, avoided being in the barn alone after dark. Amzi
never forgot what had happened there; and he often
thought, as he plodded about his work in the cow-bay,
or in the mow, that it would be a mercy if the old barn
should be struck by lightning, and burn to the ground. It
was a sort of reminder, so he thought, to the children that
might come after him. They would think of the three men
who had taken violent hands against their own lives in
that ancestral barn. He even asked himself if it were possible, that, in his old age, with mental faculties dimmed
and life a burden by reason of infirmities, he might not
be enticed to his doom by the evil influences of the place.

But Amzi Joslin lived to a good old age, and died as a
Christian should, in his own bed, surrounded by wife and
children. All but one. His oldest son, Rufus, went before
his father. The unhappy Rufus, inheriting a strain of the

"old Joslin blood," as the old women said, followed after the ill example of Elkanah, Jotham, and the first Amzi. No need for us to tell how the good man wept over the sorrowful tragedy of the young life snuffed out so needlessly, untimely. The old man aged swiftly after this happened, and not a few of the community roundabout began to shake their heads, and whisper that old Amzi would go the way of the other self-destroyers. But the farmer lived on patiently and trustfully, dying, as we have said, at a good old age and in a Christian manner.

In 188-, after more than one generation of Joslins had come and gone, the old barn had acquired a name and repute throughout the region altogether unenviable. It is not necessary nor desirable to tell here how two other men of the Joslin family, as they grew up and were old enough to take in the full significance of the doleful story of their ancestral barn, became fixed in their belief that other suicides must follow. Suffice to say that, in course of years, but at long intervals, the historic timber across the hay-mow bore evil fruit twice more. Something ailed the place, men said. There were strange lights about the farm o' nights. Sobs and whispering murmurs drifted down from the uplands on the wild March winds, or sighed in the snow-squalls that whirled around the place as the December gales came on apace.

No wonder that strangers, passing along the road, stopped and looked curiously at the barn, whose tragedy had been told by so many country firesides and in so many solitary wayside inns. It was the custom for every passenger along the road to turn his head and look at the old barn, now black with age, hoary with the gray lichens that clung to its roof, and still winking with its single evil eye in the gable. And when the Blue Hill stage drove that way, as it did when the upper road was heavy with the winter's

snow, the passengers all craned their necks from the side
of the wagon, and stared at the Joslin barn as long as it
was in sight.

These things annoyed Mrs. Joslin, widow of Stephen,
who had died in an honest and respectable manner. She
knew that Stephen had worried a good deal over the *felo de
se* of his father, and that he had had a fight within himself
to keep back from the path which had brought so many
Joslins to the fatal beam. She knew that her Stephen had
sometimes thought that the evil one was in that barn, and
that he pursued him, the eldest representative of the Joslin name, continually suggesting that this was the way out
of the world for him. And so, although her husband had
never yielded to these wicked thoughts, she had the family
history so burned into her very soul, that it fretted her to
see the gossiping people of the neighborhood whispering
and nodding their wise heads among themselves. "If I was
a Joslin, instead of a Gardner," she would say, "I just believe that these everlasting tattle-tales would drive me to
hanging myself."

Not so thought Charlie, the widow's handsome and
only son. Charlie was a prime favorite through all the
country side. None so stalwart and lithe as he. To see him
swinging his scythe as he strode down the mowing-field
with rhythmic step, leveling a mighty swath, was as good
as a heroic poem on canvas. His melodious voice resound-
ed like a trumpet when he called to his oxen, or chanted
a rural ditty as he came from afield, hearty and fresh as if
he had not passed a long and toilsome day at the plough
or with the hay-rake. And many a country lass, never quite
unmindful of the tragic story of the old barn, forgot it all
when she looked into Charlie Joslin's brown and handsome
face. His dancing blue eyes, full of fun, and mild with the
light of a cheery disposition, sent the tell-tale blush to
many a coy young maiden's cheek, as she "passed the time

o' day" with the young and thriving heir-apparent of the
Joslin place.

But of all the girls that looked with a little thrill of rapture after Charlie's lithe and graceful figure, and marked
the crisp brightness of his wavy hair, none seemed to have
the power to long arrest his roving eye. It was a pity, too,
the neighbors said, that Charlie should put off marrying.
There was no knowing what might happen. The Joslins
were a cur'ous family. There had been many mighty sing'lar
things happening at the Joslin place. And Charlie was the
last of the name. If he should live to be an old bachelor,
he might get a twist into his mind, just as so many of the
Joslins had afore him. Not that Charlie was the least bit
tetched. He was as sound as a dollar. But there's no telling.
And the wise ones shook their heads apprehensively.

If any of these croakings reached Charlie's ears, he gave
them no heed. To him the blowing of the wind, or the
fluttering of the swallows under the eaves of the old barn,
were just as worthy of a second thought as the idle gossip
he heard among his mates, about the spell that so many
thought rested on the Joslin farm. It was a wholesome
place, he thought. The sun poured down its fullness, rip-
ening the early harvest apples that hung in the dark green
leaves of the little orchard, yellowing the grain that rose
and

fell in the upper field to the wanton straying wind
from the head of the bay, and giving the thick grass in the
mowing-field a more intense emerald, day by day. It was
a cheerful place, withal, in spite of the dark frown of the
historic barn, and the evil eye that twinkled in its gable
end. The hollyhocks and sunflowers drank in and yielded
again, with a rapturous gladness of life, the warm sunshine
and the languorous summer air. The very bees that kept
up their murmurous song, as they filled themselves among
the clover tops, and hied to the warm hives at the edge of

the meadow, buzzed a cheery and satisfied hymn of peace
and comfort. There was no room in Charlie's merry heart
for foreboding of dark shadows of what might be to come.
And if the thought of what had gone before ever crossed
his mind, it was when, sinking into the tranquil slumbers
of healthy and careless youth, he whispered to his inmost
self that the jocund world was too good to leave.

Nevertheless, Master Charlie would not hear to any
suggestion that the barn should be torn down. There were
timorous spirits in the vicinity, who regarded the ancestral barn as a blot on the landscape, a rallying point, perhaps, for the phantoms and hobgoblins of the air and
earth. It is in the semi-farming and seafaring life of a region like that around the head of the Northern Bay, that
one must look for a sturdy survival of all the old English
provincial traditions and superstitions. Here it is that
one is told of death-warnings, omens, signs in the sky or
on the waters, strange noises in the forest, charms, love
potions, and occult devices of various sorts. No wonder
that the ghost-dreading folk who passed the Joslin place,
many times in the year, looked at the barn, in which so
many tragedies had been enacted, as something quite too
uncanny and unwholesome to be left standing; a standing
invitation, so to speak, for the last of the Joslins to come
in and hang himself. But the jovial master of the place
would not listen to reason. He was not only sure that he
wouldn't take the fatal leap from the traditional beam, but
that nobody else ever would.

"He just thinks the world and all of that barn," grumbled one of the neighbors, surly Major Payne, who, having
come home from the wars minus one leg and plus a pension, had set himself up as oracle of the Northern Bay and
Penobscot country.

"No, he wouldn't have a single board taken off of that
ere barn, 'cept it rotted off, for no money. I just think

that Charlie Joslin considers that barn as a sort of ancestral tomb. So many of his relations have ended their days
there, that it's got to be a sort of sacred place to him. It
may be sacred to him, but it's an infernal nuisance to the
rest of the neighborhood. And that's a fact."

But there was one member of the Joslin family who
really did wish that Charlie would tear down the fateful
barn; and that was Nelly Webber. Now Nelly was only a
hired girl in the Joslin place. Local usage forbids that we
should call her a servant. She was emphatically one of the
family, as all native-born family-helps are in the region of
which I am discoursing. The handmaid and the farm-hand
are part and parcel with the household as long as they stay,
sitting at the same board and respected as the children of
the house, provided they are worthy of respect. They are,
in fact, the children of other families whose social standing in the widely scattered community is as high as that
in which they temporarily serve; and of such was Nelly
Webber.

Nelly's head was well filled with a goodly assortment of
ghostly and supernatural lore. She could tell the stage of
the tide by the cat's eyes; knew the best time for pig-kill-
ing by the phase of the moon; had heard drowned men's
voices in the tide-rips hailing each other; was certain of
the quality of the hay crop when she had examined a bum-
ble bee's nest, and found significance in every incident
of daily routine, from the dropping of a dish-clout to the
color of the hen that had stolen her nest away.

And yet Nelly was not a sour and cross old maid, who
took a savage pleasure in revenging on her fellow-beings
the disappointments of her own life. Nelly was a merry
and winsome fresh-faced country girl, from Blue Hill. She
"lived out" because she did not like her step-mother, and
because she had views in life that included the Normal
School at Fairport, and the expenditure of more money

than her second-wife-ridden father would allow her. Never-theless, Nelly was strongly infected with superstitious no-tions; and she had a morbid aversion to the Joslin barn, and that aversion feebly extended to the Joslin family. But as her present engagement was the most eligible that had offered when she set out to "hoe her own row," as she was wont to express it, she waived the Joslin family ghosts, and accepted the situation with a lively sense of danger, which was not wholly without its charm to her adventur-ous spirit. And the cruel thing about all this was, that Charlie loved Nelly. It was a long time before this awful yet pride-compelling fact dawned on Nelly's mind. For the shrewd girl was well aware that Widow Joslin had other views for her only son, than a marriage with a portionless girl with a step-mother. Matilda Sellers, heir-presumptive to a farm on the other side of the river, and the ferry-right into the bargain, was a more eligible match for the hand-some heir of all the Joslins.

It was in secret, and in fear of his mother's wrath, that Charlie carried on his wooing of the coy Nelly. Her birthday present from the young man was a "Friendship's Offering," gorgeously bound and gilt-edged, and bear-ing on its fly-leaf, in hastily penciled secrecy, "Keep this dark." Sly Master Charlie meant to win the consent of Nelly, and then, secure in the possession of her love, brave the opposition of his mother. But the fair maid was obdu-rate. She vowed and protested that she was "keeping com-pany with no feller"; that she would "have nothing to do with beaux"; and that until she had been through at least one term of the Normal School, when she should be fit to teach, she would have nothing to do with love or lovers.

"You're a hard-hearted and calculating thing," said Charlie, regarding her with new admiration, kindled by her very refusal to listen to his suit. "You'd be a regular tearer on a farm of your own. Gosh! how you'd make the help stand round!"

But compliments and hints were wasted on the matter-of-fact handmaid. She had laid out her career, and it did not include an early marriage with anybody, least of all with one of the haunted Joslins. So she shook her dancing curls at Master Charlie, and merrily defied him to come on with the allurements which he promised to add to those already set forth. The saucy beauty was a little pained, perhaps, to be obliged to say "no" to so handsome and likely a young fellow as Charlie. But Nelly had put her foot down, and when that remarkably well-shaped member was in an attitude of figurative determination, it was immovable. She loyally kept from the suspicious mother the secret that the young man had enjoined upon her; but she inwardly burned to let the gossips know that Charlie Joslin and the well-tilled farm could be hers for the taking.

Nellie's obstinacy only strengthened the determination of the willful young man to win her heart. A more observant woman than Widow Joslin would have detected the courtship, vain as it was, that went on under her eyes. But she saw nothing. With a fierce repression, Charlie went about his round of homely tasks, laying out the work of the farm with a master's hand, and inspiring his helpers with his own cheery and lively temper, and enlivening the old place with his unfailing good-humor and blitheness. But the poor lad's heart was often heavy. Sometimes, when he caught a glimpse of the coldness that shone in Nelly's dark eyes, or was ravished anew by a sudden vision of her beauty, he made a half-choked excuse, and hurried away from the house, to forget his sorrows, if possible, in a long and impetuous walk over the wind-swept hills.

Many of the sharp-eyed women of the neighborhood noted Charlie's not unfrequent moodiness, fleeting though

the clouds were on his sunny face. But they never suspected the cause of his disquiet. Even the loving vigilance of
the mother failed to see that any serious grief moved the
young man to behavior unusual; and nobody, not even
the cause of all this perturbation, could know the anguish
with which the rejected suitor, bent on gaining a revoca-
tion that seemed hopeless, buried himself in the hay of
that fatal mow, and communed savagely with his fate. If
Nelly could, at such times, have seen the exceeding great
sorrow of her lover, mayhap she would have been moved
to relenting. More likely, she would have been confirmed
in her dread of the suicidal Joslins.

But there was no fear of Charlie. He contemplated his
future with unclouded eyes, and his wholesome nature,
hard though his lot might be, could not play tentatively on
the verge of self-destruction. Nothing short of a blow that
would be heavy enough to overturn his reason, could tempt
the lighthearted Charlie to take a desperate step. And he
yet had hope. He believed that Nelly was only trying him.
She knew that he had a right to look higher for a wife. She
would run no risks of dissatisfaction after marriage. She
would not risk any possibility of having a difference in
fortune "thrown up at her" when it should be too late to
retrace her steps. And without taking so low a view of the
case, Charlie revolved all these things in his heart, listening
ever to the siren that sung of distant but possible bliss.

Master Charlie had a rude awakening. It was in haying
time, and the last load had that afternoon been hauled
into the barn, and pitched to lofts and mows. The day's
work was done, and silence and peace reigned over the
Joslin homestead, save where the heir of the farm lightly
leaned at the window and talked with the girl who stood
dawdling within the keeping-room. The widow had gone
down the road to visit a sick neighbor. The tired farm-
hands had sought their unusually early rest. Only Nelly

and her persistent lover were left to whisper together in the fast-gathering darkness. Great masses of black cloud were rolling up in the westward, and a greenish crepuscular light was filtered over the opposite shore of the Northern Bay, suggesting a thunder-storm and a summer rain.

No matter; the hay was all under cover, and everything was made trim and snug for any change that might come in the weather. But this was not in Charlie's mind, as he stood there pleading by turns, and by turns bantering the sorely beset young girl. He would not take "no" for an answer, he said, and so he foolishly rushed on to his fate.

"I should think you might give a man a decided answer," he said, half pettishly.

The girl's eyes flashed in the deepening gloom as she tartly replied. "What do you want for an answer, Charlie Joslin?" she cried, with rising anger. "Haven't I told you fifty times that I wouldn't have you, nor any other man, for that matter? And what's more, I wouldn't marry a Joslin if he was to get down on his bended knees; and you know the reason why. So there, now!"

Master Charlie had got his answer. He went away half stunned, for the first time realizing in the cruel speech of the girl the depth that separated her from him. The flash of lightning that suddenly illumined the darkness in the western sky was not more vivid than the beam of light that had laid bare to the young man's mental vision the utter hopelessness of his lot. And, the face of nature changed to his eyes that looked without seeing, he stumbled aimlessly and with sluggish step down through the orchard, whose fragrant fruit was brushed by his beautiful bare head as he passed beneath.

Big drops of rain were falling when Charlie, having mounted the highest upland swale on the farm, turned aimlessly and made his weary way back to the homestead. Reaching it, he hesitated to go in, stood wondering which way he should next turn, to be rid of the nightmare that pressed him down, and then wandered away again into the darkness like a lost man.

The Widow Joslin was scant of breath when she came hurrying home, scolding because the chamber windows were not closed, although there was a smart shower coming over, and because Charlie had not come down the road after her, and she an old woman poking home in the dark. The rain fell in such sheets as it falls in a New England thunder shower, or in the tropics, with a whirring and seething sound. The widow was always fidgety in a thunderstorm; her brother had been killed by lightning, and she never could abide thunder from that day to this. And she went complainingly to the rear of the house to make all fast, for the rain was pelting on the western windows.

"Land sakes alive!" she screamed. "What a flash and crash! I just believe that that struck somewheres nigh here. Did you ever, Nelly?" and the frightened woman began to drag out a feather-bed, by way of shield from the electric storm.

Just then, Nelly, whose face was away from the windows, saw a bright red light on the opposite wall of the room. She quickly turned her head, and, with a throbbing heart, cried, "Oh, Mis' Joslin, the barn's all afire!" The fated hour for that ancestral edifice had come. It had been struck by lightning.

The widow Joslin's fright vanished at the awful sight of the haunted barn in flames. With something like calmness, she looked, and only said, "I calculate that Charlie is out there fighting the fire."

The two women snatched up such outer coverings as came to hand, and, while the widow went to the stairdoor to waken the men with her shrill call, Nelly rushed out into the rain, crying "Fire!" with all her small might. It was needless. The bright flames flashed far and wide the signal of a great calamity. The neighbors ran breath-lessly to the rescue, bearing the few buckets that formed the only appliance for extinguishing fires that the region boasted. It was too late to save the haunted barn. Possi-bly, the men worked with less enthusiasm than they would have if the structure had been more highly valued in their eyes. They contented themselves with trying to save the house. The barn with its rich store of hay and grain, and with the goodly stock of horses therein, must go.

There was something awesome in the sight. A fire in the country is always more terrible than in the city. The flames are uncontrollable. The best that can be done, usu-ally, is to confine the destruction to the building in which it has seated itself. But this fire raged on, while the rain fell hissing into the red ruin which it could not check. The thunderous artillery of the sky never ceased its booming volleys, as the leaping fires sprang upward into the inky blackness of the night And as the country folk saw the charred framework of the old barn stand out with startling distinctness in the lurid light, they shivered to think of the tragedies that had taken place under the roof now fly-ing from its place in red cinders, and had crept along that square stick of timber now blazing and crumbling before their eyes.

Were those fiery ghosts, or only shuddering flames, that went so swiftly off to the eastward, momently light-ing up the gloom into which they vanished? Was that a cloud of burning hay that was hurled upward by the eddy-ing draft of air? or was it some dreadful shape, some im-age of a dead and gone Joslin, hurrying away to a new rendezvous? and the fatal beam, would it never burn quite through and drop, an accursed thing? Nelly Webber wept as she looked; wept, she knew not why. And her lively imagination saw dreadful things innumerable in the burn-ing of the barn. And when the reddened skeleton fell in with a crash, and the volleying tumult of smoke and flame ascended on high, a suppressed shout that might have been a mighty sigh, and was very like a cheer, went up from the awestricken throng huddled on the rain-drenched slope before the house.

But where was the masterful Charlie while all this ruin was being wrought? The widow missed his voice cheering on the men. The men, even as they hurried about their arduous work, whispered ominously among themselves. And when the fire had died down, the other buildings saved, the horrible brightness quenched in an angry and sullen glare, and the widow had time to recover something of her scattered carefulness for other things than the ruined barn, she cried, with motherly anguish, "Where is that boy?"

Vain cry! If the flaming herald of disaster that had alarmed the country from Fairport to Blue Hill, and had lighted the sky so redly that the people fifteen miles away thought that the town at the port had been laid in ashes, had not warned homeward the absent heir of the Joslin place, of what avail was his mother's feeble call?

He never came. For days, until late into the autumn, when the sumachs burned on the hillside like live coals, and the maples flamed yellowly against the black spruces on Orphan Island, the sympathetic neighbors hunted for the lost Charlie. With chilly dread of finding him, they dragged the Northern Bay, or they searched the tangled bushes that skirted in dense growths the bluffy shores. Wherever a man could have fallen in a sudden faint or in an unwary moment, they looked.

Even in the ashes of the barn, now reduced to only a heap of almost impalpable powder, did they furtively pursue their quest. The uncontrolled fire had licked up everything so clean, that scarcely a cinder was left of the vast and massive frame-work of the barn, that had been built with so much care, and had seen so much sorrow. Here and there, however, the larger bones of the poor dumb creatures that had perished in the famous fire, were found bleached and half calcined by the fierceness of the heat that had raged around them. And one day, Hiram Grindle, holding up with an awe-struck face, as he rose from a rummage among the ashes, a fragment of ivory whiteness, said: "I swan to man! That's a human critter's bone!"

Then Obadiah Mullet, taking it from him, cast his eyes about him, and whispered to his mate: "This is just where the edge of the hay-mow must have been. Supposin' that a man had flung himself from that beam on the night of the fire—" but Obadiah did not finish his sentence. The suggestion was too awful.

"He was the seventh and the last," said Hiram. And a tear glittered in his honest eyes.

"Never mind; let's say nothin' about it. Perhaps we are mistaken; there's no tellin'." So, with a mighty effort, the two men shouldered over the tottering wall that bounded the pit, which had been a subway beneath the barn, and in which the relics lay in a heap. The stone-work fell in with a great clatter, and a cloud of dust and ashes rose like a column over the wreck. And under this tumult of masonry now lay forever hidden whatever of mystery remained of the hereditary barn.

THE HAWTHORNE FARM MYSTERY
Jeremiah L. M'Carthy
(1888)

Did I not know, beyond the shadow of a doubt, that the story I am about to tell is the plain truth and nothing but the truth, these lines would never have been written, and the strange story, of which they form a part, would be locked fast in my heart just as it has been locked for seventeen years, and not exposed to the sneers and scoffs of a doubting world. Though, when I think the matter over, I come to the conclusion that the doubting world is not to be blamed so much after all, for my story certainly does seem more like the offspring of a vivid imagination than the plain, truthful narrative that I declare it to be. Still it is annoying to feel that a statement which you make in good faith, and which you know to be the unvarnished truth, not in any way adorned with the trappings of fancy, will be received as the merest falsehood, and the maker of it an intentional deceiver. It is not pleasant, I repeat, to know this, and, therefore, I have hesitated long about giving my story to a skeptical world. However, I am now resolved to relate my strange experience, be it believed or not. I believe it to be my duty to do so. My story will prove to the reader, if he is not of a doubting disposition, how true is the saying that truth is stranger than fiction, and it will show what strange mysteries exist concealed from our knowledge in this very queer world of ours.

If anyone is qualified by experience to write about the queer sights and adventures of this life, I think I am the person, for no man, I am sure, has had a larger experience of both than the writer of these lines. Like many a man before me, who has set out to seek his fortune, I have traveled extensively in my time, and seen life in many phases and aspects. I have sought the fickle jade, fortune, in Europe and Australia, and in far off Africa and India, as well as in my native country. I have seen strange things, indeed, and met with stranger adventures, while wresting fortune from mother earth in the gold mines of California and Australia, among the rough motley adventures of the one, and the convicts and bushrangers of the other. I have sought fortune in the diamond mines of Africa, and have seen queer things there, both among the miners, and the weird savages of that benighted region; and I have met with adventures in India—that paradise of murder and super-stition—among the thugs and other fanatical demons of that accursed clime, which if related would cause people to stamp me a a romancer—not to use a stronger term—of the first water. But the strangest experience of my life was met with, not among the rough miners of California and Australia, nor among the fierce savages white and black of the South African diamond fields. nor yet the merciless Phansigars of the land of the Hindoo. It was in a plain, commonplace farmhouse, in a dull prosaic New England village, that the weird experience, which I can truly say is the strangest and most mysterious I have ever met with in all my eventful life, and which forms the subject of this story, was encountered.

It happened this way. Seventeen years ago, when I was a much younger man than I am at present, I was engaged in farming in the little town of S—, in Massachusetts. The farm on which I had lived was not a desirable one in some respects. The buildings on it were good enough, but the land was poor, being rocky and ill-adapted to agricultural purposes. I had rented it by an arrangement I had made with the owner, but I did not intend to settle on it permanently and was looking around for a more suitable location. One day, I heard of a farm which was offered at a figure which I considered very cheap. This farm was situated in the town of R—, about ten miles from the place I was living in. It was called Hawthorne Farm, owing to the profusion of hawthorne bushes growing about it, and when I examined it, in company with the agent who had charge of it, I was very much pleased with it. The farmhouse and the out-buildings connected with it were in excellent condition, and required but little repairing, while the land surrounding them was, as well as I could judge, greatly superior to that of the farm I was occupying. I was surprised at the price which I thought extremely cheap for such a place, and without further talk on the subject I purchased the farm, paying the price down. In the light of subsequent occurrences, I can see now why the place was disposed of so cheaply, but I knew nothing about it then, and grasped eagerly at what I considered a bargain. I brought my wife to see it, and she was as pleased with the farm as I was, and approved the purchase. A day or two after we moved into Hawthorne Farm. It was a warm day in June on which we moved, and like all such work, especially in the country, it was a tiresome job. It was almost dark when the last of our things was conveyed into our new domicile and we were tired enough. So after supper was eaten we retired at once to bed and were sound asleep in a few minutes. We arose early next morning much refreshed by our night's rest. We spent the following day in arranging our household effects and putting things to rights. It was pleasant labor with us, as we were delighted with our new home.

By evening we had settled about everything and were, as you may suppose, tired enough; so, when supper was eaten, we all went to bed early, looking forward to a good night's rest. Right here I will give the reader a diagram of the ground floor of Hawthorne Farm, in order that he will be able to clearly understand what follows. The rooms on the ground floor were two in number, a parlor and kitchen. The former was in the front of the house, and the latter in the back. We had a bed-room of the parlor temporarily, and it communicated with the kitchen by a door between the two apartments, which, like those in all farmhouses, were large and roomy. The kitchen was the usual kind of kitchen seen in all farmhouses, and there was a door in it leading out into an entry at the side of the kitchen, at the end of which entry was a door leading to a large cellar underneath the house. There was nothing peculiar or worthy of especial mention about the rooms, they being the plain, old-fashioned apartments to be met with in all country houses, so they do not require any extended description here. Well, I was just dropping into a doze, when I heard a noise which filled me with amazement. It came from the stairs leading down into the cellar, and as I listened in momentary astonishment, I heard the sound plain. It was the most peculiar sound I had ever heard. It was as if somebody were walking backward down the stairs dragging something after him which bumped at every step. Thinking it was some tramp who had gained access to the cellar, I got up and going out into the entry pulled the cellar door open, and in sharp tones asked who was there. No answer was returned to my question, even when I repeated it, nor could I see anything in the shape of man or animal. Yet the strange noise kept on while I stood there; bump, bump, bump, down the stairs, just as if you dragged a heavy object, such as a sack of potatoes down the stairs. When it had apparently reached the foot of the stairs, the noise culminated in a sound like that of a heavy blow, followed by a smothered shriek, and all was still.

Going back to the bedroom I found my wife awake, she having been roused from sleep by the strange sound as I was, and telling her of the mysterious occurrences on the cellar stairs, we talked it over for a while, wondering what had caused it. While we were conversing, my two children, a boy and girl, aged respectively twelve and fifteen, who slept in rooms overhead, came running down stairs, saying that a woman was crying np in their rooms, and sure enough we heard the sound of crying overhead. Hastily lighting a lamp, I went upstairs and searched about, but though I hunted everywhere I could not find trace of anything, man or beast. All the time, like the noise on the cellar stairs, the crying noise continued. It was a strange, sobbing sound, just like a woman crying. I thought it was a cat, but it could not have been caused by one, for not a trace of one could be seen, nor was there any way in which a cat could gain access to the rooms, the windows being tightly locked and shuttered. I searched both rooms thoroughly, but I was compelled at length to give up the search baffled. Suddenly, as it had commenced, the strange noise ceased, and after waiting for a few moments for it to begin again, I went down stairs, utterly mystified. I found all quiet below, although my wife and the children were much frightened, and we stayed awake an hour or two awaiting further developments. Nothing occurred, however, and we went to bed again, the children occupying temporary beds in our room, as they were afraid to go upstairs again. At breakfast next morning my wife and I talked the subject of the queer noises over. Naturally we were greatly puzzled by them, and did not know what cause to ascribe them to, for we never dreamed that the sounds were caused by other than an earthly agency. Still, we did not attach any importance to the matter, as we were plain, practical people without a particle of superstition in our natures, so concluding that the strange noises were mere temporary disturbances, caused no doubt by rats or cats, and that they would disappear finally we dismissed the subject from our minds, and soon other matters engrossed our attention.

When bed-time came we retired as usual, I having previously locked every door and seen to every fastening. I had not the slightest thought that the strange noises would disturb us again, but I was disagreeably mistaken. Scarcely had we laid down, when, as before, the bumping commenced on the cellar stairs. There it was, clearly defined. Bump, bump, bump, down the stairs as before, winding up when the invisible disturbers had arrived at the bottom, with the sound of a dull, heavy blow and then a stifled scream.

Then happened what did not happen on the first night. Just as the scream died away on the cellar stairs, the doors, which I have mentioned as standing in the entry leading down into the cellar, flew violently open, although I could have sworn I had fastened it securely five minutes before. I knew by the sound the door made that something had banged it open, although I could not see, and as I hurriedly sprang out of bed, lit a lamp and investigated, I found that my surmise was correct. There was the door, which I was almost certain I had securely locked, wide open. Going downstairs, I explored the cellar thoroughly, but could see or hear nothing, not even a mouse.

Going upstairs again I fastened the cellar door and went into the bedroom, where I found the children, having ran down a second time from their bed-rooms, overhead, disturbed and frightened by the crying sounds, which as before, had followed the bumping noise on the cellar stairs. Taking the lamp with me I hurried upstairs and searched again in every direction for the source of the mysterious sounds, but as before I was at length forced to give up, completely non-plussed by the mysterious affair. I could discover nothing to throw any light on the matter. After listening to the strange noise, which was just like the sound of a woman crying and sobbing, until it suddenly ceased, I went downstairs where I found my wife and the children very much frightened. They wanted to leave the house at once, but I quieted their fears, telling them that I would clear up the mystery soon.

And this I was determined to do. I made up my mind to solve the weird mystery if it was possible. Next night we awaited the manifestations with interest. Heretofore they had occurred soon after sundown but this time they did not occur till late. Taking a loaded pistol with me, I went upstairs, resolved to find the cause of the mysterious sounds, leaving my wife and the children below, where the bright light of a lamp served to keep up their courage. I took no light with me, thinking that I could solve the mystery just as well, if not better in the dark. It was seven o'clock when I took my position in the room overhead of the parlor, where I noticed the sounds always came from. I sat in the dark for two hours, waiting to hear the strange noise. It did not occur very soon, and I thought it would not come at all, but just as the clock below in the kitchen was striking nine it suddenly broke out. It sounded quite near me, though I could not make out from what direction of the room it came, and I had an excellent opportunity to hear it. It was a low, moaning sound, inexpressibly mournful to listen to. It seemed to be a woman who was in deep grief, and she appeared to be grieving and moaning about something. I strained my eyes through the darkness, with my weapon ready to shoot any object which presented itself, but as before I could see nothing. I felt my hands carefully along the walls of the room, but no door or opening of any kind rewarded my patient search. As before I was completely puzzled by the queer sounds, which had now ceased as abruptly as they had begun. Before I could pursue my investigation farther, piercing screams from downstairs caused me to hurriedly run below, where I found that the bumping noise had commenced on the cellar-stairs, Bump—bump, it went down to the foot of the stair case, where, as before, it finished with the sound of a heavy blow followed by a smothered scream, and it frightened the children so that they screamed with terror, while my wife was so worked up that she fainted dead away.

There was now no further use in closing our eyes to the plain truth. Hawthorne Farm was haunted. The fact was plainly apparent. What caused the strange noises if not disembodied spirits? Next day I removed my family to a cottage some distance from the haunted farmhouse which I hired for their temporary reception. I then went back to Hawthorne Farm, determined to give the place a final examination before I left it forever. I searched every room from the garret to the bottom thoroughly, but daylight revealed no more to unravel the mystery than lamplight. The farmhouse was a two-story building with two rooms on each floor, including two garrets, front and back. The garrets were dreary places, with sloping ceiling, partly lit by a scuttle overhead. I explored them thoroughly, but they contained nothing bur dust and cobwebs. I then examined the other rooms, especially the one where the crying sounds occurred, but no discovery rewarded my quest. I spent half a day exploring the rooms but to no purpose. Nothing could be found to throw any light on the mystery. I then descended to the cellar and examined it for several hours. I found nothing peculiar about the cellar. It was like the cellars in most farmhouses, excellently built. The walls which composed the foundation of the house were of strong masonry, closely cemented together so that not even a mouse could squeeze through. The floor was composed of stout planking, and two or three small windows in the walls admitted a meagre light into the cellar through their dusty and cobwebby panes. The cellar contained nothing but a few old boxes and earthenware jars. Thinking that the explanation of the strange affair could be found buried at the foot of the cellar-stairs, I had the ground dug up to the depth of several feet, but nothing was found.

I was dumbfounded; it was the most puzzling affair I had ever encountered. I kept the matter as quiet as possible, but it gradually leaked out, as such things will, and crowds of curious people came from the surrounding country to gaze at the haunted farm and glean what information they could in regard to it. I questioned the neighbors about the matter, but none of them knew anything about the farm, as they did not live very near it. All I could learn was that the last family occupying it had moved away some months ago, since which time it had remained vacant until I had taken it. Nobody could see why it should become the scene of supernatural manifestations, as there was no record of any terrible occurrence happening there. Nevertheless, Hawthorne Farm was haunted if ever a place was, and I had been shamefully swindled by a rascally real estate agent. The latter must have known the stigma on the farm, when he disposed of the farm to me at such a cheap figure. I tried to hunt him up, but he had left for parts unknown. The farm was now a white elephant on my hands, for I could not occupy it myself, and I could not dispose of it to anybody, knowing the strange mystery connected with it. But while I was debating what to do with the place, the matter was settled for me in a manner quite unexpected. A terrible thunder storm arose one night, and a bolt of lighting, striking the farmhouse, set it on fire, and it was burned to the ground, outbuildings and all. And thus was settled forever, though not in the

way it should have been, the mystery of the haunted farm.
And do I believe that Hawthorne Farm was really haunted
by disembodied spirits! Most assuredly I do; and, further-
more, although I have been a great skeptic on such matters
prior to my experience at Hawthorne Farm, ever since I
have been a firm believer in tbs supernatural, and also in
the theory advanced by Shakespeare, when the great bard
makes Hamlet say:

> "There are more things in heaven and earth,
>   Horatio, than are dreamt of in your philosophy."

THE HAUNTED ORCHARD
Richard Le Gallienne
(1912)

Spring was once more in the world. As she sang to herself in the faraway woodlands her voice reached even the ears of the city, weary with the long winter. Daffodils flowered at the entrances to the Subway, furniture removing vans blocked the side streets, children clustered like blossoms on the doorsteps, the open cars were running, and the cry of the "cash clo'" man was once more heard in the land.

Yes, it was the spring, and the city dreamed wistfully of lilacs and the dewy piping of birds in gnarled old apple-trees, of dogwood lighting up with sudden silver the thickening woods, of water-plants unfolding their glossy scrolls in pools of morning freshness.

On Sunday mornings, the outbound trains were thronged with eager pilgrims, hastening out of the city, to behold once more the ancient marvel of the spring; and, on Sunday evenings, the railway termini were aflower with banners of blossom from rifled woodland and orchard carried in the hands of the returning pilgrims, whose eyes still shone with the spring magic, in whose ears still sang the fairy music.

And as I beheld these signs of the vernal equinox, I knew that I, too, must follow the music, forsake awhile the beautiful siren we call the city, and in the green silences meet once more my sweetheart Solitude.

As the train drew out of the Grand Central, I hummed to myself,

"I've a neater, sweeter maiden, in a greener, cleaner land"—

and so I said good-by to the city, and went forth with beating heart to meet the spring.

I had been told of an almost forgotten corner on the south coast of Connecticut, where the spring and I could live in an inviolate loneliness—a place uninhabited save by birds and blossoms, woods and thick grass, and an occasional silent farmer, and pervaded by the breath and shimmer of the Sound.

Nor had rumor lied, for when the train set me down at my destination I stepped out into the most wonderful green hush, a leafy Sabbath silence, through which the very train, as it went farther on its way, seemed to steal as noiselessly as possible for fear of breaking the spell.

After a winter in the town, to be dropped thus suddenly into the intense quiet of the country-side makes an almost ghostly impression upon one, as of an enchanted silence, a silence that listens and watches but never speaks, finger on lip. There is a spectral quality about everything upon which the eye falls: the woods, like great green clouds, the wayside flowers, the still farm-houses half lost in orchard bloom—all seem to exist in a dream. Everything is so still, everything so supernaturally green. Nothing moves or talks, except the gentle susurrus of the spring wind swaying the young buds high up in the quiet sky, or a bird now and again, or a little brook singing softly to itself among the crowding rushes.

Though from the houses one notes here and there there are evidently human inhabitants of this green silence, none are to be seen. I have often wondered where the countryfolk hide themselves, as I have walked hour after hour, past farm and croft and lonely door-yards, and never caught sight of a human face. If you should want to ask the way, a farmer is as shy as a squirrel, and if you knock at a farm-house door, all is as silent as a rabbit-warren.

As I walked along in the enchanted stillness, I came at length to a quaint old farm-house—"old Colonial" in its architecture—embowered in white lilacs, and surrounded by an orchard of ancient apple-trees which cast a rich shade on the deep spring grass. The orchard had the impressiveness of those old religious groves, dedicated to the strange worship of sylvan gods, gods to be found now only in Horace or Catullus, and in the hearts of young poets to whom the beautiful antique Latin is still dear.

The old house seemed already the abode of Solitude. As I lifted the latch of the white gate and walked across the forgotten grass, and up on to the veranda already festooned with wistaria, and looked into the windows, I saw Solitude sitting by an old piano, on which no composer later than Bach had ever been played.

In other words, the house was empty; and going round to the back, where old barns and stables leaned together as if falling asleep, I found a broken pane, and so climbed in and walked through the echoing rooms. The house was very lonely. Evidently no one had lived in it for a long time. Yet it was all ready for some occupant, for whom it seemed to be waiting. Quaint old four-poster bedsteads stood in three rooms—dimity curtains and spotless linen—old oak chests and mahogany presses; and, opening drawers in Chippendale sideboards, I came upon beautiful frail old silver and exquisite china that set me thinking of a beautiful grandmother of mine, made out of old lace and laughing wrinkles and mischievous old blue eyes.

There was one little room that particularly interested me, a tiny bedroom all white, and at the window the red

roses were already in bud. But what caught my eye with
peculiar sympathy was a small bookcase, in which were
some twenty or thirty volumes, wearing the same forgotten
expression—forgotten and yet cared for—which lay like a
kind of memorial charm upon everything in the old house.
Yes, everything seemed forgotten and yet everything, curiously—even religiously—remembered. I took out book
after book from the shelves, once or twice flowers fell out
from the pages—and I caught sight of a delicate hand-
writing here and there and frail markings. It was evidently
the little intimate library of a young girl. What surprised
me most was to find that quite half the books were in
French—French poets and French romancers: a charming,
very rare edition of Ronsard, a beautifully printed edition
of Alfred de Musset, and a copy of Théophile Gautier's
Mademoiselle de Maupin. How did these exotic books come
to be there alone in a deserted New England farm-house?

This question was to be answered later in a strange way.
Meanwhile I had fallen in love with the sad, old, silent
place, and as I closed the white gate and was once more on
the road, I looked about for some one who could tell me
whether or not this house of ghosts might be rented for
the summer by a comparatively living man.

I was referred to a fine old New England farm-house
shining white through the trees a quarter of a mile away.
There I met an ancient couple, a typical New England
farmer and his wife; the old man, lean, chin-bearded, with
keen gray eyes flickering occasionally with a shrewd humor, the old lady with a kindly old face of the withered-
apple type and ruddy. They were evidently prosperous
people, but their minds—for some reason I could not at
the moment divine—seemed to be divided between their
New England desire to drive a hard bargain and their disinclination to let the house at all.

Over and over again they spoke of the loneliness of the place. They feared I would find it very lonely. No one had lived in it for a long time, and so on. It seemed to me that afterwards I understood their curious hesitation, but at the moment I only regarded it as a part of the circuitous New England method of bargaining. At all events, the rent I offered finally overcame their disinclination, whatever its cause, and so I came into possession— for four months—of that silent old house, with the white lilacs, and the drowsy barns, and the old piano, and the strange orchard; and, as the summer came on, and the year changed its name from May to June, I used to lie under the apple-trees in the afternoons, dreamily reading some old book, and through half-sleepy eyelids watching the silken shimmer of the Sound.

I had lived in the old house for about a month, when one afternoon a strange thing happened to me. I remember the date well. It was the afternoon of Tuesday, June 13th. I was reading, or rather dipping here and there, in Burton's *Anatomy of Melancholy*. As I read, I remember that a little unripe apple, with a petal or two of blossom still clinging to it, fell upon the old yellow page. Then I suppose I must have fallen into a dream, though it seemed to me that both my eyes and my ears were wide open, for I suddenly became aware of a beautiful young voice singing very softly somewhere among the leaves. The singing was very frail, almost imperceptible, as though it came out of the air. It came and went fitfully, like the elusive fragrance of sweet-brier—as though a girl was walking to and fro dreamily humming to herself in the still afternoon. Yet there was no one to be seen. The orchard had never seemed more lonely. And another fact that struck me as strange was that the words that floated to me out of the aerial music were French, half sad, half gay snatches of some long-dead

singer of old France. I looked about for the origin of the
sweet sounds, but in vain. Could it be the birds that were
singing in French in this strange orchard? Presently the
voice seemed to come quite close to me, so near that it
might have been the voice of a dryad singing to me out of
the tree against which I was leaning. And this time I distinctly caught the words of the sad little song:

> "*Chante, rossignol, chante,*
> *Toi qui as le cœur gai;*
> *Tu as le cœur à rire,*
> *Moi, je l'ai-t-à pleurer"*

But, though the voice was at my shoulder, I could see
no one, and then the singing stopped with what sounded
like a sob; and a moment or two later I seemed to hear a
sound of sobbing far down the orchard. Then there followed silence, and I was left to ponder on the strange
occurrence. Naturally, I decided that it was just a day-
dream between sleeping and waking over the pages of an
old book; yet when next day and the day after the invisible
singer was in the orchard again, I could not be satisfied
with such mere matter-of-fact explanation.

> "*A la claire fontaine,*"

went the voice to and fro through the thick orchard boughs,

> "*M'en allant promener,*
> *J'ai trouvé l'eau si belle*
> *Que je m'y suis baigné,*
> *Lui y a longtemps que je t'aime,*
> *Jamais je ne t'oubliai.*"

It was certainly uncanny to hear that voice going to and fro the orchard, there somewhere amid the bright sun-dazzled boughs—yet not a human creature to be seen—not another house even within half a mile. The most materialistic mind could hardly but conclude that here was something "not dreamed of in our philosophy." It seemed to me that the only reasonable explanation was the entirely irrational one—that my orchard was haunted: haunted by some beautiful young spirit, with some sorrow of lost joy that would not let her sleep quietly in her grave.

And next day I had a curious confirmation of my theory. Once more I was lying under my favorite apple-tree, half reading and half watching the Sound, lulled into a dream by the whir of insects and the spices called up from the earth by the hot sun. As I bent over the page, I suddenly had the startling impression that some one was leaning over my shoulder and reading with me, and that a girl's long hair was falling over me down on to the page. The book was the Ronsard I had found in the little bedroom. I turned, but again there was nothing there. Yet this time I knew that I had not been dreaming, and I cried out:

"Poor child! tell me of your grief—that I may help your sorrowing heart to rest."

But, of course, there was no answer; yet that night I dreamed a strange dream. I thought I was in the orchard again in the afternoon and once again heard the strange singing—but this time, as I looked up, the singer was no longer invisible. Coming toward me was a young girl with wonderful blue eyes filled with tears and gold hair that fell to her waist. She wore a straight, white robe that might have been a shroud or a bridal dress. She appeared not to see me, though she came directly to the tree where I was sitting. And there she knelt and buried her face in the grass and sobbed as if her heart would break. Her long hair fell over her like a mantle, and in my dream I stroked it pityingly and murmured words of comfort for a sorrow I did not understand. . . . Then I woke suddenly as one does from dreams. The moon was shining brightly into the room. Rising from my bed, I looked out into the orchard. It was almost as bright as day. I could plainly see the tree of which I had been dreaming, and then a fantastic notion possessed me. Slipping on my clothes, I went out into one of the old barns and found a spade. Then I went to the tree where I had seen the girl weeping in my dream and dug down at its foot.

I had dug little more than a foot when my spade struck upon some hard substance, and in a few more moments I had uncovered and exhumed a small box, which, on examination, proved to be one of those pretty old-fashioned Chippendale work-boxes used by our grandmothers to keep their thimbles and needles in, their reels of cotton and skeins of silk. After smoothing down the little grave in which I had found it, I carried the box into the house, and under the lamplight examined its contents.

Then at once I understood why that sad young spirit went to and fro the orchard singing those little French songs—for the treasure-trove I had found under the apple-tree, the buried treasure of an unquiet, suffering soul, proved to be a number of love-letters written mostly in French in a very picturesque hand—letters, too, written but some five or six years before. Perhaps I should not have read them—yet I read them with such reverence for the beautiful, impassioned love that animated them, and literally made them "smell sweet and blossom in the dust," that I felt I had the sanction of the dead to make myself the confidant of their story. Among the letters were little songs, two of which I had heard the strange young voice singing in the orchard, and, of course, there were many withered flowers and such like remembrances of bygone rapture.

Not that night could I make out all the story, though it was not difficult to define its essential tragedy, and later on a gossip in the neighborhood and a headstone in the churchyard told me the rest.

The unquiet young soul that had sung so wistfully to and fro the orchard was my landlord's daughter. She was the only child of her parents, a beautiful, wilful girl, exotically unlike those from whom she was sprung and among whom she lived with a disdainful air of exile. She was, as a child, a little creature of fairy fancies, and as she grew up it was plain to her father and mother that she had come from another world than theirs. To them she seemed like a child in an old fairy-tale strangely found on his hearth by some shepherd as he returns from the fields at evening—a little fairy girl swaddled in fine linen and dowered with a mysterious bag of gold.

Soon she developed delicate spiritual needs to which her simple parents were strangers. From long truancies in the woods she would come home laden with mysterious flowers, and soon she came to ask for books and pictures and music, of which the poor souls that had given her birth had never heard. Finally she had her way, and went to study at a certain fashionable college; and there the brief romance of her life began. There she met a romantic young Frenchman who had read Ronsard to her and written her those picturesque letters I had found in the old mahogany work-box. And after a while the young Frenchman had gone back to France, and the letters had ceased. Month by month went by, and at length one day, as she sat wistful at the window, looking out at the foolish sunlit road, a message came. He was dead. That headstone in the village churchyard tells the rest. She was very young to

die—scarcely nineteen years; and the dead who have died
young, with all their hopes and dreams still like unfold-
ed buds within their hearts, do not rest so quietly in the
grave as those who have gone through the long day from
morning until evening and are only too glad to sleep.

Next day I took the little box to a quiet corner of the
orchard, and made a little pyre of fragrant boughs—for so
I interpreted the wish of that young, unquiet spirit—and
the beautiful words are now safe, taken up again into the
aerial spaces from which they came.

But since then the birds sing no more little French
songs in my old orchard.

THE FARMHOUSE ON THE HILL
Algernon Blackwood
(1914)

William Beach, surveyor, arrived about midday at the small station of a south Dorchester village, and shouldered his bag and instruments to walk across to the Inn where he had already telegraphed earlier in the day for a room. His surveying, having little to do with the account of his distressing subsequent adventures, may be left at once out of the story; but the fact that the Inn was in the throes of temporary building operations is important to mention, since it led to the landlord's directing him to the only place where accommodation was likely, or possible—the farmhouse half way up the hill.

"That dark old house where you see the smoke 'anging about the trees," he pointed. "Garfit's away, but his missus'll find you a bed, no doubt, if you care for that kind of a place. That is," he added quickly, "if you ain't too partickler."

"Anything wrong, d'you mean?" asked the surveyor.

"Oh, I don't say there's nothing wrong with it," said the man, emphasising a word in every phrase, "I'm not one to criticise my neighbours at any time, and I've known of other gentlemen sleepin' there quite comfortable. Any'ow, there's no other house to take you!"

Now there was something in the tone of the disappointed inn-keeper that combined to affect the surveyor disagreeably. He slipped at once into a minor key, and when he turned a corner of the sandy path and found himself suddenly face to face with the old grey-stoned Tudor house, massive of wall and irregular of shape, its forbidding aspect produced so marked an impression on him that he instinctively hesitated, and, with the weakness peculiar to impressionable persons, Beach would probably have retired there and then, but, while his purpose was still an instinct merely, he became suddenly aware that a figure with fixed gaze had been staring at him for some time from the pillars of the deep porch where the yew trees that lined the approach threw their darkest shadow. A second glance showed him that it was a woman, a woman dressed in black. Clearly this was Mrs. Garfit, and he advanced to meet her, and explained his errand.

"We can manage something, perhaps," she said in a flat, colourless sort of voice, cutting short his explanations about the Inn, and turning slowly to enter the house. He followed her through the cold hall, stone-flagged, and up the broad stairs. Mrs. Garfit opened a door, moving aside for him to pass, and he saw a small room with a sky-light window in the sloping ceiling, a cramped brass bed in the far corner, and hooks in the wall from which a number of faded old dresses hung in a dingy row. The air smelt quite musty.

"If you have a somewhat larger room," he began, turning to her, "one with a fire-place, too, as I shall be working a bit in the evenings—"

"The fire would be a shillin' extra," she said presently, "and I could let you 'ave this room for another two shillin' more than the small room." She crossed the landing and showed him the room referred to; it was large, with two windows, an arm-chair, and a deep fire-place.

"I prefer this," said Beach shortly, and then and there clinched the bargain, making the best terms he could with her for breakfast and supper as well.

"Then you holds to the big one," repeated the woman, "because my 'usband—and he'll be back ter-morrer—'e says the little one sleeps in best."

He had a high-tea before the kitchen fire, shared—both tea and fire—by a black cat of huge proportions which insisted on rubbing against his knees. But the food was good, and the friendly attentions of the black cat soothed him so pleasantly that he passed gradually into a happy state of indifference to everything but the seductions of a good pipe and the prospect later of a refreshing sleep.

Then, midway in a stream of most pleasantly flowing reflections, his nerves answered to a startling shock, and his sensations of content were scattered suddenly to the winds of heaven. There, at the end of the room, Mrs. Garfit was bending over an open drawer and, through the smoke curling upwards from his pipe, he had caught sight unexpectedly of her face reflected in the mirror that hung upon the cupboard door. She was evidently not aware of being inspected, and her visage, sombre at any time, now wore an aspect so malefic that the sudden revelation positively horrified him. He saw it, dark and hard, with eyes at once terrible yet haunted, the mouth set, and a deep-settled gloom upon the features that was quite dreadful. The surveyor gave a sudden start that sent the cat flying from his knee, and when the woman turned again to face the kitchen she had resumed the mask of her normal expression of countenance.

"I'll take my candle and go up to read a bit," he stammered, as though surprised in an unauthorised or guilty act. "And—please let me have breakfast at eight o'clock." He was disturbed, and not a little alarmed, by the sight of that changed and evil face, and as he slowly went upstairs he could not help connecting it in his mind with the pain of a tormenting conscience. It seemed to turn the face black—black with mental pain—and the pallor of the skin had made the contrast truly horrible.

A blazing fire in his bedroom, a good novel, and a tolerably comfortable arm-chair, he hoped, would soon put to flight, however, the distressing effects of the vision. Yet, somehow, when he closed the door, it did not keep the woman out. That face came into the room with him. It perched on the table beside his book and seemed to watch him as he read. Then, as he sat there, half reading, half listening to the sounds below stairs, his thoughts took another turn: he thought of his brother, Hubert.

Now, Hubert was the antithesis of himself: practical and keen-minded. They had formerly known great arguments—visionary *versus* materialist—in which Hubert's cool and logical mind invariably gained the victory, and he wished Hubert were with him now. Then, with a fresh start, he recognised that it was this very sense of alarm that had suggested Hubert to his mind at all, and that in his subconsciousness he was already groping for help! Plainly, this was the reason of his brother's appearance upon the scene. The sinister setting of his night's lodging, the desolate hills, and above all the revelation of the woman's changed face had combined to touch his imagination with unholy suggestion.

His thoughts dwelt a good deal upon these things, but, after all, the strong Dorsetshire air was not to be denied; the fire, moreover, was comforting, and his limbs ached. The coals dropped softly into the grate and the winter wind came mournfully over the hills and sighed round the walls of the house; there was no other sound; downstairs everyone seemed to have gone to bed. He would read one more chapter and turn in himself. Good sleep would chase the phantoms effectually. But the new chapter began with wearisome description, and his thoughts wandered again—theodolite—black cat—Hubert—the woman's face.

His eyes were travelling heavily through a big paragraph when a faint sound made itself audible in the room behind him, and he turned with a quick start to look over the back of his chair. The candle threw his head and shoulders, greatly magnified, upon wall and ceiling; but the room was empty; nothing seemed to stir. Yet the moment he looked down again upon his book the sound was repeated. Instantly he was in the whirl of a genuine nervous flurry, confused a little, and thinking of a dozen things at once. Perhaps the friendly black cat had followed him up and was hiding in the room; he would get up and search. But before he could actually leave his chair a slight movement close beside him caught the corner of his eye. The brass knob of the doorhandle at his left was turning. That was where the sounds came from. There was someone at the door.

Beach caught his breath with a rush. His first instinct was to dash forward and turn the key; his second, to seize the poker; yet he found no strength to do either the one or the other. He glued his eyes to the knob, watching it slowly turn. It stopped for a moment, and then the door pushed gently open, and he saw the figure of Mrs. Garfit, partially concealed by a black shawl over the head, and wearing the very expression that he had seen reflected in the mirror downstairs a few hours before. She was staring intently into the empty room behind him. Encircled by both arms, and grasped by her great muscular hands, she carried a kind of loose bundle which she held pressed closely into her body.

The woman, thus drawn in patches of black and white, standing erect in the doorway with darkness at her back, and that face of set evil dominating the picture, presented an appearance so appalling that at once the fear in the surveyor's heart passed into terror, pure and simple, and he found himself unable to utter a sound or make the smallest movement.

Without taking the slightest notice of him, she tiptoed softly forward into the room, and Beach then became aware for the first time that she was not alone. A man crouched behind her in the darkness of the landing, holding a lantern beneath the folds of a cloak. He was kneeling; and his face, with red hair and beard, and half-opened mouth showing the teeth, was just distinguishable in the faint glimmer of the shrouded light.

Looking neither to the right nor to the left, the woman passed almost soundlessly behind him, brushing the arm of the chair with her black gown, and making obviously for the end of the room. And when Beach, fearing that any moment she might face about and come towards himself, turned his head by a supreme effort and saw that she was already at the far end beside the bed, he made at the same time the further startling discovery—a cold sweat bursting through his skin—that the bed was occupied!

For one second he saw on the pillow the face of a young girl, sleeping peacefully, with masses of light hair about her, and then the black outline of that terrible woman bent double over her, and the loose bundle she carried in her hands descended full upon the pillow with her great weight above it, and remained there motionless, like a tiger upon its prey, for the space of what seemed to him many minutes.

There was no struggle and no sound; nothing but a little convulsive movement beneath the bed-clothes lower down; and then the surveyor, still powerless to move or cry in the grip of a real terror, was aware that the man had left his post of observation in the passage and was already half way across the floor. He, too, went past him, as though unaware of his presence, but the woman, hearing the stealthy approach, straightened herself up beside the bed and turned to meet him. The lantern carried by the man, who was short and humpbacked, shed a faint upward light upon her features, and the slow smile it revealed coming into being on her fixed white face was so ghastly that it gave Beach that little extra twist of terror needed to release the frozen will and make speech and movement possible.

With a loud cry he leaped out of his chair and dashed forward upon the fiendish couple still standing beside the bed of murder—and woke with a violent start in his armchair before an extinguished fire in a room that was pitch dark and miserably cold. It was one o'clock in the morning.

He examined the bed, that awful bed where he had seen a young girl smothered in her sleep, and the horror of the nightmare remained so vividly with him that he gave up trying to persuade himself that it had been nothing more than a dream, and that two evil persons, and a third, had not vacated the room. One thing was certain, he could never sleep in such a bed. He would slip across to the other room. The dread of perhaps meeting the woman in the passage gave him pause for a moment, but after all it was a lesser terror, and he softly opened the door and crept, candle in hand, over the cold boards to the other side of the landing. He stood and listened for a moment—the house was utterly still—and then quietly turned the knob. But the door was locked. He was obliged to return to his own room, where he passed the remainder of a troubled night in what sleep he could snatch upon an arm-chair and two others.

The late daylight, cold and grey, brought no such balm to his imagination as the bright sunshine of a spring morning might have done, and the horror of his dream possessed him so painfully that he realised he could not spend another night in that room unless—yes, that was a splendid idea—unless he could get his brother, Hubert, down for the weekend to share it with him. Hubert's cold logic would work wonders. Ah, and another thought! It would be interesting to see if he felt anything odd about the house or room. He would say nothing about his own impressions, or his own experience, and would see what Hubert felt. The idea possessed him at once, and he decided to telegraph the moment he had finished breakfast. Then, having arranged for another bed to be moved into the room, he took some bread and cheese with him and spent the entire day surveying on the hills until the darkness fell over the country and it was time to meet the train.

And Hubert came, glad of the prospect of walks and talks with his brother, and seduced by the telegraphic description of the "jolly old farmhouse" among the hills. He appeared delighted, too, with the Tudor building. "You ought to advertise, ma'am, and take in summer boarders," he said briskly to Mrs. Garfit.

"You better tell my 'usband that," she replied, with something like a sigh mixed up in her sullen voice. "He'll be here to-night or to-morrer mornin'."

"Surly old cat," said Hubert, when they were alone at bed-time in their room; "she'd have to wear a veil to keep her boarders. Her face is like some of those women in the Chamber of Horrors." He laughed cheerfully, and plunged into the details of his week's work—he was a stockbroker—and of family matters that were of interest between them. William carefully manoeuvred that Hubert should occupy the large bed, but he could not repress a creeping sense of horror when the time for sleep came and he saw his brother snuggling down under the sheets and blankets and putting his head upon that haunted pillow. All through the night, as long as the firelight lasted, he lay awake and watched to see if anything would happen. But, up to the late hour when he finally fell asleep, nothing did happen. It must have been very early in the morning when he woke with a start and saw someone standing beside his bed in the darkness, and heard his name called softly. It was Hubert: "I say, Billy, is that cursed woman in the room, or what—who is calling?"

William jumped up and struck a light. Hubert's face was blanched. This was the first thing he noticed. "What's up?" he stammered, still dazed with sleep. "The door's locked; there's no one here—is there?"

Hubert stood there shivering. Then he took the candle and walked round the room, poking into corners and cupboards, and even looking under the beds. He went back to his own bed again and pulled the sheets about savagely.

"What did you hear?" asked William nervously.

"I'm not sure I heard anything. Something woke me—I couldn't breathe properly—felt suffocated—and I thought I heard that woman calling to 'hurry up.' Been dreaming, I suppose." He hesitated a moment. William saw that he had only told half, and wanted to say something else that rather stuck in his gorge.

"You'll get your death of cold standing there," he whispered.

Hubert ceased fumbling at his own bed and crossed the floor; his face was as white as chalk. "I say, old Billy, do you mind very much if I sleep with you? I think, perhaps, my sheets seem a bit damp," he whispered at length.

And when he had crawled into bed, William felt that he was shaking all over, and for a long time before sleep again overtook them he kept giving little nervous starts of fear. He knew his brother too well to ask him just then what had really happened, but next morning, when the sunshine was in the room, he pressed him for an explanation, and Hubert admitted that he had never felt so frightened in his life; horrible dreams of being stifled had haunted his sleep, and finally someone had come stealthily up to the bed and tried to suffocate him by putting a blanket over his face. For a wonder, too, when he heard his brother's story he neither argued nor scoffed, but merely remarked that it would be interesting to find out the history of the house and also to see if Mr. Garfit resembled the man with the lantern.

And the first person they met on going down to a belated breakfast was the farmer himself coming in from a gig standing in the yard. He was hump-backed and very short. Moreover he had red hair and beard, and a trick of leaving his mouth open so that the teeth showed.

The landlord of the Purbeck Arms, when suitably urged, furnished something of the required "history" of the house by stating that, some years before, Garfit's step-daughter had been found suffocated in her bed, and that the couple of them, man and wife, had only escaped the gallows because the circumstantial evidence was weak. "It was long before I came here," he said, "but you'll find the story in the papers of that date. You see," he continued, "the girl had money of her own from her mother. The Garfits got that."

THE HAUNTED COW

Bertram Munn

(1915)

I

The Irish are notoriously superstitious. They believe in all manner of things, such as fairies and leprechauns; and nearly every village has its little halo of myths. But this particular one is different from most. It is very "tall"; so tall that at times I wonder whether the villagers had not merely made a compact to pull my leg. They knew I was a sceptical Londoner, that I scribbled tales, that . . . But here is the yarn and you shall judge for yourself.

The two Flannigans, man and wife, lived in about the last spot on earth. It was a mere handful of land known as Bowles' Island, and situated in the centre of the Shannon just above Lough Rea. About an acre was raw bogland, where a few potatoes struggled manfully in a soil which was never intended for them; another acre or so, the higher ground in the centre, was grass (of a kind), and the remainder, a few perches, was given up to still more potatoes of a much healthier and larger variety.

In normal times the Flannigans lived on two staple products—milk and potatoes. Occasionally a pig came their way, spent a brief life burrowing and fattening, and then died a sudden and violent death which resulted in bacon and pork galore. But this was very seldom. Their mainstay was a cow. It was a large, quiet and affectionate animal, with a peculiar individuality of its own. It always ate its food hurriedly and jerkily, as if half ashamed of taking the scanty grass. Afterwards it ambled forward, lay down in front of the cabin door, and commenced ruminating. It ruminated slowly and thoughtfully, like all well-bred cows, and it had a peculiar knack of keeping one eye closed—the eye furthest from the door. The other one, a large, mild, pathetic affair, it kept on watch for Flannigan or his wife. Whenever one of them emerged it got up, wagged its tail, and ambled quietly after them. Nothing they did in the open ever escaped its attention, and at times, to show its affection, it even licked them! A cow's tongue is not exactly soothing when applied to the, back of one's neck. It is the very opposite. Resembling as it does a piece of wet sand-paper, it was apt to make old Flannigan half jump out of his skin.

"Ah! you brute," he would shout. "You may mane well, but, begorra, it hurts."

He would reach up with his hand and rub the back of his neck, whilst the cow stood by, peacefully chewing, with one eye half closed—as dreamy and affectionate-looking an animal as could be imagined.

Time went by. Calves came and went. But even its own offspring failed to fascinate it. For a while they were attended to in a mild, disinterested way; but its heart was really with the Flannigans, and it worshipped them with all the power of its cow-like nature. Nothing it could do for them was enough. It yielded milk with a cheerfulness which was touching. It knew that it was merely paying back in kind the generosity of its hosts, and it was proud of its function in the world.

In return, the Flannigans respected their cow. They knew it was unlike all other cows, and they treated it with the utmost kindness. They gave it morsels and tit-bits, and even granted the exceptional honour of allowing it to put its head in at the door and watch them eating their meals.

The villagers who occasionally crossed to the island invariably returned with fresh tales of its doings and touching little stories of its affection. People always spoke of "the Flannigans and their cow" as if the three were inseparable.

Under such circumstances it was inevitable that when the Great Flood came the cow should figure conspicuously. For two months the boiling and seething waters of the Shannon tore and eddied round the little island. All communication with the mainland was cut off. The Flannigans' ramshackle old boat was torn away from its moorings, dashed and splintered against the banks, and finally drifted down stream, a mass of battered wreckage. In the hurricane and the blinding rain houses and trees were rooted up and washed away like children's toys. Whole villages were destroyed; every man, woman and child in the vicinity of the Shannon rushed pell-mell inland, leaving everything behind them, only too glad to escape with their lives.

And in the centre of the howling chaos of destruction the Flannigans fought against starvation and the rising flood. With the exception of a small plot of grass and the house itself, the whole of the island was submerged.

The cow, homeless and desolate, was taken into their own house, where it watched them with piteous and understanding eyes. It knew what was in their mind—and when the fatal day arrived it forgave them.

Flannigan took it outside.

"Faith!" he said. "I'd rather kill meself."

His wife scolded him. "'Tis only a cow!" she said. "An' it has no soul at all."

"It's one o' ourselves," quavered the old man.

"Ah! Go in wi' ye!—It must be done, Mike!"

Michael rubbed his eyes with the back of his hand, whilst the cow wagged its tail and lowered its head for the sacrifice.

Then the old woman went inside and shut the door.

After awhile Michael entered. He looked a shade paler than usual.

"'Tis done," he said quietly.

The evening was drawing in, and through the window they saw the sun turning the angry waters to bright gold. For a while they stood watching the great expanse of water and sky. Then Michael spoke again.

"We'll leave it till mornin'. I've not the heart to go out again."

His wife nodded and, crossing to the door, glanced out with a shudder and closed it. . . .

The next morning they awoke to find a pool of water on the floor.

"Begor!" exclaimed Michael. "The flood's risen."

He went to the door and opened it. His eyes encountered an endless stretch of water running away from the door right up to the horizon's edge.

"Sabina!" he shouted. "'Tis gone!"

"What?" she exclaimed.

"The cow! 'Tis gone! The flood's taken it away. Faith! We're done for. 'Tis starvation we'll die of."

She hurried to his side, and together they craned their heads through the doorway. Nothing but rushing water and floating trees and wreckage met their gaze.

They stood there, hopeless and irresolute, unable to speak.

And then the unexpected happened. Right in front of their astonished gaze, a cow suddenly appeared, turned its head towards them, wagged a bedraggled tail, and slowly closed one eye.

"'Oly mother!" cried Michael. "Hasten yourself, Sabina. The pail!"

His eyes had fallen on the well-filled udder of the cow—a sight they had not encountered for four weary weeks.

His wife's trembling hands gave him the dirty old bucket which had once served as a milk pail.

"Faith!" he mumbled, as he waded knee-deep into the muddy water. "'Tis a fine animal that ye are, after the way I've treated ye. Steady, ole woman."

He stooped down, and the cow's swishing tail came to rest.

"Hasten, Mike," urged his wife. "'Tis a quare business."

Michael hastened.

At last he rose with his milk-laden pail.

"Sabina! take it while I make her fast."

He handed her the bucket, raised his hand to put it on the cow's neck—and suddenly fell forward into the water.

The cow had vanished!

After that Michael and his wife lost their heads.

"'Tis the divil himself that is in that cow!" he exclaimed, as he scrambled to his feet. "Where are ye, ye brute?"

"Ah! Don't be sayin' unseemly things, Mike," cried his wife. "Come inside and be drinking the milk."

She was a practical woman above all things, and had been without food for three days. She wanted to make certain of the milk before that vanished, too!

Michael stumbled indoors, sat down in his dripping clothes, and began to drink. . . .

II

The next morning the cow was there again—and Michael crossed himself before he milked her.

The moment he rose with the full pail she vanished.

At the end of a fortnight Michael looked upon the supernatural as one of the everyday occurrences of life.

"Sure," he said to his wife, "the cow's hauntit. But, be-gor, the milk's good, an' it's not for us to raise our voices and complain."

"There's a quare taste to it, Mike," observed his wife.

"An', woman, what d'ye expect? The poor craitur has ate not a bit nor a bite since I killed her. Bedad, I don't know where the milk comes from at all."

"'Tis not for us to be askin' where it comes from," said his wife, in a half-frightened tone.

"Ah! You're right. We'd best take it with a grateful heart, an' ask no questions . . ."

And so the "hauntit" cow and its "hauntit" milk saved the Flannigans from starvation until the flood at last receded.

This was after a month's diet on milk and nothing else; and it was not long before the villagers from the mainland could cross once more to the island and see if the Flannigans were still alive.

Pat Fleming and Barney Whelan were the two first to go, and they stated afterwards that when they got within full view of the Flannigan's house they could see the old man milking his cow, just outside the door.

When the boat grounded the cow was no longer there, and the old couple ran down to the water's edge and talked very excitedly. They looked quite well, and little the worse for their two months' imprisonment: but what struck Pat and Barney as very peculiar at the time was that the old couple did not exactly seem to walk towards them, but more to *drift*—almost as if their feet just missed touching the ground at times.

Another strange thing was that when the old people stood with the sun behind them they seemed to glow—almost as if the light were finding its way through their clothes and coming out at the other side.

Michael took them inside the cabin, made them sit down, and gave them a drink of milk.

Pat and Barney smacked their lips after the first draught.

"It tastes a bit quare," observed one of them.

"Ah!" said the old man. "It does. It's hauntit."

"What!" screamed Barney.

Then Michael told them the whole story.

They listened in a half-believing sort of way, tried to laugh it off when they emerged into the open once more, and finally received a shock which convinced them of the truth of the old man's story.

Coming up from the boat in a jerky, floating motion, was the cow. When it saw Pat and Barney it suddenly lowered its head and made for them.

With a scream they turned and fled, the cow pursuing them in big jumpy strides and hops, its tail stuck out at the back, quite straight, like a rudder.

They raced into the cabin, slammed the door to, and stood there panting in the half-darkness, scared out of their lives.

After a while they heard Michael's voice.

"Open the door! The baste's gone!"

They opened it, very tentatively, and came out into the sunshine once more. Their faces were a sickly white, and their hands were shaking with fear.

They said very little, and made straight for the boat.

When they reached it they received another shock. It was overturned, and the few packets of grocery they had so thoughtfully brought over had been ripped open and scattered in the water.

It was undoubtedly a direct hint from the cow that it had taken on the feeding of the Flannigan's—and was going to have no interference from strangers.

Pat and Barney took the hint, set the boat afloat again, and started back for the village, as hard as they could row.

The next day a half dozen adventurous (and incredulous) spirits from the village set out for the island again.

In route they were met by the cow, swimming in the water, its tail raised like a flagstaff.

Two of them jumped overboard and swam wildly for the shore. The others rowed back as hard as they could.

After that truth and fiction became hopelessly mixed. Rumours and legends sprang up like weeds in a badly-kept garden. Everybody saw the cow! It was said to have been seen in the Shannon, on the mainland, and even floating about in the sky.

The last authenticated story of the Flannigans was given by a couple of fishermen who had approached the island.

They stated that they had distinctly seen two half-transparent people emerge from the cabin, milk a substantial-looking cow—and then float away into thin air.

To-day Bowles' Island is uninhabited. The old ruin of a cabin is still to be seen, and at times, so the villagers assert, one may sometimes see the old man milking his cow at the broken-down doorway. But it happens only in flood time.

All the villagers believe in the story. Not one of them would live on the island for a king's ransom.

And, of course, they all have explanations of the strange events which happened.

Barney Whelan is most emphatic. He says that no one could drink the milk of a "hauntit" cow without becoming "hauntit" himself.

"An' mark ye," he says, "them old people never died. They just wint on gettin' lighter an' lighter until they floated away. Faith! It's a warnin' to people not to get mixin' themselves up with spirits. No one ever heard tell of any good comin' of it."

I believe he's right. . . .

WITH INTENT TO STEAL
Algernon Blackwood
(1917)

To sleep in a lonely barn when the best bedrooms in the house were at our disposal, seemed, to say the least, unnecessary, and I felt that some explanation was due to our host.

But Shorthouse, I soon discovered, had seen to all that; our enterprise would be tolerated, not welcomed, for the master kept this sort of thing down with a firm hand. And then, how little I could get this man, Shorthouse, to tell me. There was much I wanted to ask and hear, but he surrounded himself with impossible barriers. It was ludicrous; he was surely asking a good deal of me, and yet he would give so little in return, and his reason—that it was for my good—may have been perfectly true, but did not bring me any comfort in its train. He gave me sops now and then, however, to keep up my curiosity, till I soon was aware that there were growing up side by side within me a genuine interest and an equally genuine fear; and something of both these is probably necessary to all real excitement.

The barn in question was some distance from the house, on the side of the stables, and I had passed it on several of my journeyings to and fro wondering at its forlorn and untarred appearance under a regime where everything was so spick and span; but it had never once occurred to me as possible that I should come to spend a night under its roof with a comparative stranger, and undergo there an experience belonging to an order of things I had always rather ridiculed and despised.

At the moment I can only partially recall the process by which Shorthouse persuaded me to lend him my company. Like myself, he was a guest in this autumn house-party, and where there were so many to chatter and to chaff, I think his taciturnity of manner had appealed to me by contrast, and that I wished to repay something of what I owed. There was, no doubt, flattery in it as well, for he was more than twice my age, a man of amazingly wide experience, an explorer of all the world's corners where danger lurked, and—most subtle flattery of all—by far the best shot in the whole party, our host included.

At first, however, I held out a bit.

"But surely this story you tell," I said, "has the parentage common to all such tales—a superstitious heart and an imaginative brain—and has grown now by frequent repetition into an authentic ghost story? Besides, this head gardener of half a century ago," I added, seeing that he still went on cleaning his gun in silence, "who was he, and what positive information have you about him beyond the fact that he was found hanging from the rafters, dead?"

"He was no mere head gardener, this man who passed as such," he replied without looking up, "but a fellow of splendid education who used this curious disguise for his own purposes. Part of this very barn, of which he always kept the key, was found to have been fitted up as a complete laboratory, with athanor, alembic, cucurbite, and other appliances, some of which the master destroyed at once—perhaps for the best—and which I have only been able to guess at—"

"Black Arts," I laughed.

"Who knows?" he rejoined quietly. "The man undoubtedly possessed knowledge—dark knowledge—that was most unusual and dangerous, and I can discover no means by which he came to it—no ordinary means, that is. But I have found many facts in the case which point to the exercise of a most desperate and unscrupulous will; and the strange disappearances in the neighbourhood, as well as the bones found buried in the kitchen garden, though never actually traced to him, seem to me full of dreadful suggestion."

I laughed again, a little uncomfortably perhaps, and said it reminded one of the story of Giles de Rays, maréchal of France, who was said to have killed and tortured to death in a few years no less than one hundred and sixty women and children for the purposes of necromancy, and who was executed for his crimes at Nantes. But Shorthouse would not "rise," and only returned to his subject.

"His suicide seems to have been only just in time to escape arrest," he said.

"A magician of no high order then," I observed sceptically, "if suicide was his only way of evading the country police."

"The police of London and St. Petersburg rather," returned Shorthouse; "for the headquarters of this pretty company was somewhere in Russia, and his apparatus all bore the marks of the most skilful foreign make. A Russian woman then employed in the household—governess, or something—vanished, too, about the same time and was never caught. She was no doubt the cleverest of the lot. And, remember, the object of this appalling group was not mere vulgar gain, but a kind of knowledge that called for the highest qualities of courage and intellect in the seekers."

I admit I was impressed by the man's conviction of voice and manner, for there is something very compelling in the force of an earnest man's belief, though I still affected to sneer politely.

"But, like most Black Magicians, the fellow only succeeded in compassing his own destruction—that of his tools, rather, and of escaping himself."

"So that he might better accomplish his objects *elsewhere and otherwise*," said Shorthouse, giving, as he spoke, the most minute attention to the cleaning of the lock.

"Elsewhere and otherwise," I gasped.

"As if the shell he left hanging from the rafter in the barn in no way impeded the man's spirit from continuing his dreadful work under new conditions," he added quietly, without noticing my interruption. "The idea being that he sometimes revisits the garden and the barn, chiefly the barn—"

"The barn!" I exclaimed; "for what purpose?"

"Chiefly the barn," he finished, as if he had not heard me, "that is, when there is anybody in it."

I stared at him without speaking, for there was a wonder in me how he would add to this.

"When he wants fresh material, that is—he comes to steal from the living."

"Fresh material!" I repeated aghast "To steal from the living!" Even then, in broad daylight, I was foolishly conscious of a creeping sensation at the roots of my hair, as if a cold breeze were passing over my skull.

"The strong vitality of the living is what this sort of creature is supposed to need most," he went on imperturbably, "and where he has worked and thought and struggled before is the easiest place for him to get it in. The former conditions are in some way more easily reconstructed—" He stopped suddenly, and devoted all his attention to the gun. "It's difficult to explain, you know, rather," he added presently, "and, besides, it's much better that you should not know till afterwards."

I made a noise that was the beginning of a score of questions and of as many sentences, but it got no further than a mere noise, and Shorthouse, of course, stepped in again.

"Your scepticism," he added, "is one of the qualities that induce me to ask you to spend the night there with me."

"In those days," he went on, in response to my urging for more information, "the family were much abroad, and often travelled for years at a time. This man was invaluable in their absence. His wonderful knowledge of horticulture kept the gardens—French, Italian, English—in perfect order. He had carte blanche in the matter of expense, and of course selected all his own underlings. It was the sudden, unexpected return of the master that surprised the amazing stories of the countryside before the fellow, with all his cleverness, had time to prepare or conceal."

"But is there no evidence, no more recent evidence, to show that something is likely to happen if we sit up there?" I asked, pressing him yet further, and I think to his liking, for it showed at least that I was interested. "Has anything happened there lately, for instance?"

Shorthouse glanced up from the gun he was cleaning so assiduously, and the smoke from his pipe curled up into an odd twist between me and the black beard and oriental, sun-tanned face. The magnetism of his look and expression brought more sense of conviction to me than I had felt hitherto, and I realised that there had been a sudden little change in my attitude and that I was now much more inclined to go in for the adventure with him. At least, I thought, with such a man, one would be safe in any emergency; for he is determined, resourceful, and to be depended upon.

"There's the point," he answered slowly; "for there has apparently been a fresh outburst—an attack almost, it seems,—quite recently. There is evidence, of course, plenty of it, or I should not feel the interest I do feel, but—" he hesitated a moment, as though considering how much he ought to let me know, "but the fact is that three men this summer, on separate occasions, who have gone into that barn after nightfall, have been *accosted*—"

"Accosted?" I repeated, betrayed into the interruption by his choice of so singular a word.

"And one of the stablemen—a recent arrival and quite ignorant of the story—who had to go in there late one night, saw a dark substance hanging down from one of the rafters, and when he climbed up, shaking all over, to cut it down—for he said he felt sure it was a corpse—the knife passed through nothing but air, and he heard a sound up under the eaves as if someone were laughing. Yet, while he slashed away, and afterwards too, the thing went on swinging there before his eyes and turning slowly with its own weight, like a huge joint on a spit. The man declares, too, that it had a large bearded face, and that the mouth was open and drawn down like the mouth of a hanged man."

"Can we question this fellow?"

"He's gone—gave notice at once, but not before I had questioned him myself very closely."

"Then this was quite recent?" I said, for I knew Shorthouse had not been in the house more than a week.

"Four days ago," he replied. "But, more than that, only three days ago a couple of men were in there together in full daylight when one of them suddenly turned deadly faint. He said that he felt an overmastering impulse to hang himself; and he looked about for a rope and was furious when his companion tried to prevent him—"

"But he did prevent him?"

"Just in time, but not before he had clambered on to a beam. He was very violent."

I had so much to say and ask that I could get nothing out in time, and Shorthouse went on again.

"I've had a sort of watching brief for this case," he said with a smile, whose real significance, however, completely escaped me at the time, "and one of the most disagreeable features about it is the deliberate way the servants have invented excuses to go out to the place, and always after dark; some of them who have no right to go there, and no real occasion at all—have never been there in their lives before probably—and now all of a sudden have shown the keenest desire and determination to go out there about dusk, or soon after, and with the most paltry and foolish excuses in the world. Of course," he added, "they have been prevented, but the desire, stronger than their superstitious dread, and which they cannot explain, is very curious."

"Very," I admitted, feeling that my hair was beginning to stand up again.

"You see," he went on presently, "it all points to volition—in fact to deliberate arrangement. It is no mere family ghost that goes with every ivied house in England of a certain age; it is something real, and something very malignant."

He raised his face from the gun barrel, and for the first time his eye caught mine in the full. Yes, he was very much in earnest. Also, he knew a great deal more than he meant to tell.

"It's worth tempting—and fighting, *I* think," he said; "but I want a companion with me. Are you game?" His enthusiasm undoubtedly caught me, but I still wanted to hedge a bit.

"I'm very sceptical," I pleaded.

"All the better," he said, almost as if to himself. "You have the pluck; I have the knowledge—"

"The knowledge?"

He looked round cautiously as if to make sure that there was no one within earshot.

"I've been in the place myself," he said in a lowered voice, "quite lately—in fact only three nights ago—the day the man turned queer."

I stared.

"But—I was obliged to come out—"

Still I stared.

"Quickly," he added significantly.

"You've gone into the thing pretty thoroughly," was all I could find to say, for I had almost made up my mind to go with him, and was not sure that I wanted to hear too much beforehand.

He nodded. "It's a bore, of course, but I must do everything thoroughly—or not at all."

"That's why you clean your own gun, I suppose?"

"That's why, when there's any danger, I take as few chances as possible," he said, with the same enigmatical smile I had noticed before; and then he added with emphasis, "And that is also why I ask you to keep me company now."

Of course, the shaft went straight home, and I gave my promise without further ado.

Our preparations for the night—a couple of rugs and a flask of black coffee—were not elaborate, and we found no difficulty, about ten o'clock, in absenting ourselves from the billiard-room without attracting curiosity. Shorthouse met me by arrangement under the cedar on the back lawn, and I at once realised with vividness what a difference there is between making plans in the daytime and carrying them out in the dark. One's common sense—at least in matters of this sort—is reduced to a minimum, and imagination with all her attendant sprites usurps the place of judgment. Two and two no longer make four—they make a mystery, and the mystery loses no time in growing into a menace. In this particular case, however, my imagination did not find wings very readily, for I knew that my companion was the most *unmovable* of men—an unemotional, solid block of a man who would never lose his head, and in any conceivable state of affairs would always take the right as well as the strong course. So my faith in the man gave me a false courage that was nevertheless very consoling, and I looked forward to the night's adventure with a genuine appetite.

Side by side, and in silence, we followed the path that skirted the East Woods, as they were called, and then led across two hay fields, and through another wood, to the barn, which thus lay about half a mile from the Lower Farm. To the Lower Farm, indeed, it properly belonged; and this made us realise more clearly how very ingenious must have been the excuses of the Hall servants who felt the desire to visit it.

It had been raining during the late afternoon, and the trees were still dripping heavily on all sides, but the moment we left the second wood and came out into the open, we saw a clearing with the stars overhead, against which the barn outlined itself in a black, lugubrious shadow. Shorthouse led the way—still without a word—and we crawled in through a low door and seated ourselves in a soft heap of hay in the extreme corner.

"Now," he said, speaking for the first time, "I'll show you the inside of the barn, so that you may know where you are, and what to do, in case anything happens."

A match flared in the darkness, and with the help of two more that followed I saw the interior of a lofty and somewhat rickety-looking barn, erected upon a wall of grey stones that ran all round and extended to a height

of perhaps four feet. Above this masonry rose the wooden
sides, running up into the usual vaulted roof, and supported by a double tier of massive oak rafters, which stretched
across from wall to wall and were intersected by occasional
uprights. I felt as if we were inside the skeleton of some
antediluvian monster whose huge black ribs completely
enfolded us. Most of this, of course, only sketched itself
to my eye in the uncertain light of the flickering matches,
and when I said I had seen enough, and the matches
went out, we were at once enveloped in an atmosphere as
densely black as anything that I have ever known. And the
silence equaled the darkness.

We made ourselves comfortable and talked in low
voices. The rugs, which were very large, covered our legs;
and our shoulders sank into a really luxurious bed of
softness. Yet neither of us apparently felt sleepy. I certainly didn't, and Shorthouse, dropping his customary brevity
that fell little short of gruffness, plunged into an easy
run of talking that took the form after a time of personal
reminiscences. This rapidly became a vivid narration of
adventure and travel in far countries, and at any other
time I should have allowed myself to become completely
absorbed in what he told. But, unfortunately, I was never
able for a single instant to forget the real purpose of our
enterprise, and consequently I felt all my senses more
keenly on the alert than usual, and my attention accordingly more or less distracted. It was, indeed, a revelation
to hear Shorthouse unbosom himself in this fashion, and
to a young man it was of course doubly fascinating; but
the little sounds that always punctuate even the deepest
silence out of doors claimed some portion of my attention, and as the night grew on I soon became aware that
his tales seemed somewhat disconnected and abrupt—and
that, in fact, I heard really only part of them.

It was not so much that I actually heard other sounds, but that I *expected* to hear them; this was what stole the other half of my listening. There was neither wind nor rain to break the stillness, and certainly there were no physical presences in our neighbourhood, for we were half a mile even from the Lower Farm; and from the Hall and stables, at least a mile. Yet the stillness was being continually broken—perhaps *disturbed* is a better word—and it was to these very remote and tiny disturbances that I felt compelled to devote at least half my listening faculties.

From time to time, however, I made a remark or asked a question, to show that I was listening and interested; but, in a sense, my questions always seemed to bear in one direction and to make for one issue, namely, my companion's previous experience in the barn when he had been obliged to come out "quickly."

Apparently I could not help myself in the matter, for this was really the one consuming curiosity I had; and the fact that it was better for me not to know it made me the keener to know it all, even the worst.

Shorthouse realised this even better than I did. I could tell it by the way he dodged, or wholly ignored, my questions, and this subtle sympathy between us showed plainly enough, had I been able at the time to reflect upon its meaning, that the nerves of both of us were in a very sensitive and highly-strung condition. Probably, the complete confidence I felt in his ability to face whatever might happen, and the extent to which also I relied upon him for my own courage, prevented the exercise of my ordinary powers of reflection, while it left my senses free to a more than usual degree of activity.

Things must have gone on in this way for a good hour or more, when I made the sudden discovery that there was something unusual in the conditions of our environment.

This sounds a roundabout mode of expression, but I really know not how else to put it. The discovery almost rushed upon me. By rights, we were two men waiting in an alleged haunted barn for something to happen; and, as two men who trusted one another implicitly (though for very different reasons), there should have been two minds keenly alert, with the ordinary senses in active co-operation. Some slight degree of nervousness, too, there might also have been, but beyond this, nothing. It was therefore with something of dismay that I made the sudden discovery that there was something more, and something that I ought to have noticed very much sooner than I actually did notice it.

The fact was—Shorthouse's stream of talk was wholly unnatural. He was talking with a purpose. He did not wish to be cornered by my questions, true, but he had another and a deeper purpose still, and it grew upon me, as an unpleasant deduction from my discovery, that this strong, cynical, unemotional man by my side was talking—and had been talking all this time—to gain a particular end. And this end, I soon felt clearly, was to *convince himself.* But, of what?

For myself, as the hours wore on towards midnight, I was not anxious to find the answer; but in the end it became impossible to avoid it, and I knew as I listened, that he was pouring forth this steady stream of vivid reminiscences of travel—South Seas, big game, Russian exploration, women, adventures of all sorts—*because he wished the past to reassert itself to the complete exclusion of the present.* He was taking his precautions. He was afraid.

I felt a hundred things, once this was clear to me, but none of them more than the wish to get up at once and leave the barn. If Shorthouse was afraid already, what in the world was to happen to me in the long hours that lay ahead? . . . I only know that, in my fierce efforts to deny to myself the evidence of his partial collapse, the strength came that enabled me to play my part properly, and I even found myself helping him by means of animated remarks upon his stories, and by more or less judicious questions. I also helped him by dismissing from my mind any desire to enquire into the truth of his former experience; and it was good I did so, for had he turned it loose on me, with those great powers of convincing description that he had at his command, I verily believe that I should never have crawled from that barn alive. So, at least, I felt at the moment. It was the instinct of self-preservation, and it brought sound judgment.

Here, then, at least, with different motives, reached, too, by opposite ways, we were both agreed upon one thing, namely, that temporarily we would forget. Fools we were, for a dominant emotion is not so easily banished, and we were for ever recurring to it in a hundred ways direct and indirect. A real fear cannot be so easily trifled with, and while we toyed on the surface with thousands and thousands of words—mere words—our sub-conscious activities were steadily gaining force, and would before very long have to be properly acknowledged. We could not get away from it. At last, when he had finished the recital of an adventure which brought him near enough to a horrible death, I admitted that in my uneventful life I had never yet been face to face with a real fear. It slipped out inadvertently, and, of course, without intention, but the tendency in him at the time was too strong to be resisted. He saw the loophole, and made for it full tilt.

"It is the same with all the emotions," he said. "The experiences of others never give a complete account. Until a man has deliberately turned and faced for himself the fiends that chase him down the years, he has no knowledge of what they really are, or of what they can do. Imaginative authors may write, moralists may preach, and scholars may criticise, but they are dealing all the time in a coinage of which they know not the actual value. Their listener gets a sensation—but not the true one. Until you have faced these emotions," he went on, with the same race of words that had come from him the whole evening, "and made them your own, your slaves, you have no idea of the power that is in them—hunger, that shows lights beckoning beyond the grave; thirst, that fills with mingled ice and fire; passion, love, loneliness, revenge, and—" He paused for a minute, and though I knew we were on the brink I was powerless to hold him. ". . . *and fear,*" he went on—"fear . . . I think that death from fear, or madness from fear, must sum up in a second of time the total of all the most awful sensations it is possible for a man to know."

"Then you have yourself felt something of this fear," I interrupted; "for you said just now—"

"I do not mean physical fear," he replied; "for that is more or less a question of nerves and will, and it is imagination that makes men cowards. I mean an *absolute* fear, a physical fear one might call it, that reaches the soul and withers every power one possesses."

He said a lot more, for he, too, was wholly unable to stem the torrent once it broke loose; but I have forgotten it; or, rather, mercifully I did not hear it, for I stopped my ears and only heard the occasional words when I took my fingers out to find if he had come to an end. In due course he did come to an end, and there we left it, for I then knew positively what he already knew: that somewhere here in the night, and within the walls of this very barn where we were sitting, there was waiting Something of dreadful malignancy and of great power Something that we might both have to face ere morning, and Something that he had already tried to face once and failed in the attempt.

The night wore slowly on; and it gradually became more and more clear to me that I could not dare to rely as at first upon my companion, and that our positions were undergoing a slow process of reversal. I thank Heaven this was not borne in upon me too suddenly; and that I had at least the time to readjust myself somewhat to the new conditions. Preparation was possible, even if it was not much, and I sought by every means in my power to gather up all the shreds of my courage, so that they might together make a decent rope that would stand the strain when it came. The strain would come, that was certain, and I was thoroughly well aware—though for my life I cannot put into words the reasons for my knowledge—that the massing of the material against us was proceeding somewhere in the darkness with determination and a horrible skill besides.

Shorthouse meanwhile talked without ceasing. The great quantity of hay opposite—or straw, I believe it actually was—seemed to deaden the sound of his voice, but the silence, too, had become so oppressive that I welcomed his torrent and even dreaded the moment when it would stop. I heard, too, the gentle ticking of my watch. Each second uttered its voice and dropped away into a gulf, as if starting on a journey whence there was no return. Once a dog barked somewhere in the distance, probably on the Lower Farm; and once an owl hooted close outside and I could hear the swishing of its wings as it passed overhead. Above me, in the darkness, I could just make out the outline of the barn, sinister and black, the rows of rafters stretching across from wall to wall like wicked arms that pressed upon the hay. Shorthouse, deep in some involved yarn of the South Seas that was meant to be full of cheer and sunshine, and yet only succeeded in making a ghastly mixture of unnatural colouring, seemed to care little whether I listened or not. He made no appeal to me, and I made one or two quite irrelevant remarks which passed him by and proved that he was merely uttering sounds. He, too, was afraid of the silence.

I fell to wondering how long a man could talk without stopping. . . . Then it seemed to me that these words of his went falling into the same gulf where the seconds dropped, only they were heavier and fell faster. I began to chase them. Presently one of them fell much faster than the rest, and I pursued it and found myself almost immediately in a land of clouds and shadows. They rose up and enveloped me, pressing on the eyelids. . . . It must have been just here that I actually fell asleep, somewhere between twelve and one o'clock, because, as I chased this word at tremendous speed through space, I knew that I had left the other words far, very far behind me, till, at last, I could no longer hear them at all. The voice of the story-teller was beyond the reach of hearing; and I was falling with ever increasing rapidity through an immense void.

A sound of whispering roused me. Two persons were talking under their breath close beside me. The words in the main escaped me, but I caught every now and then bitten-off phrases and half sentences, to which, however, I could attach no intelligible meaning. The words were quite close—at my very side in fact—and one of the voices sounded so familiar, that curiosity overcame dread, and I turned to look. I was not mistaken; *it was*

Shorthouse whispering. But the other person, who must have been just a little beyond him, was lost in the darkness and invisible to me. It seemed then that Shorthouse at once turned up his face and looked at me and, by some means or other that caused me no surprise at the time, I easily made out the features in the darkness. They wore an expression I had never seen there before; he seemed distressed, exhausted, worn out, and as though he were about to give in after a long mental struggle. He looked at me, almost beseechingly, and the whispering of the other person died away.

"They're at me," he said.

I found it quite impossible to answer; the words stuck in my throat. His voice was thin, plaintive, almost like a child's.

"I shall have to go. I'm not as strong as I thought. They'll call it suicide, but, of course, it's really murder." There was real anguish in his voice, and it terrified me.

A deep silence followed these extraordinary words, and I somehow understood that the Other Person was just going to carry on the conversation—I even fancied I saw lips shaping themselves just over my friend's shoulder—when I felt a sharp blow in the ribs and a voice, this time a deep voice, sounded in my ear. I opened my eyes, and the wretched dream vanished. Yet it left behind it an impression of a strong and quite unusual reality.

"*Do* try not to go to sleep again," he said sternly. "You seem exhausted. Do you feel so?" There was a note in his voice I did not welcome,—less than alarm, but certainly more than mere solicitude.

"I do feel terribly sleepy all of a sadden," I admitted, ashamed.

"So you may," he added very earnestly; "but I rely on you to keep awake, if only to watch. You have been asleep for half an hour at least—and you were so still—I thought I'd wake you—"

"Why?" I asked, for my curiosity and nervousness were altogether too strong to be resisted. "Do you think we are in danger?"

"I think *they* are about here now. I feel my vitality going rapidly—that's always the first sign. You'll last longer than I, remember. Watch carefully."

The conversation dropped. I was afraid to say all I wanted to say. It would have been too unmistakably a confession; and intuitively I realised the danger of admitting the existence of certain emotions until positively forced to. But presently Shorthouse began again. His voice sounded odd, and as if it had lost power. It was more like a woman's or a boy's voice than a man's, and recalled the voice in my dream.

"I suppose you've got a knife?" he asked.

"Yes—a big clasp knife; but why?" He made no answer. "You don't think a practical joke likely? No one suspects we're here," I went on. Nothing was more significant of our real feelings this night than the way we toyed with words, and never dared more than to skirt the things in our mind.

"It's just as well to be prepared," he answered evasively. "Better be quite sure. See which pocket it's in—so as to be ready."

I obeyed mechanically, and told him. But even this scrap of talk proved to me that he was getting further from me all the time in his mind. He was following a line that was strange to me, and, as he distanced me, I felt that the sympathy between us grew more and more strained. *He knew more;* it was not that I minded so much—but that he was willing to *communicate less.* And in proportion as I lost his support, I dreaded his increasing silence. Not of words—for he talked more volubly than ever, and with a fiercer purpose—but his silence in giving no hint of what he must have known to be really going on the whole time.

The night was perfectly still. Shorthouse continued steadily talking, and I jogged him now and again with remarks or questions in order to keep awake. He paid no attention, however, to either.

About two in the morning a short shower fell, and the drops rattled sharply on the roof like shot. I was glad when it stopped, for it completely drowned all other sounds and made it impossible to hear anything else that might be going on. Something was going on, too, all the time, though for the life of me I could not say what. The outer world had grown quite dim—the house-party, the shooters, the billiard-room, and the ordinary daily incidents of my visit. All my energies were concentrated on the present, and the constant strain of watching, waiting, listening, was excessively telling.

Shorthouse still talked of his adventures, in some Eastern country now, and less connectedly. These adventures, real or imaginary, had quite a savour of the Arabian Nights, and did not by any means make it easier for me to keep my hold on reality. The lightest weight will affect the balance under such circumstances, and in this case the weight of his talk was on the wrong scale. His words were very rapid, and I found it overwhelmingly difficult not to follow them into that great gulf of darkness where they all rushed and vanished. But that, I knew, meant sleep again. Yet, it was strange I should feel sleepy when at the same time all my nerves were fairly tingling. Every time I heard what seemed like a step outside, or a movement in the hay opposite, the blood stood still for a moment in my veins. Doubtless, the unremitting strain told upon me more than I realised, and this was doubly great now that I knew Shorthouse was a source of weakness instead of strength, as I had counted. Certainly, a curious sense of languor grew upon me more and more, and I was sure that the man beside me was engaged in the same struggle. The feverishness of his talk proved this, if nothing else. It was dreadfully hard to keep awake.

But this time, instead of dropping into the gulf, I saw something come up out of it! It reached our world by a door in the side of the barn furthest from me, and it came in cautiously and silently and moved into the mass of hay opposite. There, for a moment, I lost it, but presently I caught it again higher up. It was clinging, like a great bat, to the side of the barn. Something trailed behind it, I could not make out what. . . . It crawled up the wooden wall and began to move out along one of the rafters. A

numb terror settled down all over me as I watched it. The
thing trailing behind it was apparently a rope.

The whispering began again just then, but the only
words I could catch seemed without meaning; it was almost like another language. The voices were above me,
under the roof. Suddenly I saw signs of active movement
going on just beyond the place where the thing lay upon
the rafter. There was something else up there with it! Then
followed panting, like the quick breathing that accom-
panies effort, and the next minute a black mass dropped
through the air and dangled at the end of the rope.

Instantly, it all flashed upon me. I sprang to my feet
and rushed headlong across the floor of the barn. How
I moved so quickly in the darkness I do not know; but,
even as I ran, it flashed into my mind that I should never
get at my knife in time to cut the thing down, or else
that I should find it had been taken from me. Somehow
or other—the Goddess of Dreams knows how—I climbed
up by the hay bales and swung out along the rafter. I was
hanging, of course, by my arms, and the knife was already
between my teeth, though I had no recollection of how it
got there. It was open. The mass, hanging like a side of
bacon, was only a few feet in front of me, and I could
plainly see the dark line of rope that fastened it to the
beam. I then noticed for the first time that it was swinging and turning in the air, and that as I approached it
seemed to move along the beam, so that the same distance
was always maintained between us. The only thing I could
do—for there was no time to hesitate—was to jump at it
through the air and slash at the rope as I dropped.

I seized the knife with my right hand, gave a great
swing of my body with my legs and leaped forward at it
through the air. Horrors! It was closer to me than I knew,
and I plunged full into it, and the arm with the knife
missed the rope and cut deeply into some substance that

was soft and yielding. But, as I dropped past it, the thing had time to turn half its width so that it swung round and faced me—and I could have sworn as I rushed past it through the air, that it had the features of Shorthouse.

The shock of this brought the vile nightmare to an abrupt end, and I woke up a second time on the soft hay-bed to find that the grey dawn was stealing in, and that I was exceedingly cold. After all I had failed to keep awake, and my sleep, since it was growing light, must have lasted at least an hour. A whole hour off my guard!

There was no sound from Shorthouse, to whom, of course, my first thoughts turned; probably his flow of words had ceased long ago, and he too had yielded to the persuasions of the seductive god. I turned to wake him and get the comfort of companionship for the horror of my dream, when to my utter dismay I saw that the place where he had been was vacant. He was no longer beside me.

It had been no little shock before to discover that the ally in whom lay all my faith and dependence was really frightened, but it is quite impossible to describe the sensations I experienced when I realised he had gone altogether and that I was alone in the barn. For a minute or two my head swam and I felt a prey to a helpless terror. The dream, too, still seemed half real, so vivid had it been! I was thoroughly frightened—hot and cold by turns—and I clutched the hay at my side in handfuls, and for some moments had no idea in the world what I should do.

This time, at least, I was unmistakably awake, and I made a great effort to collect myself and face the meaning of the disappearance of my companion. In this I succeeded so far that I decided upon a thorough search of the barn, inside and outside. It was a dreadful undertaking, and I did not feel at all sure of being able to bring it to a conclusion, but I knew pretty well that unless something was done at once, I should simply collapse.

But, when I tried to move, I found that the cold, and fear, and I know not what else unholy besides, combined to make it almost impossible. I suddenly realised that a tour of inspection, during the whole of which my back would be open to attack, was not to be thought of. My will was not equal to it. Anything might spring upon me any moment from the dark corners, and the growing light was just enough to reveal every movement I made to any who might be watching. For, even then, and while I was still half dazed and stupid, I knew perfectly well that someone was watching me all the time with the utmost intentness. I had not merely awakened; I had *been* awakened.

I decided to try another plan; I called to him. My voice had a thin weak sound, far away and quite unreal, and there was no answer to it. Hark, though! There was something that might have been a very faint voice near me!

I called again, this time with greater distinctness, "Shorthouse, where are you? can you hear me?"

There certainly was a sound, but it was not a voice. Something was moving. It was someone shuffling along, and it seemed to be outside the barn. I was afraid to call again, and the sound continued. It was an ordinary sound enough, no doubt, but it came to me just then as something unusual and unpleasant. Ordinary sounds remain ordinary only so long as one is not listening to them; under the influence of intense listening they become unusual, portentous, and therefore extraordinary. So, this common sound came to me as something uncommon, disagreeable. It conveyed, too, an impression of stealth. And with it there was another, a slighter sound.

Just at this minute the wind bore faintly over the field the sound of the stable clock, a mile away. It was three o'clock; the hour when life's pulses beat lowest; when poor souls lying between life and death find it hardest to resist. Vividly I remember this thought crashing through my brain with a sound of thunder, and I realised that the strain on my nerves was nearing the limit, and that something would have to be done at once if I was to reclaim my self-control at all.

When thinking over afterwards the events of this dreadful night, it has always seemed strange to me that my second nightmare, so vivid in its terror and its nearness, should have furnished me with no inkling of what was really going on all this while; and that I should not have been able to put two and two together, or have discovered sooner than I did *what* this sound was and *where* it came from. I can well believe that the vile scheming which lay behind the whole experience found it an easy trifle to direct my hearing amiss; though, of course, it may equally well have been due to the confused condition of my mind at the time and to the general nervous tension under which I was undoubtedly suffering.

But, whatever the cause for my stupidity at first in failing to trace the sound to its proper source, I can only say here that it was with a shock of unexampled horror that my eye suddenly glanced upwards and caught sight of the figure moving in the shadows above my head among the rafters. Up to this moment I had thought that it was somebody outside the barn, crawling round the walls till it came to a door; and the rush of horror that froze my heart when I looked up and saw that it was Shorthouse creeping stealthily along a beam, is something altogether beyond the power of words to describe.

He was staring intently down upon me, and I knew at once that it was he who had been watching me.

This point was, I think, for me the climax of feeling in the whole experience; I was incapable of any further sensation—that is any further sensation in the same direction. But here the abominable character of the affair showed itself most plainly, for it suddenly presented an entirely new aspect to me. The light fell on the picture from a new angle, and galvanised me into a fresh ability to feel when I thought a merciful numbness had supervened. It may not sound a great deal in the printed letter, but it came to me almost as if it had been an extension of consciousness, for the Hand that held the pencil suddenly touched in with ghastly effect of contrast the element of the ludicrous. Nothing could have been worse just then. Shorthouse, the masterful spirit, so intrepid in the affairs of ordinary life, whose power increased rather than lessened in the face of danger—this man, creeping on hands and knees along a rafter in a barn at three o'clock in the morning, watching me all the time as a cat watches a mouse! Yes, it was distinctly ludicrous, and while it gave me a measure with which to gauge the dread emotion that caused his aberration, it stirred somewhere deep in my interior the strings of an empty laughter.

One of those moments then came to me that are said to come sometimes under the stress of great emotion, when in an instant the mind grows dazzlingly clear. An abnormal lucidity took the place of my confusion of thought, and I suddenly understood that the two dreams which I had taken for nightmares must really have been sent me, and that I had been allowed for one moment to look over the edge of what was to come; the Good was helping, even when the Evil was most determined to destroy.

I saw it all clearly now. Shorthouse had overrated his strength. The terror inspired by his first visit to the barn (when he had failed) had roused the man's whole nature to win, and he had brought me to divert the deadly stream of evil. That he had again underrated the power against him was apparent as soon as he entered the barn, and his wild talk, and refusal to admit what he felt, were due to this desire not to acknowledge the insidious fear that was growing in his heart. But, at length, it had become too strong.

He had left my side in my sleep—had been overcome himself, perhaps, first in *his* sleep, by the dreadful impulse. He knew that I should interfere, and with every movement he made, he watched me steadily, for the mania was upon him and he was *determined to hang himself.* He pretended not to hear me calling, and I knew that anything coming between him and his purpose would meet the full force of his fury—the fury of a maniac, of one, for the time being, truly possessed.

For a minute or two I sat there and stared. I saw then for the first time that there was a bit of rope trailing after him, and that this was what made the rustling sound I had noticed. Shorthouse, too, had come to a stop. His body lay along the rafter like a crouching animal. He was looking hard at me. That whitish patch was bis face.

I can lay claim to no courage in the matter, for I must confess that in one sense I was frightened almost beyond control. But at the same time the necessity for decided action, if I was to save his life, came to me with an intense relief. No matter what animated him for the moment, Shorthouse was only a man; it was flesh and blood I had to contend with and not the intangible powers. Only a few hours before I had seen him cleaning his gun, smoking his pipe, knocking the billiard balls about with very human clumsiness, and the picture flashed across my mind with the most wholesome effect.

Then I dashed across the floor of the barn and leaped upon the hay bales as a preliminary to climbing up the sides to the first rafter. It was far more difficult than in my dream. Twice I slipped back into the hay, and as I scrambled up for the third time I saw that Shorthouse, who thus far had made no sound or movement, was now busily doing something with his hands upon the beam. He was at its further end, and there must have been fully fifteen feet between us. Yet I saw plainly what he was doing; he was fastening the rope to the rafter. *The other end, I saw, was already round his neck!*

This gave me at once the necessary strength, and in a second I had swung myself on to a beam, crying aloud with all the authority I could put into my voice—

"You fool, man! What in the world are you trying to do? Come down at once!"

My energetic actions and words combined had an immediate effect upon him for which I blessed Heaven; for he looked up from his horrid task, stared hard at me for a second or two, and then came wriggling along like a great cat to intercept me. He came by a series of leaps and bounds and at an astonishing pace, and the way he moved somehow inspired me with a fresh horror, for it did not seem the natural movement of a human being at all, but more, as I have said, like that of some lithe wild animal.

He was close upon me. I had no clear idea of what exactly I meant to do. I could see his face plainly now; he was grinning cruelly; the eyes were positively luminous, and the menacing expression of the mouth was most distressing to look upon. Otherwise it was the face of a chalk man, white and dead, with all the semblance of the living human drawn out of it. Between his teeth he held my clasp knife, which he must have taken from me in my sleep, and with a flash I recalled his anxiety to know exactly which pocket it was in.

"Drop that knife!" I shouted at him, "and drop after it yourself—"

"Don't you dare to stop me!" he hissed, the breath coming between his lips across the knife that he held in his teeth. "Nothing in the world can stop me now—I have promised—and I must do it. I can't hold out any longer."

"Then drop the knife and I'll help you," I shouted back in his face. "I promise—"

"No use," he cried, laughing a little, "I must do it and you can't stop me."

I heard a sound of laughter, too, somewhere in the air behind me. The next second Shorthouse came at me with a single bound.

To this day I cannot quite tell how it happened. It is still a wild confusion and a fever of horror in my mind, but from somewhere I drew more than my usual allowance of strength, and before he could well have realised what I meant to do, I had his throat between my fingers. He opened his teeth and the knife dropped at once, for I gave him a squeeze he need never forget. Before, my muscles had felt like so much soaked paper; now they recovered their natural strength, and more besides. I managed to work ourselves along the rafter until the hay was beneath us, and then, completely exhausted, I let go my hold and we swung round together and dropped on to the hay, he clawing at me in the air even as we fell.

The struggle that began by my fighting for his life ended in a wild effort to save my own, for Shorthouse was quite beside himself, and had no idea what he was doing. Indeed, he has always averred that he remembers nothing of the entire night's experiences after the time when he first woke me from sleep. A sort of deadly mist settled over him, he declares, and he lost all sense of his own identity. The rest was a blank until he came to his senses under a mass of hay with me on the top of him.

It was the hay that saved us, first by breaking the fall and then by impeding his movements so that I was able to prevent his choking me to death.

THE SCARECROW

Gwendolyn Ranger Wormser

(1918)

"Ben—"

The woman stood in the doorway of the ramshackle, tumble-down shanty. Her hands were cupped at her mouth. The wind blew loose, whitish blond wisps of hair around her face and slashed the faded blue dress into the uncorseted bulk of her body.

"Benny—oh, Benny—"

Her call echoed through the still evening.

Her eyes staring straight before her down the slope in front of the house caught sight of something blue and antiquatedly military standing waist deep and rigid in the corn field.

"That ole scarecrow," she muttered to herself, "that there old scarecrow with that there ole uniform onto him, too!"

The sun was going slowly just beyond the farthest hill. The unreal light of the skies' reflected colors held over the yellow, waving tips of the corn field.

"Benny—," she called again. "Oh—Benny!"

And then she saw him coming toward her trudging up the hill.

She waited until he stood in front of her.

"Supper, Ben," she said. "Was you down in the south meadow where you couldn't hear me call?"

145

"Naw."

He was young and slight. He had thick hair and a thin face. His features were small. There was nothing unusual about them. His eyes were deep-set and long, with the lids that were heavily fringed.

"You heard me calling you?"

"Yes, maw."

He stood there straight and still. His eyelids were lowered.

"Why ain't you come along then? What ails you, Benny, letting me shout and shout that way?"

"Nothing—maw."

"Where was you?"

He hesitated a second before answering her.

"I was to the bottom of the hill."

"And what was you doing down there to the bottom of the hill? What was you doing down there, Benny?"

Her voice had a hushed tenseness to it.

"I was watching, maw."

"Watching, Benny?"

"That's what I was doing."

His tone held a guarded sullenness.

"'Tain't no such a pretty sunset, Benny."

"Warn't watching no sunset."

"Benny—!"

"Well." He spoke quickly. "What d'you want to put it there for? What d'you want to do that for in the first place?"

"There was birds, Benny. You know there was birds."

"That ain't what I mean. What for d'you put on that there uniform?"

"I ain't had nothing else. There warn't nothing but your grand-dad's ole uniform. It's fair in rags, Benny. It's all I had to put on to it."

"Well, you done it yourself."

"Naw, Benny, naw! 'Tain't nothing but an ole uniform with a stick into it. Just to frighten off them birds. 'Tain't nothing else. Honest, 'tain't, Benny."

He looked up at her out of the corners of his eyes.

"It was waving its arms."

"That's the wind."

"Naw, maw. Waving its arms before the wind it come up."

"Sush, Benny! 'Tain't likely. 'Tain't."

"I was watching, maw. I seen it wave and wave. S'pose it should beckon—; s'pose it should beckon to me. I'd be going, then, maw."

"Sush, Benny."

"I'd fair have to go, maw."

"Leave your mammy? Naw, Ben; naw. You couldn't never go off and leave your mammy. Even if you ain't able to bear this here farm you couldn't go off from your mammy. You couldn't! Not—your—maw—Benny!"

She could see his mouth twitch. She saw him catch his lower lip in under his teeth.

"Aw—"

"Say you couldn't leave, Benny; say it!"

"I—I fair hate this here farm!" He mumbled. "Morning and night;—and morning and night. Nothing but chores and earth. And then some more of them chores. And always that there way. So it is! Always! And the stillness! Nothing alive, nothing! Sometimes I ain't able to stand it nohow. Sometimes—!"

"You'll get to like it—; later, mebbe—"

"Naw! naw, maw!"

"You will, Benny. Sure you will."

"I won't never. I ain't able to help fretting. It's all closed up tight inside of me. Eating and eating. It makes me feel sick."

She put out a hand and laid it heavily on his shoulder.

"Likely it's a touch of fever in the blood, Benny."

"Aw—! I ain't got no fever!"

"You'll be feeling better in the morning, Ben."

"I'll be feeling the same, maw. That's just it. Alway the same. Nothing but the stillness. Nothing alive. And down there in the corn field—"

"That ain't alive, Benny!"

"Ain't it, maw?"

"Don't say that, Benny. Don't!"

He shook her hand off of him.

"I was watching," he said doggedly. "I seen it wave and wave."

She turned into the house.

"That ole scarecrow!" She muttered to herself. "That there ole scarecrow!"

She led the way into the kitchen. The boy followed at her heels.

A lamp was lighted on the center table. The one window was uncurtained. Through the naked spot of it the evening glow poured shimmeringly into the room.

Inside the doorway they both paused.

"You set down, Benny."

He pulled a chair up to the table.

She took a steaming pot from the stove and emptying it into a plate, placed the dish before him.

He fell to eating silently.

She came and sat opposite him. She watched him cautiously. She did not want him to know that she was watching him. Whenever he glanced up she hurried her eyes away from his face. In the stillness the only live things were those two pair of eyes darting away from each other.

"Benny—!" She could not stand it any longer. "Benny—just—you—just—you—"

He gulped down a mouthful of food.

"Aw, maw—don't you start nothing. Not no more tonight, maw."

She half rose from her chair. For a second she leaned stiffly against the table. Then she slipped back into her seat, her whole body limp and relaxed.

"I ain't going to start nothing, Benny. I ain't even going to talk about this here farm. Honest—I ain't."

"Aw—this—here—farm—!"

"I've gave the best years of my life to it."

She spoke the words defiantly.

"You said that all afore, maw."

"It's true," she murmured. "Terrible true. And I done it for you, Benny. I wanted to be giving you something. It's all I'd got to give you, Benny. There's many a man, Ben, that's glad of his farm. And grateful, too. There's many that makes it pay—"

"And what'll I do if it does pay, maw? What'll I do then?"

"I—I—don't know, Benny. It's only just beginning, now."

"But if it does pay, maw? What'll I do? Go away from here?"

"Naw, Benny—. Not—away—. What'd you go away for, when it pays? After all them years I gave to it?"

His spoon clattered noisily to his plate. He pushed his chair back from the table. The legs of it rasped loudly along the uncarpeted floor. He got to his feet.

"Let's go on outside," he said. "There ain't no sense to this here talking—and talking."

She glanced up at him. Her eyes were narrow and hard.

"All right, Benny. I'll clear up. I'll be along in a minute. All right, Benny."

He slouched heavily out of the room.

She sat where she was, the set look pressed on her face. Automatically her hands reached out among the dishes, pulling them toward her.

Outside the boy sank down on the step.

It was getting dark. There were shadows along the ground. Blue shadows. In the graying skies one star shone brilliantly. Beyond the mist-slurred summit of a hill the full moon grew yellow.

In front of him was the slope of wind-moved corn field, and in the center of it the dim, military figure standing waist deep in the corn.

His eyes fixed themselves to it.

"Ole—uniform—with—a—stick—into—it."

He whispered the words very low.

Still—standing there—still. The same wooden attitude of it. His same, cunning watching of it.

There was a wind. He knew it was going over his face. He could feel the cool of the wind across his moistened lips.

He took a deep breath.

Down there in the shivering corn field, standing in the dark, blue shadows, the dim figure had quivered.

An arm moved—swaying to and fro. The other arm began—swaying—swaying. A tremor ran through it. Once it pivoted. The head shook slowly from side to side. The arms rose and fell—and rose again. The head came up and down and rocked a bit to either side.

"I'm here—" he muttered involuntarily. "Here."

The arms were tossing and stretching.

He thought the head faced in his direction.

The wind had died out.

The arms went down and came up and reached.

"Benny—"

The woman seated herself on the step at his side.

"Look!" He mumbled. "Look!"

He pointed his hand at the dim figure shifting restlessly in the quiet, shadow-saturated corn field.

Her eyes followed after his.

"Oh—Benny—"

"Well—" His voice was hoarse. "It's moving, ain't it? You can see it moving for yourself, can't you? You ain't able to say you don't see it, are you?"

"The—wind—" She stammered.

"Where's the wind?"

"Down—there."

"D'you feel a wind? Say, d'you feel a wind?"

"Mebbe—down—there."

"There ain't no wind. Not now—there ain't! And it's moving, ain't it? Say, it's moving, ain't it?"

"It looks like it was dancing. So it does. Like as if it was—making—itself—dance—"

His eyes were still riveted on those arms that came up and down—; up and down—; and reached.

"It'll stop soon—now." He stuttered it more to himself than to her. "Then—it'll be still. I've watched it mighty often. Mebbe it knows I watch it. Mebbe that's why—it—moves—"

"Aw—Benny—"

"Well, you see it, don't you? You thought there was something the matter with me when I come and told you how it waves—and waves. But you seen it waving, ain't you?"

"It's nothing, Ben. Look, Benny. It's stopped!"

The two of them stared down the slope at the dim, military figure standing rigid and waist deep in the corn field.

The woman gave a quick sigh of relief.

For several moments they were silent.

From somewhere in the distance came the harsh, discordant sound of bull frogs croaking. Out in the night a dog bayed at the golden, full moon climbing up over the hills. A bird circled between sky and earth hovering above the corn field. They saw its slow descent, and then for a second they caught the startled whir of its wings, as it flew blindly into the night.

"That ole scarecrow!" She muttered.

"S'pose—" He whispered. "S'pose when it starts its moving like that;—s'pose some day it walks out of that there corn field! Just naturally walks out here to me. What then, if it walks out?"

"Benny—!"

"That's what I'm thinking of all the time. If it takes it into its head to just naturally walk out here. What's going to stop it, if it wants to walk out after me; once it starts moving that way? What?"

"Benny—! It couldn't do that! It couldn't!"

"Mebbe it won't. Mebbe it'll just beckon first. Mebbe it won't come after me. Not if I go when it beckons. I kind of figure it'll beckon when it wants me. I couldn't stand the other. I couldn't wait for it to come out here after me. I kind of feel it'll beckon. When it beckons, I'll be going."

"Benny, there's sickness coming on you."

"'Tain't no sickness."

The woman's hands were clinched together in her lap.

"I wish to Gawd—" She said—"I wish I ain't never seen the day when I put that there thing up in that there corn field. But I ain't thought nothing like this could never happen. I wish to Gawd I ain't never seen the day—"

"'Tain't got nothing to do with you."

His voice was very low.

"It's got everything to do with me. So it has! You said that afore yourself; and you was right. Ain't I put it up? Ain't I looked high and low the house through? Ain't that ole uniform of your grand-dad's been the only rag I could lay my hands on? Was there anything else I could use? Was there?"

"Aw—maw—!"

"Ain't we needed a scarecrow down there? With them birds so awful bad? Pecking away at the corn; and pecking."

"'Tain't your fault, maw."

"There warn't nothing else but that there ole uniform. I wouldn't have took it, otherwise. Poor ole Pa so desperate proud of it as he was. Him fighting for his country in it. Always saying that he was. He couldn't be doing enough for his country. And that there ole uniform meaning so much to him. Like a part of him I used to think it,— and—. You wanting to say something, Ben?"

"Naw—naw—!"

"He wouldn't even let us be burying him in it. 'Put my country's flag next my skin'; he told us. 'When I die keep the ole uniform.' Just like a part of him, he thought it. Wouldn't I have kept it, falling to pieces as it is, if there'd have been anything else to put up there in that there corn field?"

She felt the boy stiffen suddenly.

"And with him a soldier—"

He broke off abruptly.

She sensed what he was about to say.

"Aw, Benny—. That was different. Honest, it was. He warn't the only one in his family. There was two brothers."

The boy got to his feet.

"Why won't you let me go?" He asked it passionately. "Why d'you keep me here? You know I ain't happy! You know all the men've gone from these here parts. You know I ain't happy! Ain't you going to see how much I want to go? Ain't you able to know that I want to fight for my country? The way he did his fighting?"

The boy jerked his head in the direction of the figure standing waist deep in the corn field; standing rigidly and faintly outlined beneath the haunting flood of moonlight.

"Naw, Benny. You can't go. Naw—!"

"Why, maw? Why d'you keep saying that and saying it?"

"I'm all alone, Benny. I've gave all my best years to make the farm pay for you. You got to stay, Benny. You

got to stay on here with me. You just plain got—to! You'll
be glad some day, Benny. Later—on. You'll be right glad."

She saw him thrust his hands hastily into his trouser
pockets.

"Glad?" His voice sounded tired. "I'll be shamed. That's
what I'll be. Nothing, d' you hear, nothing—but shamed!"

She started to her feet.

"Benny—" A note of fear shook through the words.
"You wouldn't—wouldn't—go?"

He waited a moment before he answered her.

"If you ain't wanting me to go—; I'll stay. Gawd! I
guess I plain got to—stay."

"That's a good boy, Benny. You won't never be sorry—nohow—I promise you!—I'll be making it up to you.
Honest, I will!—There's lots of ways—I'll—!"

He interrupted her.

"Only, maw—; I won't let it come after me. If it beckons I—got—to—go—!"

She gave a sudden laugh that trailed off uncertainly.

"'Tain't going to beckon, Benny."

"It if beckons, maw—"

"'Tain't going to, Benny. 'Tain't nothing but the wind
that moves it. It's just the wind, sure. Mebbe you got a
touch of fever. Mebbe you better go on to bed. You'll be
all right in the morning. Just you wait and see. You're a
good boy, Benny. You'll never go off and leave your maw
and the farm. You're a fine lad, Benny."

"If—it—beckons,—" He repeated in weary monotone.

"'Tain't, Benny!"

"I'll be going to bed," he said.

"That's it, Benny. Good night."

"Good night, maw."

She stood there listening to his feet thudding up the
stairs. She heard him knocking about in the room overhead.

A door banged. She stood quite still. There were footsteps moving slowly. A window was thrown open.

She looked up to see him leaning far out over the sill.

Her eyes went down the slope of the moonlight-bathed corn field.

Her right hand curled itself into a fist.

"Ole—scarecrow—!"

She half laughed.

She waited there until she saw the boy draw away from the window. She went into the house and bolted the door behind her. Then she went up the narrow steps.

That night she lay awake for a long time. The heat had grown intense. She found herself tossing from side to side of the small bed.

The window shade had stuck at the top of the window.

The moonlight trickled into the room. She could see the window-framed, star-specked patch of the skies. When she sat up she saw the round, reddish-yellow ball of the moon.

She must have dozed, because she woke with a start. She felt that she had had a fearful, evil dream. The horror of it clung to her.

The room was like an oven.

She thought the walls were coming together and the ceiling pressing down.

Her body was covered with sweat.

She forced herself wide awake. She made herself get out of the bed. She stood for a second uncertain. Then she went to the window.

Not a breath of air stirring.

The moon was high in the sky.

She looked out across the hills.

Down there to the left the acres of potatoes. Potatoes were paying. She counted on a big harvest. To the right the wheat. Only the second year for those five fields. She knew that she had done well with them.

She thought, with a smile running over her lips, back to the time when less than half of the place had been under cultivation. She remembered her dream of getting the whole of her farm in work. She and the boy had made good. She thought of that with savage complacency. It had been a struggle; a bitter, hard fight from the beginning. But she had made good with her farm.

And there down the slope, just in front of the house, the corn field. And in the center of it, standing waist deep in the corn, the antiquated, military figure.

The smile slid from her mouth.

The suffocating heat was terrific.

Not a breath of air.

Suddenly she began to shake from head to foot.

Her eyes wide and staring, were fixed on the moon-light-whitened corn field; her eyes were held to the moon-light-streaked figure standing in the ghostly corn.

Moving—

An arm swayed—swayed to and fro. Backwards and for-wards—backwards— The other arm—swaying— A tremor ran through it. Once it pivoted. The head shook slowly from side to side. The arms rose and fell—; and rose again. The head came up and down, and rocked a bit to either side.

"Dancing—" She whispered stupidly. "Dancing—"

She thought she could not breathe.

She had never felt such oppressive heat.

The arms were tossing and stretching.

She could not take her eyes from it.

And then she saw both arms reach out, and slowly, very slowly, she saw the hands of them, beckoning.

In the stillness of the room next to her she thought she heard a crash.

She listened intently, her eyes stuck to those reaching arms, and the hands of them that beckoned and beckoned.

"Benny—" She murmured—"Benny—!"

Silence.

She could not think.

It was his talk that had done this— Benny's talk— He had said something about it—walking out— If it should come—out—! Moving all over like that— If its feet should start—! If they should of a sudden begin to shuffle—; shuffle out of the cornfield—!

But Benny wasn't awake. He—couldn't—see—it. Thank Gawd! If only something—would—hold—it! If—only—it—would—stop—; Gawd!

Nothing stirring out there in the haunting moonlighted night. Nothing moving. Nothing but the figure standing waist deep in the corn field. And even as she looked, the rigid, military figure grew still. Still, now, but for those slow, beckoning hands.

A tremendous dizziness came over her.

She closed her eyes for a second and then she stumbled back to the bed.

She lay there panting. She pulled the sheets up across her face; her shaking fingers working the tops of them into a hard ball. She stuffed it between her chattering teeth.

Whatever happened, Benny mustn't hear her. She mustn't waken, Benny. Thank Heaven, Benny was asleep. Benny must never know how, out there in the whitened night, the hands of the figure slowly and unceasingly beckoned and beckoned.

The sight of those reaching arms stayed before her. When, hours later, she fell asleep, she still saw the slow-moving, motioning hands.

It was morning when she wakened.

The sun streamed into the room.

She went to the door and opened it.

"Benny;—" She called. "Oh, Benny."

There was no answer.

"Benny—" She called again. "Get on up. It's late, Benny!"

The house was quiet.

She half dressed herself and went into his room.

The bed had been slept in. She saw that at a glance. His clothes were not there. Down—in—the—field—because—she'd—forgotten—to—wake— him—.

In a sudden stunning flash she remembered the crash she had heard.

It took her a long while to get to the little closet behind the bed. Before she opened it she knew it would be empty.

The door creaked open.

His one hat and coat were gone.

She had known that.

He had seen those two reaching arms! He had seen those two hands that had slowly, very slowly, beckoned!

She went to the window.

Her eyes staring straight before her, down the slope in front of the house, caught sight of something blue and antiquatedly military standing waist deep and rigid in the corn field.

"You ole scarecrow—!" She whimpered. "Why're you standing there?" She sobbed. "What're you standing still for—*now?*"

IN THE BARN
Burges Johnson
(1920)

The moment we had entered the barn, I regretted the rash good nature which prompted me to consent to the plans of those vivacious young students. Miss Anstell and Miss Royce and one or two others, often leaders in student mischief, I suspect, were the first to enter, and they amused themselves by hiding in the darkness and greeting the rest of our party as we entered with sundry shrieks and moans such as are commonly attributed to ghosts. My wife and I brought up the rear, carrying the two farm lanterns. She had selected the place after an amused consideration of the question, and I confess I hardly approved her judgment. But she is native to this part of the country, and she had assured us that there were some vague traditions hanging about the building that made it most suitable for our purposes.

It was a musty old place, without even as much tidiness as is usually found in barns, and there was a dank smell about it, as though generations of haymows had decayed there. There were holes in the floor, and in the dusk of early evening it was necessary for us to pick our way with the greatest care. It occurred to me then, in a premonitory sort of way, that if some young woman student sprained her ankle in this absurd environment, I should be most embarrassed to explain it. Apparently it was a hay

barn, whose vague dimensions were lost in shadow. Rafters crossed its width about twenty feet above our heads,
and here and there a few boards lay across the rafters,
furnishing foothold for anyone who might wish to operate
the ancient pulley that was doubtless once used for lifting
bales. The northern half of the floor was covered with hay
to a depth of two or three feet. How long it had actually
been there I cannot imagine. It was extremely dusty, and
I feared a recurrence of my old enemy, hay fever; but it
was too late to offer objection on such grounds, and my
wife and I followed our chattering guides, who disposed
themselves here and there on this ancient bed of hay, and
insisted that we should find places in the center of their
circle.

At my suggestion, the two farm lanterns had been left
at a suitable distance, in fact, quite at the other side of
the barn, and our only light came from the rapidly falling
twilight of outdoors, which found its way through a little window and sundry cracks high in the eaves above the
rafters.

There was something about the place, now that we
were settled and no longer occupied with adjustments of
comfort, that subdued our spirits, and it was with much
less hilarity that the young people united in demanding a
story. I looked across at my wife, whose face was faintly
visible within the circle. I thought that even in the half-
light I glimpsed the same expression of amused incredulity
which she had worn earlier in the day when I had yielded
to the importunities of a deputation of my students for
this ghost-story party on the eve of a holiday.

"There is no reason," I thought to myself, repeating the
phrases I had used then—"there is no reason why I should
not tell a ghost story. True I had never done so before, but
the literary attainments which have enabled me to perfect my recent treatise upon the 'Disuse of the Comma'

are quite equal to impromptu experimentation in the field of psychic phenomena." I was aware that the young people themselves hardly expected serious acquiescence, and that, too, stimulated me. I cleared my throat in a prefatory manner, and silence fell upon the group. A light breeze had risen outside, and the timbers of the barn creaked persistently. From the shadows almost directly overhead there came a faint clanking. It was evidently caused by the rusty pulley-wheel which I had observed there as we entered. An iron hook at the end of an ancient rope still depended from it, and swung in the lightly stirring air several feet above our heads, directly over the center of our circle.

Some curious combination of influences—perhaps the atmosphere of the place, added to the stimulation of the faintly discernible faces around me, and my impulse to prove my own ability in this untried field of narration—gave me a sudden sense of being inspired. I found myself voicing fancies as though they were facts, and readily including imaginary names and data which certainly were not in any way premeditated.

"This barn stands on the old Creed place," I began. "Peter Creed was its last owner, but I suppose that it has always been and always will be known as the Turner barn. A few yards away to the south you will find the crumbling brickwork and gaping hollows of an old foundation, now overgrown with weeds that almost conceal a few charred timbers. That is all that is left of the old Ashley Turner house."

I cleared my throat again, not through any effort to gain time for my thoughts, but to feel for a moment the satisfaction arising from the intent attitude of my audience, particularly my wife, who had leaned forward and was looking at me with an expression of startled surprise.

"Ashley Turner must have had a pretty fine-looking farm here thirty years or so ago," I continued, "when he brought his wife to it. This barn was new then. But he was a ne'er-do-well, with nothing to be said in his favor, unless you admit his fame as a practical joker. Strange how the ne'er-do-well is often equipped with an extravagant sense of humor! Turner had a considerable retinue among the riffraff boys of the neighborhood, who made this barn a noisy rendezvous and followed his hints in much whimsical mischief. But he committed most of his practical jokes when drunk, and in his sober moments he abused his family and let his wife struggle to keep up the acres, assisted only by a half-competent man of all work. Finally he took to roving. No one knew how he got pocket-money; his wife could not have given him any. Then someone discovered that he was going over to Creed's now and then, and everything was explained."

This concise data of mine was evidently not holding the close attention of my youthful audience. They annoyed me by frequent pranks and whisperings. No one could have been more surprised at my glibness than I myself, except perhaps my wife, whose attitude of strained attention had not relaxed. I resumed my story.

"Peter Creed was a good old-fashioned usurer of the worst type. He went to church regularly one day in the week and gouged his neighbors—any that he could get into his clutches—on the other six. He must have been lending Turner drinking money, and everyone knew what the security must be.

"At last there came a day when the long-suffering wife revolted. Turner had come home extra drunk and in his most maudlin humor. Probably he attempted some drunken prank upon his overtaxed helpmate. Old Ike, the hired man, said that he thought Turner had rigged up some scare for her in the barn and that he had never heard anything so much like straight talking from his mistress, either before or since, and he was working in the woodshed at the

time, with the door shut. Shortly after that tirade Ashley
Turner disappeared, and no one saw or heard of him or
thought about him for a couple of years except when the
sight of his tired-looking wife and scrawny children re-
vived the recollection.

"At last, on a certain autumn day, old Peter Creed
turned up here at the Turner place. I imagine Mrs. Turner
knew what was in store for her when his rusty buggy came
in sight around the corner of the barn. At any rate, she
made no protest, and listened meekly to his curt statement
that he held an overdue mortgage, with plenty of back
interest owing, and it was time for her to go. She went.
Neither she nor anyone else doubted Creed's rights in the
matter, and, after all, I believe it got a better home for her
somewhere in the long run."

I paused here in my narration to draw breath and readjust my leg, which had become cramped. There was a
general readjustment and shifting of position, with some
levity. It was darker now. The rafters above us were invisible, and the faces about me looked oddly white against
the shadowy background. After a moment or two of delay
I cleared my throat sharply and continued.

"Old Creed came thus into possession of this place,
just as he had come to own a dozen others in the county.
He usually lived on one until he was able to sell it at a
good profit over his investment; so he settled down in the
Turner house, and kept old Ike because he worked for little or nothing. But he seemed to have a hard time finding
a purchaser.

"It must have been about a year later when an unexpected thing happened. Creed had come out here to the
barn to lock up—he always did that himself—when he
noticed something unusual about the haymow—this hay-
mow—which stood then about six feet above the barn
floor. He looked closer through the dusk, and saw a pair

of boots; went nearer, and found that they were fitted to a pair of human legs whose owner was sound asleep in his hay. Creed picked up a short stick and beat on one boot.

"'Get out of here,' he said, 'or I'll have you locked up.' The sleeper woke in slow fashion, sat up, grinned, and said:

"'Hello, Peter Creed.' It was Ashley Turner, beyond question. Creed stepped back a pace or two and seemed at a loss for words. An object slipped from Turner's pocket as he moved, slid along the hay, and fell to the barn floor. It was a half-filled whisky-flask.

"No one knows full details of the conversation that ensued, of course. Such little as I am able to tell you of what was said and done comes through old Ike, who watched from a safe distance outside the barn, ready to act at a moment's notice as best suited his own safety and welfare. Of one thing Ike was certain—Creed lacked his usual browbeating manner. He was apparently struggling to assume an unwonted friendliness. Turner was very drunk, but triumphant, and his satisfaction over what he must have felt was the practical joke of his life seemed to make him friendly.

"'I kept 'em all right,' he said again and again. 'I've got the proof. I wasn't working for nothing all these months. I ain't fool enough yet to throw away papers even when I'm drunk.'

"To the watchful Ike's astonishment, Creed evidently tried to persuade him to come into the house for something to eat. Turner slid off the haymow, found his steps too unsteady, laughed foolishly, and suggested that Creed bring some food to him there. 'Guess I've got a right to sleep in the barn or house, whichever I want,' he said, leering into Creed's face. The old usurer stood there for a few minutes eying Turner thoughtfully. Then he actually gave him a shoulder back onto the hay, said something about finding a snack of supper, and started out of the barn. In the doorway he turned, looked back, then walked over to the edge of the mow and groped on the floor until he found the whisky-flask, picked it up, tossed it into Turner's lap, and stumbled out of the barn again."

I was becoming interested in my own story and somewhat pleased with the fluency of it, but my audience annoyed me. There was intermittent whispering, with some laughter, and I inferred that one or another would occasionally stimulate this inattention by tickling a companion with a straw. Miss Anstell, who is so frivolous by nature that I sometimes question her right to a place in my classroom, I even suspected of irritating the back of my own neck in the same fashion. Naturally, I ignored it.

"Peter Creed," I repeated, "went into the house. Ike hung around the barn, waiting. He was frankly curious. In a few minutes his employer reappeared, carrying a plate heaped with an assortment of scraps. Ike peered and listened then without compunction.

"'It's the best I've got,' he heard Creed say grudgingly. Turner's tones were now more drunkenly belligerent.

"'It had better be,' he said loudly. 'And I'll take the best bed after to-night.' Evidently he was eating and muttering between mouthfuls. 'You might have brought me another bottle.'

"'I did,' said Creed, to the listening Ike's great astonishment. Turner laughed immoderately.

"A long silence followed. Turner was either eating or drinking. Then he spoke again, more thickly and drowsily.

"'Damn unpleasant that rope. Why don't you haul it up out of my way?'

"'It don't hurt you any,' said Creed.

"'Don't you wish it would?' said Turner, with drunken shrewdness. 'But I don't like it. Haul it away.'

"'I will,' said Creed.

"There was a longer silence, and then there came an intermittent rasping sound. A moment later Creed came suddenly from the barn. Ike fumbled with a large rake, and made as though to hang it on its accustomed peg near the barn door. Creed eyed him sharply. 'Get along to bed,' he ordered, and Ike obeyed.

"That was a Saturday night. On Sunday morning Ike went to the barn later than usual and hesitatingly. Even then he was first to enter. He found the drunkard's body hanging here over the mow, just about where we are sitting, stark and cold. It was a gruesome end to a miserable home-coming."

My audience was quiet enough now. Miss Anstell and one or two others giggled loudly, but it was obviously forced, and found no further echo. The breeze which had sprung up some time before was producing strange creakings and raspings in the old timbers, and the pulley-wheel far above us clanked with a dismal repetitious sound, like the tolling of a cracked bell.

I waited a moment, well satisfied with the effect, and then continued.

"The coroner's jury found it suicide, though some shook their heads meaningly. Turner had apparently sobered up enough to stand, and, making a simple loop around his neck by catching the rope through its own hook, had then slid off the mow. The rope which went over the pulley wheel up there in the roof ran out through a window under the eaves, and was made fast near the barn door outside, where anyone could haul on it. Creed testified the knot was one he had tied many days before. Ike was a timorous old man, with a wholesome fear of his employer, and he supported the testimony and made no reference to his eavesdropping of the previous evening, though he heard Creed swear before the jury that he did not recognize the tramp he had fed and lodged. There were no papers in Turner's pockets; only a few coins, and a marked pocket-knife that gave the first clue to his identity.

"A few of the neighbors said that it was a fitting end, and that the verdict was a just one. Nevertheless, whisperings began and increased. People avoided Creed and the neighborhood. Rumors grew that the barn was haunted. Passers-by on the road after dark said they heard the old pulley-wheel clanking when no breeze stirred, much as you hear it now. Some claim to have heard maudlin laughter. Possible purchasers were frightened away, and Creed grew more and more solitary and misanthropic. Old Ike hung on, Heaven knows why, though I suppose Creed paid him some sort of wage.

"Rumors grew. Folks said that neither Ike nor Creed entered this barn after a time, and no hay was put in, though Creed would not have been Creed if he had not sold off the bulk of what he had, ghost or no ghost. I can imagine him slowly forking it out alone, daytimes, and the amount of hay still here proves that even he finally lost courage."

I paused a moment, but though there was much uneasy stirring about, and the dismal clanking directly above us was incessant, no one of my audience spoke. It was wholly dark now, and I think all had drawn closer together.

"About ten years ago people began calling Creed crazy." Here I was forced to interrupt my own story. "I shall have to ask you, Miss Anstell, to stop annoying me. I have been aware for some moments that you are brushing my head with a straw, but I have ignored it for the sake of the others." Out of the darkness came Miss Anstell's voice, protesting earnestly, and I realized from the direction of the sound that in the general readjustment she must have settled down in the very center of our circle, and could not be the one at fault. One of the others was childish enough to simulate a mocking burst of raucous laughter, but I chose to ignore it.

"Very well," said I, graciously; "shall I go on?"

"Go on," echoed a subdued chorus.

"It was the night of the twenty-eighth of May, ten years ago—"

"Not the twenty-eighth," broke in my wife's voice, sharply; "that is to-day's date." There was a note in her voice that I hardly recognized, but it indicated that she was in some way affected by my narration, and I felt a distinct sense of triumph.

"It was the night of May twenty-eighth," I repeated firmly.

"Are you making up this story?" my wife's voice continued, still with the same odd tone.

"I am, my dear, and you are interrupting it."

"But an Ashley Turner and later a Peter Creed owned this place," she persisted almost in a whisper, "and I am sure you never heard of them."

I confess that I might wisely have broken off my story then and called for a light. There had been an hysterical note in my wife's voice, and I was startled at her words, for I had no conscious recollection of either name; yet I felt a resultant exhilaration. Our lanterns had grown strangely dim, though I was certain both had been recently trimmed and filled; and from their far corner of the barn they threw no light whatever into our circle. I faced an utter blackness.

"On that night," said I, "old Ike was wakened by sounds as of someone fumbling to unbar and open the housedoor. It was an unwonted hour, and he peered from the window of his little room. By the dim starlight—it was just before dawn—he could see all of the open yard and roadway before the house, with the great barn looming like a black and sinister shadow as its farther barrier. Crossing this space, he saw the figure of Peter Creed, grotesquely stooped and old in the obscuring gloom, moving slowly, almost gropingly, and yet directly, as though impelled, toward the barn's overwhelming shadow. Slowly he unbarred the great door, swung it open, and entered the blacker shadows it concealed. The door closed after him.

"Ike in his secure post of observation did not stir. He could not. Even to his crude imagining there was something utterly horrible in the thought of Creed alone at that hour in just such black darkness as this, with the great timbered chamber haunted at least by its dread memories. He could only wait, tense and fearful of he knew not what.

"A shriek that pierced the silence relaxed his tension, bringing almost a sense of relief, so definite had been his expectancy. But it was a burst of shrill laughter, ribald, uncanny, undeniable, accompanying the shriek that gave him power of motion. He ran half naked a quarter of a mile to the nearest neighbor's and told his story.

"They found Creed hanging, the rope hooked simply around his neck. It was a silent jury that filed from the barn that morning after viewing the body. 'Suicide,' said they, after Ike, shivering and stammering, had testified, harking back to the untold evidence of that other morning years before. Yes, Creed was dead, with a terrible look on his wizen face, and the dusty old rope ran through its pulley-wheel and was fast to a beam high above.

"'He must of climbed to the beam, made the rope fast, and jumped,' said the foreman, solemnly. 'He must of, he must of,' repeated the man, parrotlike, while the sweat stood out on his forehead, 'because there wasn't no other way; but as God is my judge, the knot in the rope and the dust on the beam ain't been disturbed for years.'"

At this dramatic climax there was an audible sigh from my audience. I sat quietly for a time, content to allow the silence and the atmosphere of the place, which actually seemed surcharged with influences not of my creation, to add to the effect my story had caused. There was scarcely a movement in our circle; of that I felt sure. And yet once more, out of the almost tangible darkness above me, something seemed to reach down and brush against my head. A slight motion of air, sufficient to disturb my rather scanty locks, was additional proof that I was the butt of some prank that had just missed its objective. Then, with a fearful suddenness, close to my ear burst a shrill discord of laughter, so uncanny and so unlike the usual sound of student merriment that I started up, half wondering if I had heard it. Almost immediately after it the heavy darkness was torn again by a shriek so terrible in its intensity as completely to differentiate it from the other cries which followed.

"Bring a light!" cried a voice that I recognized as that of my wife, though strangely distorted by emotion. There was a great confusion. Young women struggled from their places and impeded one another in the darkness; but finally, and it seemed an unbearable delay, someone brought a single lantern.

Its frail light revealed Miss Austell half upright from her place in the center of our circle, my wife's arms sustaining her weight. Her face, as well as I could see it, seemed darkened and distorted, and when we forced her clutching hands away from her bared throat we could see, even in that light, the marks of an angry, throttling scar entirely encircling it. Just above her head the old pulley-rope swayed menacingly in the faint breeze.

My recollection is even now confused as to the following moments and our stumbling escape from that gruesome spot. Miss Anstell is now at her home, recovering from what her physician calls mental shock. My wife will not speak of it. The questions I would ask her are checked on my lips by the look of utter terror in her eyes. As I have confessed to you, my own philosophy is hard put to it to withstand not so much the community attitude toward what they are pleased to call my taste in practical joking, but to assemble and adjust the facts of my experience.

IN THE WHEAT
Maurice Level
[transl. Alys Eyre Machlin]
(1920)

With long strokes, slow and rhythmic, Jean Madek thrust his scythe into the wheat, and at the touch of the blade the sheaths that quivered at the end of the stalks fell down softly with a long *froufrou* like silk.

He advanced, measuring his steps by the supple balance of his arm, and behind him the ground showed itself brown, spotted here and there by groups of stones, bristling with thickset sprigs of reddish straw.

His old mother followed close behind him, her back bent as she gathered up the scattered stalks, and seeing only her feet dragging their heavy sabots, her two wrinkled, knotted hands and her body covered with rags, one might have imagined she was some animal crouching on its four feet.

The sun mounted in the horizon. A heavy heat weighed on everything, wrapping the country in torpor, and the field looked like a large piece of ripe fruit, its sap rising in a penetrating perfume.

Gleaning steadily, the old woman grumbled:

"What's your wife doing as late as this? When's she coming!"

"She'll bring dinner at twelve o'clock."

The old woman shrugged her shoulders:

"At least she's not overtiring herself! . . ."

"She's like every one else. Whether she's here or at the farm, she's at work."

"Oh! Work of that sort! . . ."

Then, as if talking to herself as she continued to scrape the ground:

"Our master isn't here either this morning. Perhaps he stayed behind to give her a hand? . . ."

The man held back his scythe:

"What do you mean by that?"

"Me? . . . Nothing . . . Words . . . Something to say . . ."

Jean went on with his work. The old woman began again as if speaking to herself:

"My dead husband wouldn't have had it . . . When he went to the fields, I didn't stay behind to keep the master company."

A second time the reaper raised his head.

"Why are you telling me that?"

"I was thinking, inside me, that your father was more suspicious than you are . . ."

The son straightened himself with a jerk.

"What is it? What do you mean? You must have some reason for talking like this . . ."

"If you must have it, then," blurted the old woman from her stooping position, "people are gossiping about you and about Celine . . . Nasty gossip, too!"

"Who gossips!"

"No one . . . and every one . . . What's more, you can't blame them: they can't help seeing what's under their noses."

"Lies!"

Without seeming to hear him, the old woman pushed aside a clod of earth with her foot and continued:

"I'm telling you for your good. I'm your mother, and I oughtn't to hide anything from you . . . You can be angry if you like. But you've had your warning."

"I tell you it's all lies. Celine is a good housewife, never tired of work; she has everything she wants . . . Why should she be unfaithful! Why! . . ."

The old woman made a vague gesture:

"Who can tell!"

Changing her tone, she went on:

"Besides, I'm not saying she is . . . I'm only speaking for the good of both of you. She is young, she likes to amuse herself, to dress smartly, to go to market on Saturdays. Temptation often takes people quickly. At the beginning they see no harm in it. They let some one give them a ribbon, a fichu, a comb for the hair, a watch-chain . . . And to be able to wear them, they say they were bargains, got for next to nothing . . . that they picked them up on the road. Perhaps it's true . . ."

Every one of the slow words struck into the husband's brain. He thought of his wife's return one evening after she had accompanied the master to the town. He pictured her as he saw her the following Sunday with her lace fichu and moiré ribbons. Above all, he saw the gold chain she said she had picked up on the road . . .

The monotonous voice of the old woman continued:

"It's not her that I'm meaning, of course! But a husband isn't always there: he's in the fields: he goes off to do his month's military service . . ."

The man was no longer listening. His two hands crossed on his scythe, his eyes vague, he was absorbed in the recollections that crowded into his mind. All kinds of little incidents gave weight to the insinuations of the old woman: the master, a known libertine, very hard on all his workers, but always particularly amiable to him: the wife coquettish. And suddenly he remembered that in a week he would have to leave for a long month with his regiment.

At the bottom of the field, under the big trees, a call rang out, and raising himself, Jean Madek saw the head and shoulders of his wife emerging from the gold of the plain, and a few steps behind her, swinging his short, thick stick among the corn, the master with his red face and big, shady-brimmed hat.

And a laughing voice cried:

"Here's the pittance!"

One by one the workers rose out of the corn, sat down under a tree and began to eat their dinner.

Jean sat silent, slowly cutting his black bread into pieces.

"Why are you so quiet, Madek?" said the farmer.

"Are you ill?" added the wife.

"No, but the sun strikes hard. It must have been better in the house?"

The master broke into a laugh:

"You're about right there!"

The meal finished, every one lay down for a nap. They would start work again when the sun had lost a little of its ardor. Madek did not sleep. Lying on his stomach, his chin in his hands, he was lost in thought . . .

As two o'clock struck, the men got up, went back to the field, and once more over the gold of the corn, unruffled by any breeze, there sang the rhythmic sound of the scythes.

When they were all at work the master stretched himself slowly, and in a sleepy voice shouted to the wife of Madek:

"Come and give an eye here, Celine; have you by any chance a needle with you!"

"Yes, master."

"Then come and put a stitch in my blouse. The cows are in the meadow. There's plenty of time before you need fetch them. The sun has turned. It's too hot here just now. I'm going over there under the apple tree. Come to me when you've finished your sheaf. Come by the path so as not to beat down the corn."

They smiled stealthily at each other. But Madek, who was watching, had seen. He made a movement as if to speak, then he lowered his head and went on with the reaping.

The old woman had gone. It was now his wife who was following him. When she had tied up her sheaf he said, without turning:

"Didn't you hear what the master said to you!"

"Yes, I did . . ."

"Then what are you waiting for!"

"I'm just going . . ."

She fastened up her hair which had come undone while she stooped; and, her two hands flat on her hips, her waist swaying under her bright petticoat, she strolled along the path, a cornflower between her teeth.

He watched her being swallowed up in the verdure as one is swallowed up in the sea, and when she had quite disappeared in the shadow of the apple tree that stood out on the horizon, he set to work again.

His movements had lost their quiet ease of the morning. He went forward in jerks, stopping sharply, then on again, his head lowered, his jaw clenched, an ugly frown on his forehead.

All the old woman had said was fermenting in him like new wine, fizzing in his temples, filling him with a sort of drunken rage. At first there had been doubt; then had followed certainty which had taken deeper root because of the incidents that had just happened.

He was advancing, and before him he seemed to see his wife and the master laughing and kissing each other in the shadow of the apple tree.

He was advancing, throwing the weight of his whole body into his arms. Behind him the sheaves fell, and the field that his scythe devoured seemed to grow larger. Never

in the earliest vigor of his manhood had he been able to
work like that.

From a distance, a fellow-worker called:

"Are you going to cut it all to-day?"

Without looking up, he replied: "Perhaps."

When he was only a few yards from the apple tree he
stopped, listening intently; murmurs reached him. A voice,
the voice of his wife, said:

"No . . . He might be able to see us . . ."

And another rougher one replied:

"Keep still! He's at the other end of the field. It'll be
half an hour before he gets here . . . Come closer! . . ."

For some seconds he stood as if transfixed, livid under
his sunburn; then, with a sharp gesture of decision, he
went on reaping. But he had slowed down. The sweep of
the scythe was almost noiseless. The wheat fell to the earth
without a sound. When he was almost under the tree he
heard the sound of kisses. Pulling himself up to his fullest
height, with a furious movement he lifted the scythe. The
blade leapt up, gleaming white in the sun, came down and
plunged . . . Two horrible shrieks rang out, and two frightful things, two heads, bounded up and fell again, be-spat-
tering the stalks that broke with a grating sound . . .

The scythe flew up out of the corn-waves, all red . . .

Madek threw it away, and waving his bloody hands in
the air, roared:

"Help! . . . An accident . . . They were there! . . ."

AT THE FARMHOUSE

E. F. Benson

(1922)

The dusk of a November day was falling fast when John Aylsford came out of his lodging in the cobbled street and started to walk briskly along the road which led eastwards by the shore of the bay. He had been at work while the daylight served him at his painting, and now, when the gathering darkness weaned him from his easel, he was accustomed to go out for air and exercise and cover half a dozen miles before he returned to his solitary supper.

To-night there were but few folk abroad, and those scudded along before the strong southwesterly gale which had roared and raged all day, or, leaning forward, beat their way against it. No fishing-boats had put forth on that maddened sea, but had lain moored behind the quay-wall, tossing uneasily with the backwash of the great breakers that swept by the pier-head. The tide was low now, and they rested on the sandy beach, black blots against the smooth wet surface which somberly reflected the last flames in the west. The sun had gone down in a wrack of broken and flying clouds, angry and menacing with promise of a wild night to come.

For many days past, at this hour John Aylsford had started eastwards for his tramp along the rough coast road by the bay. The last high tide had swept shingle and sand over sections of it, and fragments of seaweed, driven by

the wind, bowled along the ruts. The heavy boom of the
breakers sounded sullenly in the dusk, and white towers
of foam appearing and disappearing showed how high they
leaped over the reefs of rock beyond the headland. For half
a mile or so, slanting himself against the gale he pursued
this road, then turned up a narrow muddy lane sunk deep
between the banks on either side of it. It ran steeply up-
hill, dipped down again, and joined the main road inland.
Having arrived at the junction, John Aylsford went eastwards no more, but turned his steps to the west, arriving,
half an hour after he had set out, on the top of the hill
above the village he had quitted, though five minutes'
ascent would have taken him from his lodgings to the spot
where he now stood looking down on the scattered lights
below him. The wind had blown all wayfarers indoors, and
now in front of him the road that crossed this high and
desolate table-land, sprinkled here and there with lonely
cottages and solitary farms, lay empty and greyly glim-
mering in the wind-swept darkness, not more than faintly
visible.

Many times during this past month had John Aylsford
made this long detour, starting eastwards from the village
and coming back by a wide circuit, and now, as on these
other occasions, he paused in the black shelter of the hedge
through which the wind hissed and whistled, crouching
there in the shadow as if to make sure that none had followed him, and that the road in front lay void of passengers, for he had no mind to be observed by any on these
journeyings. And as he paused he let his hate blaze up,
heartening him for the work the accomplishment of which
alone could enable him to recapture any peace or profit
from life. To-night he was determined to release himself
from the millstone which for so many years had hung
round his neck, drowning him in bitter waters. From long
brooding over the idea of the deed, he had quite ceased to

feel any horror of it. The death of that drunken slut was not a matter for qualms or uneasiness; the world would be well rid of her, and he more than well.

No spark of tenderness for the handsome fisher-girl who once had been his model and for twenty years had been his wife pierced the blackness of his purpose. Just here it was that he had seen her first when on a summer holiday he had lodged with a couple of friends in the farmhouse towards which his way now lay. She was coming up the hill with the late sunset gilding her face, and, breathing quickly from the ascent, had leaned on the wall close by with a smile and a glance for the young man. She had sat to him, and the autumn brought the sequel to the summer in his marriage. He had bought from her uncle the little farmhouse where he had lodged, adding to its modest accommodation a studio and a bedroom above it, and there he had seen the flicker of what had never been love, die out, and over the cold ashes of its embers the poisoned lichen of hatred spread fast. Early in their married life she had taken to drink, and had sunk into a degradation of soul and body that seemed bottomless, dragging him with her, down and down, in the grip of a force that was hardly human in its malignity.

Often during the wretched years that followed he had tried to leave her; he had offered to settle the farm on her and make adequate provision for her, but she had clung to the possession of him, not, it would seem, from any affection for him, but for a reason exactly opposite, namely, that her hatred of him fed and glutted itself on the sight of his ruin. It was as if, in obedience to some hellish power, she set herself to spoil his life, his powers, his possibilities, by tying him to herself. And by the aid of that power, so sometimes he had thought, she enforced her will on him, for, plan as he might to cut the whole dreadful business and leave the wreck behind him, he had never been able to consolidate his resolve into action. There, but a few miles away, was the station from which ran the train that would bear him out of this ancient western kingdom, where the beliefs in spells and superstitions grew rank as the herbage in that soft enervating air, and set him in the dry hard light of cities. The way lay open, but he could not take it; something unseen and potent, of grim inflexibility, held him back. . . .

He had passed no one on his way here, and satisfied now that in the darkness he could proceed without fear of being recognised if a chance wayfarer came from the direction in which he was going, he left the shelter of the hedge, and struck out into the stormy sea of that stupendous gale. Even as a man in the grip of imminent death sees his past life spread itself out in front of him for his final survey before the book is closed, so now, on the brink of the new life from which the deed on which he was determined alone separated him, John Aylsford, as he battled his advance through this great tempest, turned over page after page of his own wretched chronicles, feeling already strangely detached from them; it was as if he read the sordid and enslaved annals of another, wondering at them, and half-pitying, half-despising him who had allowed himself to be bound so long in this ruinous noose.

Yes; it had been just that, a noose drawn ever tighter round his neck, while he choked and struggled all unavailingly. But there was another noose which should very soon now be drawn rapidly and finally tight, and the drawing of that in his own strong hands would free him. As he dwelt on that for a moment, his fingers stroked and patted the hank of whipcord that lay white and tough in his pocket. A noose, a knot drawn quickly taut, and he would have paid her back with justice and swifter mercy for the long strangling which he had suffered.

Voluntarily and eagerly at the beginning had he allowed her to slip the noose about him, for Ellen Trenair's beauty in those days, so long past and so everlastingly regretted, had been enough to ensnare a man. He had been warned at the time, by hint and half-spoken suggestion, that it was ill for a man to mate with a girl of that dark and ill-famed family, or for a woman to wed a boy in whose veins ran the blood of Jonas Trenair, once Methodist preacher, who learned on one All-Hallows' Eve a darker gospel than he had ever preached before. What had happened to the girls who had married into that dwindling family, now all but extinct? One, before her marriage was a year old, had gone off her head, and now, a withered and ancient crone, mewed and gibbered about the streets of the village, picking garbage from the gutter and munching it in her toothless jaws. Another, Ellen's own mother, had been found hanging from the banister of her stairs, stark and grim. Then there was young Frank Pencarris, who had wed Ellen's sister. He had sunk into an awful melancholy, and sat tracing on sheets of paper the visions that beset his eyes, headless shapes, and foaming mouths, and the images of the spawn of hell. . . . John Aylsford, in those early days, had laughed to scorn these old-wife tales of spells and sorceries: they belonged to ages long past, whereas fair Ellen Trenair was of the lovely present, and had lit desire in his heart which she alone could assuage. He had no use, in the brightness of her eye, for such shadows and superstitions; her beams dispelled them.

Bitter and black as midnight had his enlightenment been, darkening through dubious dusks till the mirk of the pit itself enveloped him. His laughter at the notion that in this twentieth century spells and sorceries could survive, grew silent on his lips. He had seen the cattle of a neighbour who had offended one whom it was wiser not to cross, dwindle and pine, though there were rich pastures

for their grazing, till the rib-bones stuck out like the timbers of stranded wrecks. He had seen the spring on another
farm run dry at lambing-time because the owner, sceptic
like himself, had refused that bounty, which all prudent
folk paid to the wizard of Mareuth, who, like Ellen, was
of the blood of Jonas Trenair. From scorn and laughter he
had wavered to an uneasy wonder, and from wonder his
mind had passed to the conviction that there were powers occult and terrible which strove in darkness and prevailed, secrets and spells that could send disease on man
and beast, dark incantations, known to few, which could
maim and cripple, and of these few his wife was one. His
reason revolted, but some conviction, deeper than reason,
held its own. To such a view it seemed that the deed he
contemplated was no crime, but rather an act of obedience
to the ordinance, "Thou shalt not suffer a witch to live."
And the sense of detachment was over that, even as over
the memories that oozed up in his mind. Somebody—not
he—who had planned everything very carefully was in the
next hour going to put an end to his bondage.

So the years had passed, he floundering ever deeper
in the slough into which he was plunged, out of which
while she lived he could never emerge. For the last year,
she, wearying of his perpetual presence at the farm, had
allowed him to take a lodging in the village. She did not
loose her hold over him, for the days were few on which
she did not come with demands for a handful of shillings
to procure her the raw spirits which alone could slake
her thirst. Sometimes as he sat at work there in the north
room looking on to the small garden-yard, she would come
lurching up the path, with her bloated crimson face set
on the withered neck, and tap at his window with fingers
shrivelled like bird's claws. Body and limbs were no more
than bones over which the wrinkled skin was stretched,
but her face bulged monstrously with layers of fat. He

would give her whatever he had about him, and if it was
not enough, she would plant herself there, grinning at him
and wheedling him, or with screams and curses threaten-
ing him with such fate as he had known to overtake those
who crossed her will. But usually he gave her enough to
satisfy her for that day and perhaps the next, for thus she
would the more quickly drink herself to death. Yet death
seemed long in coming. . . .

He remembered well how first the notion of killing
her came into his head, just a little seed, small as that
of mustard, which lay long in barrenness. Only the bare
idea of it was there, like an abstract proposition. Then
imperceptibly in the fruitful darkness of his mind, it must
have begun to sprout, for presently a tendril, still soft and
white, prodded out into the daylight. He almost pushed it
back again, for fear that she, by some divining art, should
probe his purpose. But when next she came for supplies,
he saw no gleam of surmise in her red-rimmed eyes, and
she took her money and went her way, and his purpose
put forth another leaf, and the stem of it grew sappy. All
autumn through it had flourished, and grown tree-like,
and fresh ideas, fresh details, fresh precautions, flocked
there like building birds and made it gay with singing. He
sat under the shadow of it and listened with brightening
hopes to their song; never had there been such peerless
melody. They knew their tunes now, there was no need for
any further rehearsal.

He began to wonder how soon he would be back on the
road again, with face turned from this buffeting wind, and
on his way home. His business would not take him long;
the central deed of it would be over in a couple of minutes, and he did not anticipate delay about the setting to
work on it, for by seven o'clock of the evening, as well he
knew, she was usually snoring in the oblivion of complete
drunkenness, and even if she was not as far gone as that,

she would certainly be incapable of any serious resistance.
After that, a quarter of an hour more would finish the
job, and he would leave the house secure already from any
chance of detection. Night after night during these last
ten days he had been up here, peering from the darkness
into the lighted room where she sat, then listening for her
step on the stairs as she stumbled up to bed, or hearing her
snorings as she slept in her chair below. The outhouse, he
knew, was well stocked with paraffin; he needed no further
apparatus than the whipcord and the matches he carried
with him. Then back he would go along the exact route by
which he had come, re-entering the village again from the
eastwards, in which direction he had set out.

This walk of his was now a known and established
habit; half the village during the last week or two had
seen him every evening set forth along the coast road, for
a tramp in the dusk when the light failed for his painting,
and had seen him come back again as they hung about
and smoked in the warm dusk, a couple of hours later.
None knew of his detour to the main road which took him
westwards again above the village and so to the stretch of
bleak upland along which now he fought his way against
the gale. Always round about the hour of eight he had
entered the village again front the other side, and had
stopped and chatted with the loiterers. To-night, no later
than was usual, he would come up the cobbled road again,
and give "good night" to any who lingered there outside
the public-house. In this wild wind it was not likely that
there would be such, and if so, no matter; he had been
seen already setting forth on his usual walk by the coast of
the bay, and if none outside saw him return, none could
see the true chart of his walk. By eight he should be back
to his supper, there would be a soused herring for him,
and a cut of cheese, and the kettle would be singing on the
hob for his hot whisky-toddy. He would have a keen edge

for the enjoyment of them to-night; he would drink long healths to the damned and the dead. Not till to-morrow, probably, would the news of what had happened reach him, for the farmhouse lay lonely and sheltered by the wood of firs. However high might mount the beacon of its blazing, it would scarcely, screened by the tall trees, light up the western sky, and be seen from the village nestling below the steep hill-crest.

By now John Aylsford had come to the fir wood which bordered the road on the left, and, as he passed into its shelter, cut off from him the violence of the gale. All its branches were astir with the sound of some vexed, over-head sea, and the trunks that upheld them creaked and groaned in the fury of the tempest. Somewhere behind the thick scud of flying cloud the moon must have risen, for the road glimmered more visibly, and the tossing blackness of the branches was clear enough against the grey tumult overhead. Behind the tempest she rode in serene skies, and in the murderous clarity of his mind he likened himself to her. Just for half an hour more he would still grope and scheme and achieve in this hurly-burly, and then, like a balloon released, soar through the clouds and find seren-ity. A couple of hundred yards now would take him round the corner of the wood; from there the miry lane led from the highroad to the farm.

He hastened rather than retarded his going as he drew near, for the wood, though it roared with the gale, began to whisper to him of memories. Often in that summer before his marriage had he strayed out at dusk into it, certain that before he had gone many paces he would see a shadow flitting towards him through the firs, or hear the crack of dry twigs in the stillness. Here was their tryst; she would come up from the village with the excuse of bringing fish to the farmhouse, after the boats had come in, and deserting the high-road make a short cut through the wood. Like some distant blink of lightning the memory of those evenings quivered distantly on his mind, and he quickened his step. The years that followed had killed and buried those recollections, but who knew what stirring of corpses and dry bones might not yet come to them if he lingered there? He fingered the whipcord in his pocket, and launched out, beyond the trees, into the full fury of the gale.

The farmhouse was near now and in full view, a black blot against the clouds. A beam of light shone from an uncurtained window on the ground-floor, and the rest was dark. Even thus had he seen it for many nights past, and well knew what sight would greet him as he stole up nearer. And even so it was to-night, for there she sat in the studio he had built, betwixt table and fireplace with the bottle near her, and her withered hands stretched out to the blaze, and the huge bloated face swaying on her shoulders. Beside her tonight were the wrecked remains of a chair, and the first sight that he caught of her was to show her feeding the fire with the broken pieces of it. It had been too troublesome to bring fresh logs from the store of wood; to break up a chair was the easier task.

She stirred and sat more upright, then reached out for the bottle that stood beside her, and drank from the mouth of it. She drank and licked her lips and drank again, and staggered to her feet, tripping on the edge of the hearthrug. For the moment that seemed to anger her, and with clenched teeth and pointing finger she mumbled at it; then once more she drank, and, lurching forward, took the lamp from the table. With it in her hand she shuffled to the door, and the room was left to the flickering firelight. A moment afterwards, the bedroom window above sprang into light, an oblong of bright illumination.

As soon as that appeared he crept round the house to the door. He gently turned the handle of it, and found it unlocked. Inside was a small passage entrance, on the left of which ascended the stairs to the bedroom above the studio. All was silent there, but from where he stood he could see that the door into the bedroom was open, for a shaft of light from the lamp she had carried up with her was shed on to the landing there. . . . Everything was smoothing itself out to render his course most easy. Even the gale was his friend, for it would be bellows for the fire. He slipped off his shoes, leaving them on the mat, and drew the whipcord from his pocket. He made a noose in it, and began to ascend the stairs. They were well-built of seasoned oak, and no creak betrayed his advancing footfall.

At the top he paused, listening for any stir of movement within, but there was nothing to be heard but the sound of heavy breathing from the bed that lay to the left of the door and out of sight. She had thrown herself down there, he guessed, without undressing, leaving the lamp to burn itself out. He could see it through the open door already beginning to flicker; on the wall behind it were a couple of water-colours, pictures of his own, one of the little walled garden by the farm, the other of the pinewood of their tryst. Well he remembered painting them: she would sit by him as he worked, with prattle and singing. He looked at them now quite detachedly; they seemed to him wonderfully good, and he envied the artist that fresh, clean skill. Perhaps he would take them down presently and carry them away with him.

Very softly now he advanced into the room, and, looking round the corner of the door, he saw her, sprawling and fully dressed on the broad bed. She lay on her back, eyes closed and mouth open, her dull grey hair spread over the pillow. Evidently she had not made the bed that day, for she lay stretched on the crumpled back-turned blankets. A hair-brush was on the floor beside her; it seemed to have fallen from her hand. He moved quickly towards her.

He put on his shoes again when he came to the foot of
the stairs, carrying the lamp with him and the two pictures which he had taken down from the wall, and went
into the studio. He set the lamp on the table and drew
down the blinds, and his eye fell on the half-empty whisky bottle from which he had seen her drinking. Though
his hand was quite steady and his mind composed and
tranquil, there was yet at the back of it some impression
that was slowly developing, and a good dose of spirits
would no doubt expunge that. He drank half a tumbler
of it raw and undiluted, and though it seemed no more
than water in his mouth, he soon felt that it was doing its
work and sponging away from his mind the picture that
had been outlining itself there. In a couple of minutes he
was quite himself again, and could afford to wonder and
laugh at the illusion, for it was no less than that, which
had been gaining on him. For though he could distinctly
remember drawing the noose tight, and seeing the face
grow black, and struggling with the convulsive movements
of those withered limbs that soon lay quiet again, there
had sprung up in his mind some unaccountable impression that what he had left there huddled on the bed was
not just the bundle of withered limbs and strangled neck,
but the body of a young girl, smooth of skin and golden
of hair, with mouth that smiled drowsily. She had been
asleep when he came in, and now was half-awake, and was
stirring and stretching herself. In what dim region of his
mind that image had formed itself, he had no idea; all he
cared about now was that his drink had shattered it again,
and he could proceed now with order and method to make
all secure. Just one drop more first: how lucky it was that
this morning he had been liberal with his money when she
came to the village, for he would have been sorry to have
gone without that fillip to his nerves.

He looked at his watch, and saw to his satisfaction that it was still only a little after seven o'clock. Half an hour's walking, with this gale to speed his steps, would easily carry him from door to door, round the detour which approached the village from the east, and a quarter of an hour, so he reckoned, would be sufficient to accomplish thoroughly what remained to be done here. He must not hurry and thus overlook some precaution needful for his safety, though, on the other hand, he would be glad to be gone from the house as soon as might be, and he proceeded to set about his work without delay. There was brushwood and fire-kindling to be brought in from the woodshed in the yard, and he made three journeys, returning each time with his arms full, before he had brought in what he judged to be sufficient. Most of this he piled in a loose heap in the studio; with the rest he ascended once more to the bedroom above and made a heap of it there in the middle of the floor. He took the curtains down from the windows, for they would make a fine wick for the paraffin, and stuffed them into the pile. Before he left, he looked once more at what lay on the bed, and marvelled at the illusion which the whisky had dispelled, and as he looked, the sense that he was free mounted and bubbled in his head. The thing seemed scarcely human at all; it was a monster from which he had delivered himself, and now, with the thought of that to warn him, he was no longer eager to get through with his work and be gone, for it was all part of that act of riddance which he had accomplished, and he gloried in it. Soon, when all was ready, he would come back once more and soak the fuel and set light to it, and purge with fire the corruption that lay humped on the bed.

The fury of the gale had increased with nightfall, and as he went downstairs again he heard the rattle of loosened

tiles on the roof, and the crash as they shattered themselves on the cobbles of the yard. At that a sudden misgiv-
ing made his breath to catch in his throat, as he pictured
to himself some maniac blast falling on the house and
crashing in the walls that now trembled and shuddered.
Supposing the whole house fell, even if he escaped with
his life from the toppling ruin, what would his life be
worth? There would be search made in the fallen debris
to find the body of her who lay strangled with the whipcord round her neck, and he pictured to himself the slow,
relentless march of justice. He had bought whipcord only
yesterday at a shop in the village, insisting on its strength
and toughness . . . would it be wiser now, this moment,
to untie the noose and take it back with him or add it to
his brushwood? . . . He paused on the staircase, pondering
that; but his flesh quaked at the thought, and master of
himself though he had been during those few struggling
minutes, he distrusted his power of making himself handle
once more that which could struggle no longer. But even
as he tried to screw his courage to the point, the violence
of the squall passed, and the shuddering house braced itself again. He need not fear that; the gale was his friend
that would blow on the flames, not his enemy. The blasts
that trumpeted overhead were the voices of the allies who
had come to aid him.

All was arranged then upstairs for the pouring of the
paraffin and the lighting of the pyre; it remained but to
make similar dispositions in the studio. He would stay
to feed the flames till they raged beyond all power of
extinction; and now he began to plan the line of his retreat. There were two doors in the studio: one by the fire-
place which opened on to the little garden; the other gave
into the passage entrance from which mounted the stairs
and so to the door through which he had come into the
house. He decided to use the garden-door for his exit; but

when he came to open it, he found that the key was stiff
in the rusty lock, and did not yield to his efforts. There
was no use in wasting time over that; it made no difference
through which door he finally emerged, and he began pil-
ing up his heap of wood at that end of the room. The lamp
was burning low; but the fire, which only so few minutes
ago she had fed with a broken chair, shone brightly, and
a flaming ember from it would serve to set light to his
conflagration. There was a straw mat in front of it, which
would make fine kindling, and with these two fires, one in
the bedroom upstairs and the other here, there would be
no mistake about the incineration of the house and all that
it contained. His own crime, if crime it was, would perish,
too, and all evidence thereof, victim and whipcord, and
the very walls of the house of sin and hate. It was a great
deed and a fine adventure, and as the liquor he had drunk
began to circulate more buoyantly through his veins, he
gloried at the thought of the approaching consummation.
He would slip out of the sordid tragedy of his past life, as
from a discarded garment that he threw into the bonfire
he would soon kindle.

All was ready now for the soaking of the fuel he had
piled with the paraffin, and he went out to the shed in the
yard where the barrel stood. A big tin ewer stood beside
it, which he filled and carried indoors. That would be sufficient for the soaking of the pile upstairs, and, fetching
the smoky and flickering lamp from the studio, he went
up again, and like a careful gardener watering some bed
of choice blossoms, he sprinkled and poured till his ewer
was empty. He gave but one glance to the bed behind him,
where the huddled thing lay so quietly, and as he turned,
lamp in hand, to go down again, the draught that came in
through the window against which the gale blew, extinguished it. A little blue flame of burning vapour rose in
the chimney and went out; so, having no further use for it,

he pitched it on to the pile of soaked material. As he left the room he thought he heard some small stir of movement behind him, but he told himself that it was but something slipping in the heap he had built there.

Again he went out into the storm. The clouds that scudded overhead were thinner now, though the gale blew not less fiercely, and the blurred, watery moonlight was brighter. Once for a moment, as he approached the shed, he caught sight of the full orb plunging madly among the streaming vapours; then she was hidden again behind the wrack. Close in front of him were the fir trees of the wood where those sweet trysts had been held, and once again the vision of her as she had been broke into his mind and the queer conviction that it was no withered and bloated hag, who lay on the bed upstairs but the fair, comely limbs and the golden head. It was even more vivid now, and he made haste to get back to the studio, where he would find the trusty medicine that had dispelled that vision before. He would have to make two journeys at least with his tin ewer before he transported enough oil to feed the larger pyre below, and so, to save time, he took the barrel off its stand, and rolled it along the path and into the house. He paused at the foot of the stairs, listening to hear if anything stirred, but all was silent. Whatever had slipped up there was steady again; from outside only came the squeal and bellow of the wind.

The studio was brightly but fitfully lit by the flames on the hearth; for a moment a noonday blazed there, the next but the last smoulder of some red sunset. It was easier to decant from the barrel into his ewer than carry the heavy keg and sprinkle from it, and once and once again he filled and emptied it. One more application would be sufficient, and after that he could let what remained trickle out on to the floor. But by some awkward movement he managed to spill a pint of it down the front of his trousers: he must be sure, therefore (how quickly his brain responded with counsels of precautions), to have some accident with his lamp when he came in to his supper, which should account for this little misadventure. Or, probably, the wind through which he would presently be walking would dry it before he reached the village.

So, for the last time, with matches ready in his hand, he mounted the stairs to set light to the fuel piled in the room above. His second dose of whisky sang in his head, and he said to himself, smiling at the humour of the notion, "She always liked a fire in her bedroom; she shall have it now." That seemed a very comical idea, and it dwelt in his head as he struck the match which should light it for her. Then, still grinning, he gave one glance to the bed, and the smile died on his face, and the wild cymbals of panic crashed in his brain. The bed was empty; no huddled shape lay there.

Distraught with terror, he thrust the match into the soaked pile and the flame flared up. Perhaps the body had rolled off the bed. It must, in any case, be here some- where, and when once the room was alight there would be nothing more to fear. High rose the smoky flame, and, banging the door, he leaped down the stairs to set light to the pile below and be gone from the house. Yet, whatever monstrous miracle his eye had assured him of, it could not be that she still lived and had left the place where she lay, for she had ceased to breathe when the noose was tight round her neck, and her fight for life and air had long been stilled. But, if by some hideous witchcraft, she was not dead, it would soon be over now with her in the stupefaction of the smoke and the scorching flames. Let be; the door was shut and she within, for him it remained to be finished with the business, and flee from the house of terror, lest he leave the sanity of his soul behind him.

The red glare from the hearth in the studio lit his steps down the passage from the stairway, and already he could hear from above the dry crack and snap from the fire that prospered there. As he shuffled in, he held his hands to his head, as if pressing the brain back into its cool case, from which it seemed eager to fly out into the welter of storm and fire and hideous imagination. If he could only control himself for a few moments more, all would be done and he would escape from this disordered haunted place into the night and the gale, leaving behind him the blaze that would burn away all perilous stuff. Again the flames broke out in the embers on the hearth, bravely burning, and he took from the heart of the glare a fragment on which the fire was bursting into yellow flowers. He heeded not the scorching of his hand, for it was but for a moment that he held it, and then plunged it into the pile that dripped with the oil he had poured on it. A tower of flame mounted, licking the rafters of the low ceiling, then died away as if suffocated by its own smoke, but crept onwards, nosing its way along till it reached the straw mat, which blazed fiercely. That blaze kindled the courage in him; whatever trick his imagination had played on him just now, he had nothing to fear except his own terror, which now he mastered again, for nothing real could ever escape from the conflagration, and it was only the real that he feared. Spells and witchcrafts and superstitions, such as for the last twenty years had battened on him, were all enclosed in that tight-drawn noose.

It was time to be gone, for all was safe now, and the room was growing to oven-heat. But as he picked his way across the floor over which runnels of flames from the spilt barrel were beginning to spread this way and that, he heard from above the sound of a door unlatched, and footsteps light and firm tapped on the stairs. For one second the sheer catalepsy of panic seized him, but he recovered his control, and with hands that groped through the thick smoke he found the door. At that moment the fire shot up in a blaze of blinding flame, and there in the doorway stood Ellen. It was no withered body and bloated face that confronted him, but she with whom he had trysted in the wood, with the bloom of eternal youth upon her, and the smooth soft hand, on which was her wedding-ring, pointed at him.

It was in vain that he called on himself to rush forward out of that torrid and suffocating air. The front door was open, he had but to pass her and speed forth safe into the night. But no power from his will reached his limbs; his will screamed to him, "Go, go! Push by her: it is but a phantom which you fear!" But muscle and sinew were in mutiny, and step by step he retreated before that pointing finger and the radiant shape that advanced on him. The flames that flickered over the floor had discovered the paraffin he had spilt, and leaped up his leg.

Just one spot in his brain retained lucidity from the encompassing terror. Somewhere behind that barrier of fire there was the second door into the garden. He had but cursorily attempted to unlock its rusty wards; now, surely, the knowledge that there alone was escape would give strength to his hand. He leaped backwards through the flames, still with eyes fixed on her who ever advanced in time with his retreat, and turning, wrestled and strove with the key. Something snapped in his hand, and there still in the keyhole was the bare shaft.

Holding his breath, for the heat scorched his throat, he groped towards where he knew was the window through which he had first seen her that night. The flames licked fiercely round it, but there, beneath his hand, was the hasp, and he threw it open. At that the wind poured in as through the nozzle of a plied bellows, and Death rose high and bright around him. Through the flames, as he sank to the floor, a face radiant with revenge scowled and smiled on him.

DEARTH'S FARM
Gerald Bullett
(1923)

I

It is really not far: our fast train does it in eighty minutes. But so sequestered is the little valley in which I have made my solitary home that I never go to town without the delicious sensation of poising my hand over a lucky-bag full of old memories. In the train I amuse myself by summoning up some of those ghosts of the past, a past not distant but sufficiently remote in atmosphere from my present to be invested with a certain sentimental glamour. "Perhaps I shall meet you—or you." But never yet have I succeeded in guessing what London held up her sleeve for me. She has that happiest of tricks—without which paradise will be dull indeed—the trick of surprise. In London, if in no other place, it is the unexpected that happens. For me Fleet Street is the scene *par excellence* of these adventurous encounters, and it was in Fleet Street, three months ago, that I ran across Bailey, of Queens', whom I hadn't seen for five years. Bailey is not his name, nor Queens' his college, but these names will serve to reveal what is germane to my purpose and to conceal the rest.

His recognition of me was instant; mine of him more slow. He told me his name twice; we stared at each other, and I struggled to disguise the blankness of my memory.

The situation became awkward. I was the more embarrassed because I feared lest he should too odiously misinterpret my nonrecognition of him, for the man was shabby and unshaven enough to be suspicious of an intentional slight. Bailey, Bailey . . . now who the devil was Bailey? And then, when he had already made a gesture of moving on, memory stirred to activity.

"Of course, I remember. Bailey. Theosophy. You used to talk to me about theosophy, didn't you? I remember perfectly now." I glanced at my watch. "If you're not busy let's go and have tea somewhere."

He smiled, with a hint of irony in his eyes, as he answered: "I'm not busy." I received the uncomfortable impression that he was hungry and with no ordinary hunger, and the idea kept me silent, like an awkward schoolboy, while we walked together to a tea-shop that I knew.

Seated on opposite sides of the tea-table we took stock of each other. He was thin, and his hair greying; his complexion had a soiled unhealthy appearance; the cheeks had sunk in a little, throwing into prominence the high cheekbones above which his sensitive eyes glittered with a new light, a light not of heaven. Compared with the Bailey I now remembered so well, a rather sleek young man with an almost feline love of luxury blossoming like a tropical plant in the exotic atmosphere of his Cambridge rooms, compared with that man this was but a pale wraith. In those days he had been a flaming personality, suited well—too well, for my plain taste—to the highly-coloured orientalism that he affected in his mural decorations. And co-existent in him with this lust for soft cushions and chromatic orgies, which repelled me, there was an imagination that attracted me: an imagination delighting in highly-coloured metaphysical theories of the universe. These theories, which were as fantastic as *The Arabian*

Nights and perhaps as unreal, proved his academic undo-
ing: he came down badly in his Tripos, and had to leave
without a degree. Many a man has done that and yet prospered, but Bailey, it was apparent, hadn't prospered. I
made the conventional inquiries, adding, "It must be six
or seven years since we met last."

"More than that," said Bailey morosely, and lapsed into
silence. "Look here," he burst out suddenly, "I'm going to
behave like a cad. I'm going to ask you to lend me a pound
note. And don't expect it back in a hurry."

We both winced a little as the note changed hands.
"You've had bad luck," I remarked, without, I hope, a hint
of pity in my voice. "What's wrong?"

He eyed me over the rim of his teacup. "I look a lot
older to you, I expect?"

"You don't look very fit," I conceded.

"No, I don't." His cup came down with a nervous slam
upon the saucer. "Going grey, too, aren't I?" I was forced
to nod agreement. "Yet, do you know, a month ago there
wasn't a grey hair in my head. You write stories, don't you?
I saw your name somewhere. I wonder if you could write
my story. You may get your money back after all . . . By
God, that would be funny, wouldn't it!"

I couldn't see the joke, but I was curious about his story.
And after we had lit our cigarettes he told it to me, to the
accompaniment of a driving storm of rain that tapped like
a thousand idiot fingers upon the plate-glass windows of
the shop.

II

A few weeks ago, said Bailey, I was staying at the house of
a cousin of mine. I never liked the woman, but I wanted
free board and lodging, and hunger soon blunts the edge

of one's delicacy. She's at least ten years my senior, and all I could remember of her was that she had bullied me when I was a child into learning to read. Ten years ago she married a man named Dearth—James Dearth, the resident owner of a smallish farm in Norfolk, not far from the coast. All her relatives opposed the marriage. Relatives always do. If people waited for the approval of relatives before marrying, the world would be depopulated in a generation. This time it was religion. My cousin's people were primitive and methodical in their religion, as the name of their sect confessed; whereas Dearth professed a universal toleration that they thought could only be a cloak for indifference. I have my own opinion about that, but it doesn't matter now. When I met the man I forgot all about religion: I was simply repelled by the notion of any woman marrying so odd a being. Rather small in build, he possessed the longest and narrowest face I have ever seen on a man of his size. His eyes were set exceptionally wide apart, and the nose, culminating in large nostrils, made so slight an angle with the rest of the face that seen in profile it was scarcely human. Perhaps I exaggerate a little, but I know no other way of explaining the peculiar revulsion he inspired in me. He met me at the station in his dog-cart, and wheezed a greeting at me. "You're Mr. Bailey, aren't you? I hope you've had an agreeable journey. Monica will be delighted." This seemed friendly enough, and my host's conversation during that eight-mile drive did much to make me forget my first distaste of his person. He was evidently a man of wide reading, and he had a habit of polite deference that was extremely flattering, especially to me who had had more than my share of the other thing. I was cashiered during the war, you know. Never mind why. Whenever he laughed, which was not seldom, he exhibited a mouthful of very large regular teeth.

Dearth's Farm, to give it the local name, is a place with a personality of its own. Perhaps every place has that. Sometimes I fancy that the earth itself is a personality, or a community of souls locked fast in a dream from which at any moment they may awake, like volcanos, into violent action. Anyhow Dearth's Farm struck me as being peculiarly personal, because I found it impossible not to regard its climatic changes as changes of mood. You remember my theory that chemical action is only psychical action seen from without? Well, I'm inclined to think in just the same way of every manifestation of natural energy. But you don't want to hear about my fancies. The farmhouse, which is approached by a narrow winding lane from the main road, stands high up in a kind of shallow basin of land, a few acres ploughed but mostly grass. The countryside has a gentle prettiness more characteristic of the southeastern counties. On three sides wooded hills slope gradually to the horizon; on the fourth side grassland rises a little for twenty yards and then curves abruptly down. To look through the windows that give out upon this fourth side is to have the sensation of being on the edge of a steep cliff, or at the end of the world. On a still day, when the sun is shining, the place has a languid beauty, an afternoon atmosphere. You remember Tennyson's Lotus Isles, "in which it seemed always afternoon": Dearth's Farm has something of that flavour on a still day. But such days are rare; the two or three I experienced shine like jewels in the memory. Most often that stretch of fifty or sixty acres is a gathering ground for all the bleak winds of the earth. They seem to come simultaneously from the land and from the sea, which is six miles away, and they swirl round in that shallow basin of earth, as I have called it, like maddened devils seeking escape from a trap. When the storms were at their worst I used to feel as though I were

perched insecurely on a gigantic saucer held a hundred
miles above the earth. But I am not a courageous person.
Monica, my cousin, found no fault with the winds. She
had other fears, and I had not been with her three days
before she began to confide them to me. Her overtures
were as surprising as they were unwelcome, for that she
was not a confiding person by nature I was certain. Her
manners were reserved to the point of diffidence, and we
had nothing in common save a detestation of the family
from which we had both sprung. I suppose you will want
to know something of her looks. She was a tall, full-fig-
ured woman, handsome for her years, with jet black hair,
a sensitive face, and a complexion almost Southern in its
dark colouring. I love beauty and I found pleasure in her
mere presence, which did something to lighten for me the
gloom that pervaded the house; but my pleasure was inno-
cent enough, and Dearth's watchdog airs only amused me.
Monica's eyes—unfathomable pools—seemed troubled
whenever they rested on me: whether by fear or by some
other emotion I didn't at first know.

She chose her moment well, coming to me when Dearth
was out of the house, looking after his men, and I, pleading a headache, had refused to accompany him. The mala-
dy was purely fictitious, but I was bored with the fellow's
company, and sick of being dragged at his heels like a dog
for no better reason than his too evident jealousy afforded.

"I want to ask a kindness of you," she said. "Will you
promise to answer me quite frankly?" I wondered what the
deuce was coming, but I promised, seeing no way out of
it. "I want you to tell me," she went on, "whether you see
anything queer about me, about my behaviour? Do I say or
do anything that seems to you odd?"

Her perturbation was so great that I smiled to hide
my perception of it. I answered jocularly: "Nothing at all

odd, my dear Monica, except this question of yours. What makes you ask it?"

But she was not to be shaken so easily out of her fears, whatever they were. "And do you find nothing strange about this household either?"

"Nothing strange at all," I assured her. "Your marriage is an unhappy one, but so are thousands of others. Nothing strange about that."

"What about him?" she said. And her eyes seemed to probe for an answer.

I shrugged my shoulders. "Are you asking for my opinion of your husband? A delicate thing to discuss."

"We're speaking in confidence, aren't we!" She spoke impatiently, waving my politeness away.

"Well, since you ask, I don't like him. I don't like his face: it's a parody on mankind. And I can't understand why you threw yourself away on him."

She was eager to explain. "He wasn't always like this. He was a gifted man, with brains and an imagination. He still is, for all I know. You spoke of his face—now how would you describe his face, in one word?"

I couldn't help being tickled by the comedy of the situation: a man and a woman sitting in solemn conclave seeking a word by which to describe another man's face, and that man her husband. But her air of tragedy, though I thought it ridiculous, sobered me. I pondered her question for a while, recalling to my mind's eye the long narrow physiognomy and the large teeth of Dearth.

At last I ventured the word I had tried to avoid. "Equine," I suggested.

"Ah!" There was a world of relief in her voice. "You've seen it too."

She told me a queer tale. Dearth, it appears, had a love and understanding of horses that was quite unparalleled.

His wife too had loved horses and it had once pleased her to see her husband's astonishing power over the creatures, a power which he exercised always for their good. But his benefactions to the equine race were made at a hideous cost to himself of which he was utterly unaware. Monica's theory was too fantastic even for me to swallow, and I, as you know, have a good stomach for fantasy. You will have already guessed what it was. Dearth was growing, by a process too gradual and subtle for perception, into the likeness of the horses with whom he had so complete sympathy. This was Mrs. Dearth's notion of what was happening to her husband. And she pointed out something significant that had escaped my notice. She pointed out that the difference between him and the next man was not altogether, or even mainly, a physical difference. In effect she said: "If you scrutinize the features more carefully, you will find them to be far less extraordinary than you now suppose. The poison is not in his features. It is in the psychical atmosphere he carries about with him: something which infects you with the idea of horse and makes you impose that idea on his appearance, magnifying his facial peculiarities." Just now I mentioned that in the early days of her marriage Monica had shared this love of horses. Later, of course, she came to detest them only one degree less than she detested her husband. That is saying much. Only a few months before my visit matters had come to a crisis between the two. Without giving any definite reason, she had confessed, under pressure, that he was unspeakably offensive to her; and since then they had met only at meals and always reluctantly. She shuddered to recall that interview, and I shuddered to imagine it. I was no longer surprised that she had begun to entertain doubts of her own sanity.

But this wasn't the worst. The worst was Dandy, the white horse. I found it difficult to understand why a white horse should alarm her, and I began to suspect that the nervous strain she had undergone was making her inclined to magnify trifles. "It's his favourite horse," she said. "That's as much as saying that he dotes on it to a degree that is unhuman. It never does any work. It just roams the fields by day, and at night sleeps in the stable." Even this didn't, to my mind, seem a very terrible indictment. If the man were mad on horses, what more natural than this petting of a particular favourite?—a fine animal, too, as Monica herself admitted. "Roams the fields," cried my poor cousin urgently. "Or did until these last few weeks. Lately it has been kept in its stable, day in, day out, eating its head off and working up energy enough to kill us all." This sounded to me like the language of hysteria, but I waited for what was to follow. "The day you came, did you notice how pale I looked? I had had a fright. As I was crossing the yard with a pail of separated milk for the calves, that beast broke loose from the stable and sprang at me. Yes, Dandy. He was in a fury. His eyes burned with ferocity. I dodged him by a miracle, dropped the pail, and ran back to the house shrieking for help. When I entered the living-room my husband feigned to be waking out of sleep. He didn't seem interested in my story, and I'm convinced that he had planned the whole thing. It was past my understanding how Dearth could have made his horse spring out of his stable and make a murderous attack upon a particular woman, and I said so. "You don't know him yet," retorted Monica. "And you don't know Dandy. Go and look at the beast. Go now, while James is out."

The farmyard, with its pool of water covered in green slime, its manure and sodden straw, and its smell of pigs, was a place that seldom failed to offend me. But on this occasion I picked my way across the cobblestones thinking of nothing at all but the homicidal horse that I was

about to spy upon. I have said before that I'm not a courageous man, and you'll understand that I stepped warily as
I neared the stable. I saw that the lower of the two doors
was made fast and with the more confidence unlatched the
other.

I peered in. The great horse stood, bolt upright but
apparently in a profound sleep. It was indeed a fine creature, with no spot or shadow, as far as I could discern, to
mar its glossy whiteness. I stood there staring and brooding for several minutes, wondering if both Monica and I
were the victims of some astounding hallucination. I had
no fear at all of Dandy, after having seen him; and it didn't
alarm me when, presently, his frame quivered, his eyes
opened, and he turned to look at me. But as I looked into
his eyes an indefinable fear possessed me. The horse stared
dumbly for a moment, and his nostrils dilated. Although
I half-expected him to tear his head out of the halter and
prance round upon me, I could not move. I stared, and as
I stared, the horse's lips moved back from the teeth in a
grin, unmistakably a grin, of malign intelligence. The gesture vividly recalled Dearth to my mind. I had described
him as equine, and if proof of the word's aptness were
needed, Dandy had supplied that proof.

"He's come back," Monica murmured to me, on my return to the house. "Ill, I think. He's gone to lie down.
Have you seen Dandy?"

"Yes. And I hope not to see him again."

But I was to see him again, twice again. The first time
was that same night, from my bedroom window. Both my
bedroom and my cousin's looked out upon that grassy hill
of which I spoke. It rose from a few yards until almost
level with the second story of the house and then abruptly
curved away. Somewhere about midnight, feeling restless
and troubled by my thoughts, I got out of bed and went to
the window to take an airing.

I was not the only restless creature that night. Standing not twenty yards away, with the sky for background, was a great horse. The moon light made its white flank gleam like silver, and lit up the eyes that stared fixedly at my window.

III

For sixteen days and nights we lived, Monica and I, in the presence of this fear, a fear none the less real for being non-susceptible to definition. The climax came suddenly, without any sort of warning, unless Dearth's idiotic hostility towards myself could be regarded as a warning. The utterly unfounded idea that I was making love to his wife had taken root in the man's mind, and every day his manner to me became more openly vindictive. This was the cue for my departure, with warm thanks for my delightful holiday; but I didn't choose to take it. I wasn't exactly in love with Monica, but she was my comrade in danger and I was reluctant to leave her to face her nightmare terrors alone.

The most cheerful room in that house was the kitchen, with its red-tiled floor, its oak rafters, and its great open fireplace. And when in the evenings the lamp was lit and we sat there, listening in comfort to the everlasting gale that raged round the house, I could almost have imagined myself happy, had it not been for the presence of my reluctant host. He was a skeleton at a feast, if you like! By God, we were a genial party. From seven o'clock to ten we would sit there, the three of us, fencing off silence with the most pitiful of small talk. On this particular night I had been chaffing him gently, though with intention, about his fancy for keeping a loaded rifle hanging over the kitchen mantelpiece; but at last I sickened of the pastime, and the conversation, which had been sustained only by my efforts, lapsed. I stared at the red embers in the grate, stealing a glance now and again at Monica to see how she was enduring the discomfort of such a silence. The cheap alarm clock ticked loudly, in the way that cheap alarm clocks have. When I looked again at Dearth he appeared to have fallen asleep. I say 'appeared,' for I instantly suspected him of shamming sleep in order to catch us out. I knew that he believed us to be in love with each other, and his total lack of evidence must have occasioned him hours of useless fury. I suspected him of the most melodramatic intentions: of hoping to see a caress pass between us that would justify him in making a scene. In that scene, as I figured it, the gun over the mantelpiece might play an important part. I don't like loaded guns.

The sight of his closed lids exasperated me into a bitter speech designed for him to overhear. "Monica, your husband is asleep. He is asleep only in order that he may wake at the chosen moment and pour out the contents of his vulgar little mind upon our heads."

This tirade astonished her, as well it might. She glanced up, first at me, then at her husband; and upon him her eyes remained fixed. "He's not asleep," she said, rising slowly out of her chair.

"I know he's not," I replied.

By now she was at his side, bending over him. "No," she remarked coolly. "He's dead."

At those words the wind outside redoubled its fury, and it seemed as though all the anguish of the world was in its wail. The spirit of Dearth's Farm was crying aloud in a frenzy that shook the house, making all the windows rattle. I shuddered to my feet. And in the moment of my rising the wail died away, and in the lull I heard outside the window a sudden sound of feet, of pawing, horse's feet. My horror found vent in a sort of desperate mirth.

"No, not dead. James Dearth doesn't die so easily."

Shocked by my levity, she pointed mutely to the body in the chair. But a wild idea possessed me, and I knew that my wild idea was the truth. "Yes," I said, "that may be dead as mutton. But James Dearth is outside, come to spy on you and me. Can't you hear him?"

I stretched out my hand to the blind cord. The blind ran up with a rattle, and, pressed against the window, looking in upon us, was the face of the white horse, its teeth bared in a malevolent grin. Without losing sight of the thing for a moment, I backed towards the fire. Monica, divining my intention, took down the gun from its hook and yielded it to my desirous fingers. I took deliberate aim, and shot.

And then, with the crisis over, as I thought, my nerves went to rags. I sat down limply, Monica huddled at my feet; and I knew with a hideous certitude that the soul of James Dearth, violently expelled from the corpse that lay outside the window, was in the room with me, seeking to re-enter that human body in the chair. There was a long moment of agony during which I trembled on the verge of madness, and then a flush came back into the dead pallid cheeks, the body breathed, the eyes opened. . . . I had just enough strength left to drag myself out of my seat. I saw Monica's eyes raised to mine; I can never for a moment cease to see them. Three hours later I stumbled into the arms of the stationmaster, who put me in the London train under the impression that I was drunk. Yes, I left alone. I told you I wasn't a courageous man. . . .

IV

Bailey's voice abruptly ceased. The tension in my listening mind snapped, and I came back with a jerk, as though released by a spring, to my seat in the teashop. Bailey's queer eyes glittered across at me for a moment, and then, their light dying suddenly out, they became infinitely weary of me and of all the sorry business of living. A rationalist in grain, I find it impossible to accept the story quite as it stands. Substantially true it may be, probably is, but that it has been distorted by the prism of Bailey's singular personality I can hardly doubt. But the angle of that distortion must remain a matter for conjecture.

No such dull reflections came then to mar my appreciation of the quality of the strange hush that followed his last words. Neither of us spoke. An agitated waitress made us aware that the shop was closing, and we went into the street without a word. The rain was unremitting. I shrank back into the shelter of the porch while I fastened the collar of my mackintosh, and when I stepped out upon the pavement again, Bailey had vanished into the darkness.

I have never ceased to be vexed at losing him, and never ceased to fear that he may have thought the loss not unwelcome to me. My only hope is that he may read this and get into touch with me again, so that I may discharge my debt to him. It is a debt that lies heavily on my conscience—the price of this story, less one pound.

THE GHOST FARM
Susan Andrews Rice
(1925)

When Steven was killed we did not know it until nearly thirty days afterward. He went overseas in April, and it was the last of June before we knew he went out with a party of engineers to repair the railroad track, and was blown to pieces by a German shell.

We could not tell Maidie the truth. She knew he was dead, but concerning the manner of his going she was ignorant. They were engaged. Her love for him amounted to adoration. She was an intense, emotional girl, bound to be unhappy because of her sensitive nature and strong feelings.

She was under my professional care for several weeks the latter part of the summer, suffering from a broken ankle.

"It is the silence, the awful blank wall between Steven and me, that drives me frantic," she burst out one day, when I was making her a visit.

She had been reading a letter from Steven, and it lay in her lap. She had a little package of his letters always near her.

"I know," I returned, with a sigh. I, too, had lost my nearest and dearest.

"I wish I could consult a medium," she said, lowering her voice. "How wonderful it would be to receive a message from him! I could hardly bear it, I'm afraid."

"Don't do it, Maidie," I said. "Better leave such people alone."

"The ouija board, then? It seems rather like a silly game, but—"

I shook my head.

"'That way madness lies'," I quoted. "I wouldn't, Maidie. Steven lives in your heart, in your memories of him."

She smiled that pathetic little smile she had worn when she wished to appear cheerful.

"You are right," she answered, and changed the subject.

In spite of what she had said I discovered she was reading everything she could find about spirit communication, although I never heard of her making any attempt to reach Steven in that way.

I was very busy that fall with influenza cases, and Maidie went into Red Cross work, and when the epidemic was over I heard she had gone to California. She returned early the following summer looking haggard and ill. I prescribed for her, but could find nothing really wrong with her. She took long walks, and, her mother told me, she always went alone and resented any offer of companionship. She thought it queer, and said she feared Maidie was drifting into melancholia.

Maidie came into my office one afternoon, and I was struck with the change in her expression: she looked happy and young; the strained misery had vanished from her face. I was puzzled. Could she have fallen in love? I ran over in my mind a list of her young men acquaintances, but none of them could I see as Maidie's lover.

Her mother had informed me her walks were always in one direction. Thinking of that, I asked, "Why do you always walk along the river road, Maidie?"

She turned a vivid pink.

"You won't understand, I know, but I'm going to tell you," she replied, twisting her gloves in her hands. "In the first place, you must know Steven and I used to plan that when we were married we would own a little farm. Just a little summer place, you know. He used to say every man wanted to have a farm. Doctor, when I go up the river road, just past the school house, on the bank, where the road turns into the woods, I see a little farm. The fields are neat and cultivated. The house is painted white with green blinds and the door is open into the hall, as if people lived there. Hollyhocks are growing around the kitchen door. On a table milk-pans are turned up to dry in the sun. There are some dish-towels drying on a line. And at any moment I expect to see Steven come around the corner of the house. I feel he is there, out of my sight. I wait, and listen. He hasn't come yet, but he will, some day, and when he comes, I shall go with him."

Her face was luminous with joy. What could I say? What ought I to say?

"Do you think I could see the farm if I were with you?" I asked, speaking slowly.

"I'm afraid you couldn't," she replied. "No one knows it is there but Steven and me."

"Then, my dear Maidie, it exists only in your imagination," I told her, gently.

She smiled, as one smiles at a child who doubts one's word, and she went away.

I studied her case carefully. A good psychanalyst might have helped her, but I was not skilful in that method of treatment. I see now that we did wrong in circumventing her. In accordance with my advice her friends attempted to divert her attention from her daily walk. She was taken on automobile excursions; visitors came at that hour of the day; she was invited to go to moving pictures; duties were crowded upon her, in the hope of altering the fixed

idea in her mind of Steven's waiting at the ghost farm.
She was very sweet about acceding to the demands and
requests, though sometimes she would obstinately refuse
to listen to them.

August brought hot weather. The extreme heat wore upon
our nerves; everybody relaxed. Released from vigilant
watchfulness, Maidie left the house, unnoticed.

A terrific thunder storm came up, and Maidie's mother
was beside herself. She had been lying down taking a nap
when Maidie slipped away. She telephoned to me when the
shower was over, as Maidie was not missed until then.

I got out of my car and started up the river road, a
sense of foreboding in the back of my mind. I had not
proceeded far when a tire blew out. Impatiently I left the
machine and hurried on foot past the weather-beaten old
schoolhouse a short distance. Suddenly I stopped in my
tracks. The sun had come out, and I saw the ghost farm. It
was exactly as Maidie had described it: a stretch of green
fields; a small white house with green blinds; hollyhocks
growing by the kitchen door; milk-pans glistening in the
sun, drying on a table; towels fluttering on a line. I was
struck dumb, and stood motionless, hardly able to draw
my breath at the strangeness of the scene.

In a few minutes the vision, or mirage, vanished. Then
I perceived a tall oak tree split in half by a bolt of lightning. At the foot of the tree lay Maidie, on the wet ground,
a smile of rapture on her upturned face.

I knelt beside her and examined heart and pulse. Nothing could be done, her spirit had left its earthly body. She
had gone to be with Steven.

AT SIMMEL ACRES FARM
Eleanor Scott
(1929)

I must explain first that I didn't know Markham very well. We lived on the same stair at Cornyn (I don't think I'll give the real name of our college), but he was one of those large, vigorous people who live for Rugger and rowing, and I am no good at games on account of my short sight. I want to lay some stress on my sight, because it may account for other things. I don't believe it does, but it may. I hope it may.

It happened late in the Hilary term of our second year that Markham got rather badly damaged in a Rugger match. It was some injury to the back, not very serious, but it meant that he had to lie up for some weeks; and as we were of the same year and on the same stair, it also happened that I used to go in and see him a good deal; so when he asked me to come down to the Cotswolds with him for part of the vac. I rather jumped at it. I haven't many friends of my own—I am dull and priggish—and I expect he didn't want any of his own hefty pals about while he was so badly out of it. So, odd as we were as a pair, we fitted in rather well.

He chose the place—said his family used to come from those parts, and he had a liking for the country. It was a farmhouse, standing alone in wide, prosperous fields. We went there by car, on account of Markham's back, and

I shall never, even now, look back on that evening with
anything but pleasure. It was the twentieth of March, I remember, and there was a kind of green bloom on the bare
fields and a purple bloom on the bare woods that lay on
the hill behind the farm. The house itself was like a dozen
others in that country—long and low, built of the yellow
Cotswold stone, with a beautifully pitched roof and mul-
lioned windows. The stone barns grouped about it showed
the same beauty of perfect proportion. The whole thing
was as simple and direct as the country it stood in.

I said something of this to Markham, but he hardly
answered. He seemed fidgety and uneasy; I thought he was
probably in pain, or overtired with the journey. Anyhow,
he only growled, rather shortly, that it was all rot, one
farm was like another, and he hoped they'd give us decent meals. But he threw a queer, almost suspicious glance
round as he was being helped in. I dismissed it as of no
importance.

In the morning he was more cheerful. It was a lovely
day, soft as April, with a tender blue sky that showed up
the bursting leaf-buds. It was not a day to be in, ill or well;
so I consulted Mrs. Stokes as to the possibility of getting
Markham out. She had a sofa long and broad enough for
him, and was perfectly willing that I should take it out;
but when I asked her about a suitable spot to establish him
in she rather hesitated.

"Haven't you a small garden or a patch of grass somewhere near the house?" I asked.

She looked quite troubled and confused.

"Well, of course," she said at last, "there's the plot in
there," and she jerked her head at a high stone wall with
a wooden door in it at one end of the yard; "but I don't
think your friend would like it, sir," she added hurriedly.
"Nobody's been there for years, and it's likely all choked
wi' nettles and rubbish."

I was surprised to hear this. The farm was so well-ordered and the fields so clean that it seemed odd that a piece of ground so near the dwelling-house should be neglected.

"May I look at it?" I asked: and again I couldn't help seeing that she went for the key of the door with considerable reluctance.

While she was gone I studied the outside of this yard. It ran on to one end of the farmhouse, as if it had once been the flower-garden of some bygone farmer's wife; but instead of coming right up to the house wall, a high wall of its own cut it off from the house. This seemed absurd and ridiculously inconvenient, since of course it meant that the rooms on that side of the house could have no windows, whereas they might have looked out pleasantly on to a garden. The high wall ran round three sides of the little plot and at the fourth end, opposite the house, I could see the pointed end of a stone barn.

I'm sorry if I'm tedious, but I must explain this still more. This fourth wall was apparently the end of a ruined barn which had at one time, before the garden was made, run straight on to the house. You could tell this because a bit of the roof remained, projecting over the plot of grass like a penthouse roof. I had never seen traces of a large stone barn built straight on to a farmhouse before, and I was interested. I supposed that rats had made it inconvenient to have a barn on to the house, and that it had been destroyed and a garden made on its floor space; though why later farmers had abandoned the garden I could not imagine—still less why they had erected that wall between the grass plot and the house.

Mrs. Stokes returned with the key. She still looked "put about," as country people say, and I apologised for putting her to the trouble of opening the place.

"Oh, it isn't any trouble, sir," she said, as she fitted the key into the big lock. "Only—well, I'll tell you the truth, sir," she burst out suddenly, standing upright and facing me. "They do say as this place isn't—chancy. It's not the farm, it's just this one place. That's why they've walled it off. I don't know nothing myself," she added hastily. "I come from Dorset myself, and I've never heard nor seen a thing. But my husband's people, they've farmed this land for centuries, so they say, and there's not one of 'em as'll go anigh this plot."

"Is there a story about it?" I asked. I am very keen on folk-lore and legends, and thought there might be something here.

"N—no," she answered, rather reluctantly. And then, "But if I was you, sir, I'd keep out o' Simmel Acres Plot."

"Well, let's look at it, anyway," I said; and with no more words we opened the door—the lock shrieked dismally, I remember—and went in.

It was by no means as bad as Mrs. Stokes had painted it. The grass was long and rank, but the nettles had confined themselves to the shelter of the high stone walls. But the thing that drew my attention was the old gabled end of the barn. It was perhaps sixteen feet high, rounded off in a curiously rough and archaic form of arch. The roof, as I have said, projected in a kind of rugged penthouse, about two feet deep, and about halfway up the wall there was a niche with a stone bust of a man.

It was a very odd piece of work, worn by time and exposure, but quite complete enough for me. The top part of the head was the most disfigured; I could see some kind of fillet or crown, and some clumsy, conventional indications of hair. The blank eye-sockets were rather large, oddly rounded at the corners, and had in consequence an expression of ruthlessness. The nose was too worn to be in any way remarkable; but the mouth had the most subtle expression—at once cynical, suffering, cruel, undaunted and callous. The chin was square, but weak; the neck powerful, in a conventional manner. It was altogether a remarkable thing—almost savage in its clumsiness and crudity, and yet conveying a singular impression of truth to an original.

At first I thought it was a piece of decadent Roman sculpture; then I dismissed that as absurd. How could a Roman bust be in a barn in the Cotswolds? It might have been an eighteenth-century copy, but I didn't think so; it was too crude, too strong, too—I must use the word again—too archaic. Besides, when the eighteenth century copied Roman busts they were put in little pseudo-classical temples, not in niches in barns.

This was not quite all. Below the bust was a small semi-circular basin, floored with smooth pebbles, through which welled up water so clear as to be almost invisible—exactly like the Holy Wishing Wells one finds occasionally, decorated with pins and rags and other tributes to the presiding deity. But here there were no offerings.

The loveliness of the morning was even more apparent in the little enclosure. The soft sky gained colour from the grey walls, the grass smelt fresh and wet, the water mirrored the tiny white clouds. It was exactly the place for an invalid, I thought, restful, open and quiet. I told Mrs. Stokes my decision, and she protested no more. Together we brought the sofa out into the plot; and Markham and I settled down there for the morning.

We had set the sofa against the farmhouse wall, at the end of the little plot away from the old barn-end with its bubbling spring. When he was established I went into the house for some books and notes—I had a lot of work to do that vac.—and it was some minutes before I came out again. When I did, I noticed that Markham was not lying, as he should have been, flat on his back; he had rolled over on to his side and was staring with a frowning, puzzled look at the bust above the well.

"Hullo," I said, "oughtn't you to be on your back?"

He paid no attention. Indeed, I don't think he heard me. He was muttering something, like a man trying to remember a half-forgotten phrase.

"Damn it all, how did it go?" he broke out suddenly. *"Et te simulacrum . . . Et te . . .* Damn it! What was it?"

"What was what?" I asked, putting my books down on the table.

He looked round at me, and his face cleared a little.

"I—something came into my head—a sentence or something . . . I can't remember. I read it once—or heard it—when I was a kid . . . Some old book that belonged to some bloomin' ancestor. Dashed if I can remember . . . *Et te simulacrum . . .* Curse it! How did it go?"

"What about it?" I asked.

Again he made no answer—just lay, frowning a little and muttering. At last he said,

"What is it written under that head over there?"

"Under the bust? Nothing."

"There is," he insisted. "What is it?"

Just to satisfy him I went and looked. He was quite right—there were words there.

"There is something," I said, "but I can't read it. I can only see bits of words here and there—nothing consecutive. *Simul,* I think that is—"

"*Simulacrum, et te—requiro . . .*" muttered Markham.

I was very much surprised—for several reasons. First I was surprised that he should be interested at all; then that he should be quoting, however scrappily, a Latin sentence; and last that he could see that there was an inscription, let alone read the words. Kneeling on the ground before it, I could only just make out the defaced letters; and he was twenty yards away, lying flat.

"Can you read it right over there?" I called in astonishment.

"No—is it written there?" he cried back, wriggling
round eagerly. "Read it out, Norton—I can't remember
how it goes."

"I can't make out more than a word or two," I said.
"And I don't know all the words—must be late Latin, I
think. *Simul*—or perhaps you're right, *simulacrum*—something about water—and I think that's *lunae*—and—no, I
can't read it."

Markham seemed dissatisfied.

"There's more of it than that," he insisted.

"Yes, there is," I agreed, "but it's so worn. But, I say,
how did you know what it was? How did you know it was
there?"

He looked puzzled.

"Damned if I know," he began. He spoke slowly, like a
man groping for words, or for ideas. "I just knew . . . We
come from these parts, you know . . . used to have a big
place in the eighteenth century, or something. Rather rips,
I believe we were—Hellfire Club and all that tosh . . ."

He suddenly broke off. He made a quick gesture, like
that of a man who remembers. His face cleared and his
eyes shone. His lips moved a little as if he had caught the
words he had been seeking.

"Got it?" I asked. I was rather thrilled; it was, I thought,
a very interesting example of an inherited memory—something long forgotten and now recalled by equally forgotten
associations.

He made no reply, so I asked again—"Remembered it?"

He looked up at me, grinning, and wouldn't answer.
It was a queer look, half ashamed, half malicious, wholly
triumphant. Every now and then throughout that morning
I caught him moving his lips as if he were repeating something he was anxious not to forget—like an amateur actor

learning his part—and there was an odd, excited air about him like that of a small boy with a mischievous secret. He looked as if he were up to something recklessly silly, like an extra mad "Cupper" rag. Of course I knew he couldn't be really, but I felt uneasy somehow. He'd always had the reputation for such daredevil games, and though he was tied to his couch he might be all the more restless, planning any monkey tricks. And he had a mocking light in his eye that irritated me badly. I know I'm not his type, but open mockery was a bit more than I could stick. I decided I'd leave him to himself in the afternoon and clear out for a good walk on my own.

He seemed quite pleased when I mentioned this. All he said was, just as I looked in to the little enclosure to say I was starting,

"Right. I say, you might just give me a drink before you go, will you? Some of that spring by the wall there."

I said I'd go in and get him a drink; the spring looked good enough, but you never know, especially near a farmyard. But that wouldn't do him at all. He wanted the water from that well and nothing else. And when I said I wouldn't get it for him, he actually moved as if to get up and get it for himself.

Well, he wasn't a kid. He knew the risks of drinking the stuff as well as I did; so, still protesting, I scooped up about a spoonful of the water for him.

"I want to drink the old lad's health," he said, half apologetically, when I handed it to him; and he held the glass up as if he really were drinking a health, and muttered some more nonsense about *"libatio aquae."* It was too low for me to hear, and anyhow I was fed up with his nonsense. He still had the daring, wild expression I'd noticed in the morning, and he grinned at me in an absolutely impish way. I cleared out, annoyed and just a trifle uneasy.

I enjoyed my walk. Markham had ruffled me, and it was a real relief to be by myself for a bit. We hadn't anything in common, really. I'm a plodder by nature, and I had no sympathy with his wild outbursts of spirits and the mad enterprises that he alternated with training of a rigorous kind. Even since his illness, when we had seen a good deal of each other, I had never understood him much. I'd been surprised, for instance, to hear him quote Latin simply because I had taken it for granted that he was the ordinary beefy, brainless type; but I realised now that I had not the smallest reason, really, to think so. I knew nothing, quite literally nothing, of his mind. I began thinking of his queer behaviour that morning—his puzzled face, his relief at remembering some half-forgotten tag of dog-Latin seen in an old book, the dancing mockery of his eyes, that absurd business of the "libation." I began to wonder how long our companionship would last, and I thought that probably it would not be very long. There, at least, I was right.

I got in about six, perhaps a little earlier. I know dusk had not yet fallen; but the warmth was gone from the air, and the shadows were chill. I went out to the little grass plot at once to see if Markham had been moved in yet. I thought it might be risky for him after his illness to be lying out so late when April was not yet in.

He was still there, lying flat and rigid under the grey rug on the couch; and the dim colour of the rug and the stillness of his pose gave me quite a shock. He didn't look alive at all; he looked like a figure carved in grey stone on a tomb. It was the merest momentary impression, but for the instant it seemed to me as if even his face were—fixed. And there was something else about it . . .

Then he opened his eyes and looked at me with the dazed sort of look a man has when he wakes suddenly—puzzled, rather appealing—you know what I mean, rather

childlike somehow. And I suddenly had the oddest sort of
guilty feeling, as if I'd been thinking something treacher-
ous—planning some evil to him—I can't explain, it was all
so vague, mixed up with that swiftly-lost impression of his
set, still face and figure, like a debased statue on an evil
tomb.

We had a door between our rooms in the farm. At first
I used to leave it ajar, in case Markham should wake and
want some small attention; but that night I closed it. I
can't explain why, for I'd quite lost the irritation I'd felt
earlier in the day; instead I had a queer sort of feeling,
equally irrational, of pity, almost of grief; and yet I shut
the door with a feeling of half-shamed relief such as one
feels when one leaves a mourner one can't help.

I woke quite suddenly. Perhaps it was the big, bright
moon, nearly full for Easter, that awakened me; but I had
the impression that it was a voice. I sat up and listened.
I thought I could hear it again—a voice (or was it two
voices?) speaking quick and quiet in the next room.

"Want anything, Markham?" I called; and my voice
sounded odd—anxious, and a little unsteady.

There was immediate and deathly silence—the kind of
silence that follows on a furtive sound. I strained my ears
to listen. I remember now how the flood of strong moonlight washed my room, and the look of the queer, sharp
shadows that edged it. I could hear my own heart beating
in the dead silence.

Nothing—not a whisper, not a rustle. Only that
strained, aching, unnatural void, so different from real
quiet, that you hear when you listen intently.

I waited a little, more uneasy than I liked to admit. I
had, half unconsciously, in my mind the vision of Markham
as I had seen him that afternoon, grey and rigid, with a
set, altered, familiar, dreadful face . . .

I twisted my legs round over the edge of my bed. The room had that half-familiar, half-magic look you get in full moonlight— solid and yet ethereal, real and still dream-like . . . I felt as if minutes passed in that dead, unnatural silence. It took more effort than I should have imagined possible to break through it.

"Markham!" I said again; and, though I pitched my voice low, it sounded horribly loud. It cracked upwards unexpectedly; and I knew then—and not till then—that I was— terrified.

No sound. Only the echo of that breaking, frightened, stranger's voice that had come from my own dry throat.

I got up and opened the door between our rooms.

The window, uncurtained, let the moonlight stream in. The shadows were massive, hard-edged, like odd shapes cut in a solid substance. I could see the bed, a patchwork of black and white, cut by the shadows of things in the room. One shadow was humped, rounded—I thought it moved, and spun round to see what threw it. There was nothing. When I turned back it had gone. Perhaps it had never been there . . .

The pillow was, as it were, cut off from the whiteness of the bed by the straight, solid shadow of the curtain hanging beside the window. I could just see dimly in the blackness the blacker blot made by Markham's head. He lay as motionless as stone . . .

I stood there in the chequered black and white. I don't think I *thought* at all. I just stood there, resisting with all my strength a wave of sheer panic that swept over me. It was as if in that silent room I stood on the verge of something too evil, too fearful, to understand. I could see nothing, hear nothing, but I felt evil, malignant, appalling, in the very air. And then quite silently the curtain at the window waved in some mysterious breath of night air—lifted for a second, and fell as silently. But in that single instant I had seen . . .

Markham's head lay as if carved in stone on the pillow; the eyes were blankly lidded, the features altered—something twisted in the roughened hair, like a fillet—he smiled a little, an enigmatic, cruel and anguished smile . . . Markham, yet not Markham . . .

I forget what happened. A black wave seemed to engulf me. I heard the rush of it in my ears—I couldn't breathe for it . . . Then I was standing in my own room, backing up to the open window, deadly cold, seeing that dreadful face. And then panic seized me— not for myself, but for Markham. What had happened? He was helpless . . . I must go back —must help him—I couldn't let It . . .

If there had been some sound it wouldn't have been so bad. A groan, a cry for help, even a whisper would have been more—more human. I should have known then that Markham really was there . . .

I lit a candle. It took me, I knew, a very long time, I fumbled so. But at last I had a warm, friendly light instead of the mocking fantasy of moonlight. I went back.

The room looked just as usual. Markham lay, his brows a little drawn down, his mouth a little open, as if he were puzzled or expostulating—but it was Markham. There was no doubt of that. I felt a warm gush of sheer relief as I saw his familiar face. Oddly enough, I didn't, even then, feel at all ashamed of my terror. There *had* been something wrong, something appalling, ghastly, in that room. It was gone now, but it had been there . . .

I went back to bed, but I did not sleep again. I listened, achingly, for a sound that never came.

I felt oddly embarrassed at the idea of meeting Markham in the morning. It was as if I had unwittingly surprised him in some secret, shameful and intimate. And I noticed that he, too, when we met, seemed unwilling to meet my eye. We were both conscious of something—some bond of knowledge that was at the same time a bar. And I think we both wondered what the other knew.

After a pretence of a meal I tried, feebly enough, to get something out of him.

"I don't think you'd better go out to-day," I said, looking at him straight.

He changed colour at once.

"What d'you mean?" he asked, almost defiantly.

"I mean," I said—carefully, because I wasn't myself sure of my own meaning—"that I think Mrs. Stokes is right. That enclosure isn't—healthy."

He laughed, rather a mirthless, sneering sound.

"Too late to think of that now," he said; and as our eyes met I saw a difference— his face looked strange, yet familiar, with its cynical, suffering mouth and expressionless eyes.

"Markham!" I cried, dropping all pretence. "Markham—what is it? What have you done? Can't we . . . ?"

My voice died away.

He had said nothing. His whole face was set, rigid in that blank, cynical, anguished look. It was as if stricken to stone before my eyes. We sat, the spring sun on us, facing each other in horror and despair.

I said no more. I knew he was right—it was too late to avoid the enclosure, with its well and terrible bust. I stayed with Markham all that day, pretending to read as he lay motionless and silent in the air and sunshine of that haunted plot called Simmel Acre. I was tense the whole time, listening with strained ears, stealing furtive glances now at Markham's set face, now at the marred bust above the clear water of the spring. But nothing happened, except that once I thought I saw on the grass near the couch a crouching shadow . . . It was not there when I looked sharply up. I had imagined it, perhaps.

But as evening drew on I felt we could not leave it like that. We must do something.

"Markham," I said, as firmly as I could, "I think I'd better sleep in your room to-night."

He said nothing. He only turned his head a little and looked at me.

"You were restless last night," I said feebly. "You might need me."

"Restless?" he half whispered, mockery in his tone.

I remembered that rigid form and terrible set face.

"You might need me," I repeated.

"No. It's decent of you, Norton—but—no. I—I'd rather you didn't—I mean—I'm better alone."

I don't know what made me say it.

"Where did you get the words from?" I asked.

He stared at me as if he would read my thoughts.

"I don't know," he whispered; and his whole face was suddenly transfigured with sheer appalling panic. "Norton—Norton," he babbled, clutching at me, "if I knew! If only I knew! I might find others—to undo it—Norton, can't you think? Where can I find out? What was the book?"

I was immensely relieved. It was far less dreadful put into words.

"I'll find out," I said boldly. "There'll be books—people must know . . . I'll ask old Henderson, he's always working at these things, rites and old magic and things. He'll know, Markham, sure to. I'll go over to Oxford first thing to-morrow . . ."

"No! No! To-night, Norton, it must be tonight. The moon's full to-night. You must, you simply must. You don't know—I—I can't . . ."

He was nearly beside himself.

"I will," I promised. "I'll go now. I'll be in Oxford before eight. I'll find Henderson. It'll be all right, Markham, he's sure to know. It'll be all right . . ."

I shall never forget that mad journey to Oxford. I cycled, as there was no quicker way to go; and it took me two hours, panting up hills, sweating as if I were on an errand of life and death. It was, I knew, even more serious than that . . . And I had no clue—nothing but that Markham's family had once been connected with the village—that some ancestor had worshipped with the Hellfire Club . . . that there had been a book . . . Would it, could it be the faintest use? Could old Henderson—could anyone, pedant or priest, help us?

It seemed hours and hours before I got into the long roads of conventional houses that lie like a web about Oxford. The clocks were striking nine as I reached Carfax.

Henderson was away. Of course he was, in the vac. I stood stunned as the porter carefully explained it to me—I think he thought I was drunk. I could not take it in. Our last chance! . . . The porter saw that it was something serious.

"Something urgent was it, sir?" he asked at last.

"Yes," I whispered. My lips were almost too dry to speak.

"Well, sir—seein' as it's urgent . . . Mr. 'Enderson 'as a little 'ouse out near Kingston Bagpuize. 'E don't like visitors there, not in vacation, but seein' as it's urgent . . . It ain't on the 'phone, but if you'd care to run out . . ."

I was down the steps before he finished. He shouted the name of the house after me as I raced off. The moon, moving majestically and remorselessly up the sky, filled me with desperation. I should never, never be in time . . .

I don't know what I said to Henderson. I thought I should never make him understand. I don't know why he listened—why he didn't write me down as mad, or drunk. But, thank God, he didn't; he made me sit down and drink something—I don't know what, I couldn't taste it, and my hands were shaking so that I couldn't drink without

spilling the stuff—while he listened and nodded and consulted old books. He moved with the slowness of a very
old man, taking down one book after another, consulting
manuscripts, reading passages, while the minutes ticked
away and the night crept on . . . I can see him now, so
old and bent, with his careful gestures clear in the steady
lamplight, and the smell of old books in the air . . .

The clocks were striking eleven as we rushed, in a hired
car, out of the dim Oxford streets and struck up the glim-
mering white road to Simmel Acre Farm. I don't think we
said a word. I know I sat with every muscle taut, straining
with impatience, wild hope alternating with despair as I
watched the moon rise higher and higher in the clear sky.
We should never do it!

The moon was almost at the zenith when at last we
reached the farm. I could not stand when I got out—old
Henderson had to put his hand under my arm to keep me
from falling.

I was making for the door, but he stopped me.

"No," he said, "the enclosure—the well. We must go
there."

He was muttering to himself, like a man saying prayers,
but I knew that he was not praying to any Christian God.

The outer door was shut, but the key was in the lock,
and we opened it easily.

The little yard looked quite empty. The royal moonlight flooded the young grass and the trees with leaves just
unfolding. Only at the end the penthouse of stone threw a
dark, menacing shadow. Beneath it came the tiny tinkle of
water in the stone-edged spring. And, half in the shadow,
half in the moonlight, I saw Markham lying—Markham,
with a white, set face turned up to the moon. And his face
was that of the sneering bust above him.

BROWDEAN FARM

A. M. Burrage

(1929)

Most people with limited vocabularies such as mine would describe the house loosely and comprehensively as picturesque. But it was more than beautiful in its venerable age. It had certain subtle qualities which are called Atmosphere. It invited you, as you approached it along the rough and narrow road which is ignored by those maps which are sold for the use of motorists. In the language of very old houses it said plainly: "Come in. Come in."

It said, "Come in" to Rudge Jefferson and me. In one of the front windows there was a notice, inscribed in an illiterate hand, to the effect that the house was to be let, and that the keys were to be obtained at the first cottage down the road. We went and got them. The woman who handed them over to us remarked that plenty of people looked over the house but nobody ever took it. It had been empty for years.

"Damp and falling to pieces, I suppose," said Rudge as we returned. "There's always a snag about these old places."

The house—Browdean Farm it was called—stood some thirty yards back from the road, at the end of a strip of garden not much wider than its façade. Most of the building was plainly Tudor, but part of it was even earlier. Time was when it had been the property of prosperous yeomen, but now its acres had been added to those of another farm, and it stood shorn of all its land save the small untended gardens in front and behind, and half an acre of apple orchard.

As in most houses of that description the kitchen was the largest room. It was long and lofty and its arched roof was supported by mighty beams which stretched across its breadth. There was a huge range with a noble oven. One could fancy, in the old days of plenty, a score of harvesters supping there after their work, and beer and cider flowing as freely as spring brooks.

To our surprise the place showed few signs of damp, considering the length of time it had been untenanted, and it needed little in the way of repairs. There was not a stick of furniture in the house, but we could tell that its last occupants had been people of refinement and taste. The wallpapers upstairs, the colours of the faded paints and distempers, the presence of a bathroom—that great rarity in old farmhouses—all pointed to the probability of its having been last in the hands of an amateur of country cottages.

Jefferson told me that he knew in his bones—and for once I agreed with his bones—that Nina would love the farm. He was engaged to my sister, and they were waiting until he had saved sufficient money to give them a reasonable material start in matrimony. Like most painstaking writers of no particular reputation Jefferson had to take care of the pence and the shillings, but like Nina's, his tastes were inexpensive, and it was an understood thing that they were to live quietly together in the country.

We inquired about the rent. It was astonishingly low. Jefferson had to live somewhere while he finished a book, and he was already paying storage for the furniture which he had bought. I could look forward to some months of idleness before returning to India. There was a trout stream in the neighbourhood which would keep me occupied and out of mischief. We laid our heads together.

Jefferson did not want a house immediately, but bargains of that sort are not everyday affairs in these hard times. Besides, with me to share expenses for the next six months, the cost of living at Browdean Farm would be very low, and it seemed a profitable speculation to take the house then and there on a seven years' lease. This is just what Jefferson did—or rather, the agreement was signed by both parties within a week.

Rudge Jefferson and I were old enough friends to understand each other thoroughly, and make allowances for each other's temperaments. We were neither of us morose but often one or both of us would not be anxious to talk. There were indefinite hours when Rudge felt either impelled or compelled to write. We found no difficulty in coming to a working agreement. We did not feel obliged to converse at meals. We could bring books to the table if we so wished. Rudge could go to his work when he chose, and I could go off fishing or otherwise amuse myself. Only when we were both inclined for companionship need we pay any attention to each other's existence.

And, from the April evening when we arrived half an hour after the men with the furniture, it worked admirably.

We lived practically in one room, the larger of the two front sitting-rooms. There we took our meals, talked and smoked and read. The smaller sitting-room Rudge commandeered for a study. He retired thither when the spirit moved him to invoke the muses and tap at his type-writer. Our only servant was the woman who had lately had charge of the keys. She came in every day to cook our meals and do the housework, and, as for convenience we dined in the middle of the day, we had the place to ourselves immediately after tea. The garden we decided to tend ourselves, but although we began digging and planting with the early enthusiasm of most amateurs we soon tired of the job and let wild nature take its course.

Our first month was ideal and idyllic. The weather was kind, and everything seemed to go in our favour. The trout gave me all the fun I could have hoped for, and Rudge was satisfied with the quality and quantity of his output. I had no difficulty in adapting myself to his little ways, and soon discovered that his best hours for working were in the mornings and the late evenings, so I left him to himself at those times. We took our last meal, a light cold supper, at about half-past nine, and very often I stayed out until that hour.

You must not think that we lived like two recluses under the same roof. Sometimes Rudge was not in the mood for work and hinted at a desire for companionship. Then we went out for long walks, or he came to watch me fish. He was himself a ham-handed angler and seldom attempted to throw a fly. Often we went to drink light ale at the village inn, a mile distant. And always after supper we smoked and talked for an hour or so before turning in.

It was then, while we were sitting quietly, that we discovered that the house, which was mute by day, owned strange voices which gave tongue after dark. They were the noises which, I suppose, one ought to expect to hear in an old house half full of timber when the world around it is hushed and sleeping. They might have been nerve-racking if one of us had been there alone, but as it was we took little notice at first. Mostly they proceeded from the kitchen, whence we heard the creaking of beams, sobbing noises, gasping noises, and queer indescribable scufflings.

While neither of us believed in ghosts we laughingly agreed that the house ought to be haunted, and by something a little more sensational than the sounds of timber contracting and the wind in the kitchen chimney. We knew ourselves to be the unwilling hosts of a colony of rats, which was in itself sufficient to account for most nocturnal noises. Rudge said that he wanted to meet the ghost of an eighteenth-century miser, who couldn't rest until he had shown where the money was hidden. There was some practical use in that sort of bogie. And although, as time went on, these night noises became louder and more persistent, we put them down to "natural causes" and made no effort to investigate them. It occurred to us both that some more rats had discovered a good home, and although we talked of trapping them our talk came to nothing.

We had been at the farm about a month before Rudge Jefferson began to show symptoms of "nerves." All writers are the same. Neurotic brutes! But I said nothing to him and waited for him to diagnose his own trouble and ease up a little with his work.

It was at about that time that I, walking homewards one morning just about lunch-time, with my rod over my shoulder, encountered the local policeman just outside the village inn. He wished me a good day which was at once hearty and respectful, and at the same time passed the back of his hand over a thirsty-looking moustache. The hint was obvious, and only a heart of stone could have refrained from inviting him inside. Besides, I believe in keeping in with the police.

He was one of those country constables who become fixtures in quiet, out-of-the-way districts, where they live and let live, and often go into pensioned retirement without bringing more than half-a-dozen cases before the petty sessions. This worthy was named Hicks, and I had already discovered that everybody liked him. He did not look for trouble. He had rabbits from the local poachers, beer from local cyclists who rode after dark without lights, and more beer from the landlord who chose to exercise his own discretion with regard to closing time.

P.C. Hicks drank a pint of bitter with me and gave me his best respects. He asked me how we were getting on up at the farm. Admirably, I told him; and then he looked at me closely, as if to see if I were sincere, or, rather, to search my eyes for the passing of some afterthought.

Having found me guileless, as it seemed, he went on to tell me of his length of service—he had been eighteen years on the one beat—and of how little trouble he had been to anybody. There was something pathetic in the protestations of the middle-aged Bobby that, to all the world, he had been a man and a brother. He seemed tacitly to be asking for reciprocity, and his own vagueness drew me out of my depth.

You know those beautifully vague men, who pride themselves for being diplomatists on the principle that a nod is as good as a wink to a blind horse? The people who will hint and hint and hint, the asses who will wander round and round and round the haystack with hardly a nibble at it? He was one of them. He wanted to tell me something without actually telling me, to exact from me a promise about something he chose not to mention.

I found myself in dialectical tangles with him, and at last I laughingly gave up the task of trying to follow his labyrinthine thoughts. I ordered two more bitters and then he said:

"Well, sir, if anything 'appens up at the farm, you needn' get talkin' about it. We done our best. What's past is past, and can't be altered. There isn't no sense in settin' people against us."

I knew from his inflection on the word that "us" was the police. He did not look at me while he spoke. He was staring at something straight across the counter, and I happened by sheer chance to follow the direction of his gaze.

Opposite us, and hanging from a shelf so as to face the customers, was a little tear-off calendar. The date recorded there was the nineteenth of May.

Two evenings later—which is to say the evening of May the twenty-first—I returned home at half-past nine full of suppressed excitement. I had a story to tell Rudge, and I was yet not sure if I should be wise in telling it. His nerves had grown worse during the past two days, but after all there are nerves and nerves, and my tale might interest without harming him.

It was only just dusk and not a tithe of the stars were burning as I walked up the garden path, inhaling the rank scents of those hardy flowers which had sprung up untended in that miniature wilderness. The sitting-room window was dark, but the subdued light of an oil lamp burned behind the curtains of Rudge's study. I found the door unbarred, walked in, and entered the study. You see, it was supper-time, and Rudge might safely be intruded upon.

Rather to my surprise the room was empty, but I surmised that Rudge had gone up to wash. That he had lately been at work was evident from the fact that a sheet of paper, half used, lay in the roller of the typewriter. I sat down in the revolving chair to see what he had written—I was allowed that privilege—and was astonished to see that he had ended in the middle of a sentence. In some respects he was a methodical person, and this was unlike him. The last word he had written was "the," and the last letter of that word was black and prominent as if he had slammed down the key with unnecessary force.

Two minutes later, while I was still reading, a probable explanation was revealed to me. I heard the gate click and footfalls on the path. Naturally I guessed that Rudge, temperamental as he was, had suddenly tired of his work and

gone out for a walk. I heard the footsteps come to within a
few yards of the house, when they left the path, fell softer
on grass and weeds, and approached the window. The curtain obscured my view, but on the glass I heard the tap of
finger-tips and the clink of nails.

I did not pause to reflect that Rudge, if he had gone
out, must know that he had left the door on the latch, or
that he could have no reason to suppose that I was already
in the house. One does not consider these things in so
brief a time. I just called out, "Right ho," and went round
to the front door to let him in.

Having opened the front door I leaned out and saw
him—Rudge, I imagined—peering in at the study window. He was no more than a dark, bent shadow in the
dusk, crowned by a soft felt hat, such as he generally wore.
"Right ho," I said again, and, leaving the door wide for
him, I hurried into the kitchen. There was some salad left
in soak which had to be shaken and wiped before bringing
it to the table. I remember that, as I walked through to the
sink, one of the beams over my head creaked noisily.

I washed the salad and returned towards the dining-
room. As I turned into the hall a gust of air from the still
open door passed like a cool caress across my face. Then,
before I had time to enter the dining-room, I heard the
gate click at the end of the garden path, and footfalls on
the gravel. I waited to see who it was. It was Rudge—and
he was bareheaded.

He produced a book at supper, and sat scowling at it
over his left arm while he ate. This was permitted by our
rules, but I had something to tell him, and after a while I
forced my voice upon his attention.

"Rudge," I said, "I've made a discovery this evening. I
know how you got this place so cheap."

He sat up with a start, stared at me, and winced.

"How?" he demanded.

"This is Stanley Stryde's old house. Don't you remember Stanley Stryde?"

He was pale already, but I saw him turn paler still.

"I remember the name vaguely," he said. "Wasn't he a murderer?"

"He was," I answered. "I didn't remember the case very well. But my memory's been refreshed to-day. Everybody here thought we knew, and the curious delicacy of the bucolic mind forbade mentioning it to us. It was rather a grisly business, and the odd thing is that local opinion is all in favour of Stryde's innocence, although he was hanged."

Rudge's eyes had grown larger.

"I remember the name," he said, "but I forget the case. Tell me."

"Well, Stanley Stryde was an artist who took this place. He was what we should call in common parlance a dirty dog. He'd got himself entangled with the daughter of a neighbouring farmer—the family has left here since—and then he found himself morally and socially compelled to marry her. At the same time he fell in love with another girl, so he lured the old one here and did her in. Don't you remember now?"

Rudge wrinkled his nose.

"Yes, vaguely," he said. "Didn't he bury the body and afterwards try to make out that she'd committed suicide? So this is the house, is it? Funny nobody told us before."

"They thought we knew," I repeated, "and nobody liked to mention it. As if it were some disgrace to *us,* you know! Oh, and, of course, the house is haunted."

Rudge stared at me and frowned.

"I don't know about 'haunted,'" he said, "but it's been a damned uncomfortable house to sit in for the past few evenings. I mean at twilight, when I've been waiting for you. My nerves have been pretty raw lately. To-night I couldn't stand it, so I went out for a stroll."

"Left in the middle of a sentence," I remarked.

"Oh, so you noticed that, did you?"

"By the way," I asked, "what made you go out a second time?"

"I didn't."

"But my dear chap, you did! Because the first time you came in you wore a hat, and two minutes later I saw you walking up the garden path without one."

"That's when I did come back. I haven't worn a hat at all this evening."

"Then who—" I began.

"And that reminds me," he continued quickly, "when *you* come in of an evening you needn't sneak up to the window and tap on it with your fingers.

It doesn't frighten me, but it's disconcerting. You can always walk into the room to let me know you've come back."

I sat and looked at him and laughed.

"But, my dear chap, I haven't done such a thing yet."

"You old liar!" he exclaimed with an uneasy laugh, "you've been doing it every evening for the past week—until to-night, when I didn't give you the chance."

"I swear I haven't, Rudge. But if you thought that, it explains why you did the same thing to me to-night."

I saw from his face that I had made some queer mistake, and interrupted his denial to ask:

"Then who was the man I saw peering in at the window? I saw him from the door. I thought you'd tapped at the window to be let in, not knowing that the door was open. So I went round and saw—I thought it was you—and called out, 'Right ho.'"

We looked at each other again and laughed uneasily.

"It seems we've got our ghost after all," Rudge said half jestingly.

"Or somebody's trying to pull our leg," I amended.

"I don't know that I should fancy meeting the ghost of a murderer. But, joking apart, the house *has* been getting on my nerves of late. And those noises we've always heard have been getting louder and more mysterious lately."

As if to corroborate a statement which needed no evidence so far as I was concerned we heard a scuffling sound from the kitchen followed by the loud creaking of timber. We laughed again, puzzled uneasy laughter, for the thing was still half a joke.

"There you are!" said Rudge, and got upon his legs. "I'm going to investigate this."

He crossed the room and suddenly halted. I knew why. Then he turned about with an odd, shamed chuckle.

"No," he said, "there's no sense in it. I shall find nothing there. Why should I pander to my nerves?"

I had nothing to say. But I knew that in turning back he was pandering to cowardice, because just then I would have done almost anything rather than enter that kitchen. Had anybody asked me then where the murder was done I could have told them with as much certainty as if I had just been reading about it in the papers.

Rudge sat down again.

"Don't laugh at me," he said. "I know this is all rot, but I've got a hideous feeling that things hidden and unseen around us are moving steadily to a crisis."

"Cheerful brute," I said smiling.

"I know. It's only my nerves, of course. I don't want to infect you with them. But the noises we hear, and the fellow who comes and taps at the window—they want some explaining away, don't they?"

"Especially now that we know that somebody was murdered here," I agreed. "I'm beginning to wish we didn't know about that."

Rudge went early to bed that night, but I sat up reading. As often happens to me I fell asleep over my book, and when I woke I was almost in darkness, for the lamp needed filling. The last jagged, blue flame swelled and dwindled, fluttering like a moth and tapping against the glass. And as I watched it I became suddenly aware of the cause of my waking. I had heard the latch snap on the garden gate. And in that moment I began to hear them—the footfalls.

I heard the rhythmic crunch of gravel and then the swish of long grass and plantains, and then a shadow nodded on the blind. It loomed up large and suddenly became stationary. A loose pane rattled under the impact of fingers.

Perhaps there was a moon, perhaps not, but there was at least bright starlight in the world outside. The drawn blind looked like dim bluish glass, and the shadow of something outside was cut as cleanly as a silhouette clipped away with scissors. I saw only the head and shoulders of a man, who wore a dented felt hat. His head lolled over on to his left shoulder, just as I had always imagined a man's head would loll if—well, if he had been hanged. And I knew in my blood that he was a Horror and that he wanted me for something.

I felt my hair bristle and suddenly I was streaming with sweat. I don't remember turning and running, but I have a vague recollection of cannoning off the door post and stumbling in the hall. And when I reached my bed I don't know if I fainted or fell asleep.

No, I didn't tell Rudge next day. His nerves were in a bad enough state already. Besides, in the fresh glory of a May morning it was easy to persuade myself that the episode had been an evil dream. But I did question Mrs. Jaines, our charwoman, when she arrived, and I saw a look half stubborn and half guilty cross her face.

Yes, of course, she remembered the murder happening, but she didn't remember much about it. Mr. Stryde was quite a nice gentleman, although rather a one for the ladies, and she had worked for him sometimes. Stryde's defence was that the poor girl had committed suicide and that he'd lost his head and buried the body when he found it. Lots of people thought that was true, but they'd hanged Mr. Stryde for it all the same. And that was all I could get out of Mrs. Jaines.

I smiled grimly to myself. As if the woman didn't remember every detail! As if the neighbourhood had talked of anything else for the two following years! And then I remembered the policeman's strange words and how he had been staring at the calendar while he spoke.

So that morning when I called at the inn for my usual glass of beer, I, too, looked at the calendar and asked the landlord if he could tell me the date of the murder.

"Yes, sir," he said, "it was May the—" And then he stopped himself. "Why, it was eight years ago, to-night!" he said.

I went out again that evening and came in at the usual hour. But that evening Rudge came down the path to meet me. He was white and sick-looking.

"He's been here again," he said, "half an hour ago."

"You saw him this time?" I asked jerkily.

"Yes, I did as you did and went round to the door." He paused and added quite soberly: "He is a ghost, you know."

"What happened?" I asked, looking uneasily around me.

"Oh! I went round to the door when I heard him tapping at the window, and there he was, as you saw him yesterday evening, trying to look through into the room. He must have heard me for he turned and stared. His head was drooping all on one side, like a poppy on a broken stem. He came towards me, and I couldn't stand that, so I turned and ran into the house and locked the door."

He spoke in a tone half weary, half matter of fact, and suddenly I knew that it was all true. I don't mean that I knew that just his story was true. I knew that the house was haunted and that the thing which we had both seen was part of the man who had once been Stanley Stryde.

When once one has accepted the hitherto incredible it is strange how soon one can adapt oneself to the altered point of view.

"This is the anniversary of the—the murder," I said quietly. "I should think something—something worse will happen to-night. Shall we see it through or shall we beat it?"

And almost in a whisper Rudge said:

"Poor devil! Oughtn't one to pity? He wants to tell us something, you know."

"Yes," I agreed, "or show us something."

Together we walked into the house. We were braver in each other's company, and we did not again discuss the problem of going or staying. We stayed.

I can pass over the details of how we spent that evening. They are of no importance to the story. We were left in peace until just after eleven o'clock, when once more we heard the garden gate being opened, and footfalls which by this time we were able to recognize came up the path and through the long grass to the window. We could see nothing, for our lamp was alight, but I knew what it looked like—the thing that stood outside and now tapped softly upon the glass. And in spite of having Rudge for company I lost my head and screamed at it.

"Get back to hell! Get back to hell, I tell you!" I heard myself shout.

And it was Rudge, Rudge the sensitive neurotic, who kept his head, for human psychology is past human understanding.

"No," he called out in a thin quaver, "come in. Come in, if we can help you."

And then, as if regretting his courage on the instant, he caught my hand and held it, drawing me towards him.

The front door was locked, but it was no barrier to that which responded to the invitation. We heard slow footfalls shuffling through the hall, the footfalls, it seemed to me, of a man whose head was a burden to him. I died a thousand deaths as they approached the door of our room, but they passed and died away up the passage. And then I heard a whisper from Rudge.

"He's gone through into the kitchen. I think he wants us to follow."

I shouldn't have gone if Rudge hadn't half dragged me by the hand. And as I went the sweat from the roots of my stiffened hair ran down my cheeks.

The kitchen door was closed, and we halted outside it, both of us breathing as if we had been running hard. Then Rudge held his breath for a moment, lifted the latch, and took a quick step across the threshold. And in that same instant he froze my chilled blood with a scream such as I had heard in war-time from a wounded horse.

He had almost fainted when he fell into my arms, but he had the presence of mind to pull the door after him, so that I saw nothing. I half dragged, half carried him into the dining-room and gave him brandy. And suddenly I became aware that a great peace had settled upon the house. I can only liken it to the freshness and the sweetness of the earth after a storm has passed. Rudge felt it, too, for presently he began to talk.

"What was he—doing?" I asked in a whisper.

"He? He wasn't there—not in the kitchen."

"Not in the kitchen? Then what—who—"

"It was She. Only She. She was kicking and struggling. From the middle beam, you know. And there was an overturned chair at her feet."

He shuddered convulsively.

"She was worse than he," he said presently—"far worse."

And then later:

"Poor devil! So he didn't do it, you see!"

Next morning we had it out with Mrs. Jaines, and we did not permit her memory to be hazy or defective. She must have known that we had seen something and presently she burst into tears.

"He said he'd found her hanging in the kitchen, poor gentleman, and that he'd buried her because he was afraid people would say he'd done it. But the jury wouldn't believe him, and the doctors all said that it wasn't true, and that the marks on her neck were where he'd strangled her with a rope. I don't believe to this day he did it, I don't! But nothing can't ever bring him back." She paused at that and added. "Not back to life, I mean—real life, like you and me, I mean."

And that was all we heard and all we wished to hear.

Afterwards Rudge said to me:

"For his sake, the truth as we know it ought to be told to everybody. I suppose the police know?"

"Yes," I said, "the police know—-now. But as Mrs. Jaines said, it can't bring him back."

"Who wants to bring him back?" exclaimed Rudge with a shudder. "But perhaps if people knew—as we know—it might let him rest. I am sure that was what he wanted—just that people should know."

He paused and drew a long breath through his lips.

"You write it," he said jerkily. "I can't!"

And so I have.

CREWE

Walter de la Mare

(1929)

When misty winter dusk begins to settle on the railway station at Crewe the waiting-room grows steadily more stagnant. Particularly if one is alone in it. The long windows hardly do more than sift the failing light that slopes in on them from the glass roof outside—too feeble to penetrate into the recesses beyond. And the grained-massive, black-leathered furniture becomes less and less inviting. It appears to have been made for a scene of extreme and diabolical violence that has never occurred. One can hardly at any rate imagine it to have been designed by a really good man!

Little things like that of course are apt to get exaggerated in memory, and I may be doing the Company an injustice. But whether this is so or not (and the afternoon I have in mind is now many years distant) I certainly became more acutely conscious of the defects of my surroundings when the few fellow-travellers who had been sharing the faint murk of the room with me had hurried out at the sound of the bell for the down train, leaving me to wait for the up. And nothing and nobody, as I supposed, but a great drowsy fire of cinders in the iron grate for company.

The almost animated talk that had sprung up before we separated, never probably in this world to meet again, had been started by an account in the morning's newspapers of

249

the last voyage of a ship called the *Hesper*. She had arrived
the evening before, and some days overdue, from the West
Indies, with a cargo of sugar, and was now berthed safely
in the Southampton Docks. This must have been something of a relief to those concerned. For even her master had not refused to admit that certain mysterious and
tragic events had recently occurred on board, though he
preferred not to discuss them with a reporter. And there
was little doubt (a) that there had been a full moon at the
time, (b) that apart from a heavy swell, the sea was "as
calm as a millpond," and (c) that his ship was at present
in want of a second mate.

But the *Hesper* is now, of course, an old and familiar
tale. Indeed I had myself by that time supped my fill of
her mysteries, and had decided to seek the lights and joys
and colored bottles of the "refreshment room," when a
voice from behind me suddenly broke the hush. It was an
unusual voice, rapid, incoherent and internal, like that of
a man in his dreams or under the influence of a drug.

I shifted my ungainly chair and turned to look. Evidently the only other occupant of the room had until that
moment been as little aware of my presence there as I of
his. Indeed from what I could see of him he appeared to
have been quite taken aback by the noise I had made—had
started up and was positively staring at me from out of the
gloom.

"I am sorry," I said, "I thought—"

But he interrupted me, and not as if my company, now
that he had recognized me as a fellow-creature, was any
the less welcome for being unexpected. "Merely what I was
saying, sir," he explained, "is that those gentlemen there
who have just left us hadn't no more of a notion of what
they were talking about than an infant in its cradle."

This elegant paraphrase, I must confess, bore only the
feeblest resemblance to the language I had just overheard.

I looked at him. "How so?" I said, "I am only a landsman myself, and . . ." It seemed unnecessary to finish the sentence, particularly as he too was devoid of any obvious trace of the marine. But then at the moment little else than his flat white face was clearly discernible. He sat on the edge of a vast settee, muffled up in a very respectable overcoat a size or two too large for him, his hands thrust into its pockets.

"You don't have to go to sea for things like that," he went on. "And there is no need to argue about them if you do. But it wasn't my place to interfere. They'll find out all right—all in good time. They go their ways. And talking of that, sir, have you ever heard that there is less risk sitting in a railway carriage at sixty miles an hour than in laying alone, safe, as you might suppose, in your own bed? That's true, too. You know where you are in a spot like this. It's solid, though—" I couldn't catch the words that followed, but they seemed to be uncomplimentary to things in general.

"Yes," I agreed, "it certainly looks solid."

"Ah, looks!" he broke in rather cantankerously, "but what is your 'solid,' come to that? I thought so myself once." He seemed to be pondering over the "once." "But now," he added, "I know different."

Whereupon he sallied out of the obscurity under the high window, and after warming his veined shrunken hands at the heap of smouldering cinders in the grate and his head little more than topped the black marble mantel-piece—he seated himself opposite to me.

In deference to my own none too acute faculties of observation, let me confess at once that I didn't much care for the appearance of this stranger. I fancied at first he was about to solicit a small loan. In spite of his greatcoat he looked in need of the barber as well as of medicine and sleep, and that might presently manifest itself in a hankering for alcohol. But I was mistaken. He asked for nothing, not even for sympathy, not even advice. He merely, it seemed, wanted to talk about himself, and perhaps in certain circumstances strangers make better receptacles for such confidences than one's intimates. They tell no tales.

None the less—and, as near as I can, in his own peculiar idiom—I shall attempt to tell his. It impressed me at the time; and I have occasionally speculated since whether his statistics regarding railway travelling proved to him to be just. "Safety first" is a sound principle so far as it goes, but we are all of us outmanoeuvred in the end. And I still wonder what end was his.

He began by asking me if I had ever lived in the country: "in the depps" of the country; but soon discovering that I was more inclined to listen than to talk, he suddenly plunged into his past, and as if it might refresh him to do so.

"I was a gentleman's servant when I began," he set off, "first boot-boy, then washing up and helping at table, then in the pantry and so on. Never married or anything of that; they are nothing but encumbrances in the house; and I must say if you keep yourself *to* yourself, it sees you through—in time. What you have to beware of is those of your own party. That's the same everywhere; nobody's got much past the dog-and-cat stage in that. Not if you look close enough: high or low. I lost one or two nice easy places all through that. And if you don't stay where you are put there's precious little chance of pickings when the funeral's at the door. But that's mostly changed now, so I'm told. High wages and no work being the order of the day. They are all rolling stones, and never mind the moss."

As a philosopher this muffled-up, old white-faced creature certainly tended toward realism, though his reservations on the "solid" had fallen a little short of it. Not

that he seemed to care much about my reality. For though
in the memories he proceeded to share with me he inter-
polated many questions, he very seldom waited for an
answer, and then ignored it. I see now this was not to be
wondered at. We happened to be sharing at the moment
this (for my part) chance resort—the waiting-room on the
between-platform (midway, that is betwixt the worlds of
west and east) at Crewe; and seldom the time and the place
and any sort of listener together.

"The last situation I was in," (he was going on to tell
me), "was with the Reverend W. Somers—with an 'o.' In
the depps of the country, as I say. Just myself and another
manservant, and a woman who came in from the village to
char and cook and get things ready, though I did the best
part of that myself. The finishing touches, I mean. How
long the Reverend hadn't cared for females in the house I
never knew; though parsons get their share of them, I'm
thinking. Not that I'd say he wasn't attached enough to
his sister. They had grown up together, and that covers a
multitude of sins.

"Like *him, she* was, but more of the parrot in appearance; a high face with a beaky nose. Quite a nice lady, too,
except that she was mighty slow in being explained to.
No interference otherwise in spite of her nose. But don't
mistake me; we had to look alive when she came. Oh, yes.
But that, thank God, was seldom. And in the end it made
no difference.

"She didn't like the Vicarage. Who would? Too dark,
too shut in. And in winter freezing cold; lying low maybe. Trees all in front, everlastings; though open behind,
with a stream and cornfields and hills in the distance; in
summer, of course. They went up and down and dim or
dark, according to the weather. You could see for miles
from the corridor windows, small panes that take a lot of
cleaning. But George did the windows. George had come

from the village, too, if you could call it a village. But he was a permanency. Nothing much but a few cottages, and a farmhouse here and there. What they built a church a mile away from it for I can't say. Give the Roaring Lion a trot, perhaps. The Reverend had private means, of course. I knew that before it came out in the will, but it was a fat living notwithstanding; worked out at ten pounds to the pigsty, I shouldn't wonder, and the Vicarage thrown in. You get what you've got in this world, that's the truth; and some of us a large slice more than we deserve. But the Reverend, I must say, never took advantage of it. Give him his books, and to-morrow like yesterday, and he grumbled no more than a cat in a fish shop.

"Mind you, he liked things as they should be, and he had some of the finest silver I've ever used rouge and shammy on—all the Georges, and furniture to match. I don't mean picked up at sales and from dealers and suchlike, but real old family stuff. That's where the parrot in their noses came from. And everything punctual to the minute and the good things *good*. Soup or fish, a cutlet, a savory, and a glass of sherry or Madeira. No sweets. And I have never seen choicer fruit than was grown in his garden, though it was there that the trouble began. Cherries, gages, peaches, nectarines—old red sunbaked walls nine or ten feet high; a sight like wonder in the spring. I used to go out specially to have a look at it. He had his fancies, mind you, had the Reverend. If we smoked it had to be in the shrubbery with the blackbirds, not under the roof.

"But tobacco's not my trouble. Never was. Keep off what you don't need and you'll never want it when you can't get it. That's my feeling. It was, as I say, an easy place, if you forgot how quiet it was; no company, and not a petticoat to be seen. Good prospects, too, if you could wait. He didn't like change, did the Reverend; made no concealment of it. He told me himself that he had remembered me in his will—'if still in his service'; you know how these lawyers put it. As a matter of fact he gave me to understand that if in the meantime for any reason any of us went elsewhere, the one left was to have the lot. There, as it turned out, I was in error.

"But I'm not complaining of that now; oh, no! I've got enough to see me through however long I'm left. And that might be for a good many years yet."

His intonation suggested a question, but he made no pause for an answer and added argumentatively: "Who *wants* to go, I should like to ask? Early or late. And knowing nothing of what's on the other side?" He lifted his gray eyebrows a little to glance up at me, as he sat stooped up by the fire. But again I couldn't enlighten him.

"Well, there, as I say, I might have stayed to this day if the old gentleman's gardener had cared to stay too. *He* began it. Him gone we all went. Like ninepins. You might hardly credit it, sir, but I am the only one left of that complete establishment. Gutted. And that's where these gentlemen here were talking round their hats. What I say is, keep on this side of the tomb as long as you can. Don't meddle with that hole. Why? Because while some fine day you will have to go down into it, you can never be quite sure what mayn't come back out of it.

"*There'll be no partings there*—I have heard them singing the tune out like missel thrushes in the spring. But they seem to forget there may be some mighty unpleasant *meetings*. They talk of the further shore as if once there, friend or foe, there's no returning. But it's my belief there is some kind of a ferry plying on that river. All depends on your want to get back.

"Anyhow the Vicarage reeked of it. A low old house, with lots of little windows and much too many doors; and,

as I say, the trees too close up on one side, almost brushing the panes. No wonder they said it was what they call
haunted. You could feel that with your eyes shut; and like
breeds like. The Vicar—two or three I mean, before my
own, my last gentleman—had even gone to the trouble of
having the place exorcised. Candles and holy water, that
kind of thing. Sheer flummummery *I* call it. But if what
I've heard—and long before that gowk of a George came
to work in the house—was anything more than mere age
and owls and birds in the ivy, it must badly have needed it. And when you get accustomed to noises, you can
tell which from which. By usual, I mean. Though more
and more I'm getting to ask myself if anything's anything
much more than what you think it is—for the time being.

"Same with noises, of course. What's this voice of conscience that they talk about but something you needn't
hear if you don't like? I am not complaining of that. If
at the beginning there was anything in that house that
was better out than in, it never troubled me; at least, not
at first. And the Reverend, even though you could often
count his congregation on your ten fingers, except at Harvest Festival, was so wove up in his books that I doubt
if he'd have been roused up out of 'em even by the Last
Trump. It's my belief that in those last few months, when
I stepped in to see to the fire, as often as not he'd been
sitting asleep over them.

"No, I'm not complaining. Live at peace with who you
can, I say. But when it comes to as crusty a customer, and
a Scotchman at that, as was the Reverend's gardener, then
there's a limit. Mengus he called himself, though I can't
see how, if you spell it with a 'z.' When I first came into
the place it was all gold that glitters. I'm not the man for
contentiousness, left alone. But afterward, when the rift
came, I don't suppose we ever hardly exchanged the time
of day but what there came words of it. A long-legged

man, he was—this Mr. Menzies; too long I should have thought for strict comfort in grubbing and hoeing and weeding. He had ginger hair, scanty, and the same on his face, whiskers—and a stoop. He lived down at the lodge; and his widowed daughter kept house for him, with one little boy as fair as she was dark. Harmless enough as children go, but noisy, and not for the house.

"Now why, I ask you, shouldn't I gather a little of this gentleman's fruit or a cucumber for a salad, if need be, and him not there? What if I wanted a few grapes for dessert or a nice apricot tart for the Reverend's luncheon, and our Mr. Menzies gone home or busy with the frames? I don't hold with all these hard and fast restrictions, at least outside the house. Not he, though! We wrangled about it week in, week out. And he with a temper when roused that was past all Masoning.

"Not that I ever took much notice of him until it came to a point past bearing. I let him rave. But duty is duty, there's no getting away from it. And when, besides all that fuss about his fruit, a man takes advantage of what is meant in pure friendliness, well one's bound to make a move.

"What I mean to say is, I used occasionally—window wide open and all that, the pantry being on the other side of the house and away from the old gentleman's study—I say I used occasionally and all in the way of friendliness to offer our friend a drink. Like as with many of Old Adam's trade, drink was a little weakness of his, though I don't mean I hold with it because of that. But peace and quietness is the first thing, and to keep an easy face to all appearance, even if you do find it a little hard at times to forgive and forget.

"When he was civil, as I say, and as things should be, he could have a drink, and welcome. When not, not. It came to a kind of habit; and to be expected; which is always a bad condition of things. Oh, it was a thousand pities! There was the Reverend, growing feeble as you could see, and him believing all the while that everything around him was calm and sweet as the new Jerusalem, while there was nothing but strife and acrimony, as they call it, underneath. There's many a house looks as snug and cosey as a nut. But crack it and look inside! Mildew.

"Well, there came along at last a mighty hot summer; two years ago, you may remember. Two years ago, next August, an extraordinary hot summer. And

see the stones in the stubble fields shivering in the sun. And gardening is thirsty work, I will say that for it. Which being so, better surely virgin water from the tap or a drop of cider, same as the harvesters have, than ardent spirits; whether it is what you are bred up to or not. It stands to reason.

"Besides, we had had words again, and though I can stretch a point with a friend and no harm done, I'm not a man to come coneying and currying favor. Let him get his own drinks, was my feeling in the matter. And you can hardly call me to blame if he did. *There* was the pantry window hanging wide open in the shade of the trees—and day after day of scorching sun and not a breath to breathe. And there was the ruin of him within arm's reach from outside, and a water tap handy too. Very inviting, I'll allow.

"I'm not attesting, mind you, that he was confirmed at it, no more than I'm a man to be measuring what's given me to take charge of by tenths of inches. It's the principle of the thing. You might have thought too, that a simple honest pride would have kept him back. Nothing of the sort; and no matter, wine or spirits. I'd watch him there, though he couldn't see me, being behind the door. And practices like that, sir, as you will agree with me, can't go on. They couldn't go on, Vicarage or no Vicarage. Besides

from being secret it began to be open. It had gone too
far. Brazen it out; that was the lay. I came down one fine
morning to find one of my best decanters smashed to
smithereens on the stone floor, Irish glass and all. Cats and
sherry, who ever heard of it? And out of revenge he filled
the pantry with wasps by bringing in over-ripe plums,
petty waste of time like that; and some of the greenhouses
thick with blight!

"And so things went, from bad to worse, and at such
a pace as I couldn't have credited. A widower, too; with a
married daughter dependent on him; which is worse even
than a wife, who *expects* to take the bad with the good. No,
sir, I had to call halt to it. A friendly word in his ear, or
keeping everything out of his reach, you may be thinking,
might have been of use. Believe me, not from me. And how
can you foster such a weakness by taking steps out of the
usual to prevent it? It wouldn't be proper to your self-re-
spect. Then I thought of George, not demeaning myself in
any way, of course, in so doing. George had a face half as
long as your arm, pale and solemn, enough to make a cat
laugh. Dress him in a surplice and so on, he might have
been the Reverend's curate. Strange that, for a youth born
in the country. But curate or no curate, he had eyes in his
head and must have seen what there was to be seen.

"I said to him one day, and I remember him standing
there, in his black coat, against the white of the cupboard
paint, I said to him: 'George, a word in time saves nine,
but it would come better from you than from me. You
take me? Hold your time till our friend's sober again and
can listen to reason. Then hand it over to him—a word of
warning, I mean. Say we are muffling things up as well as
we can from the old gentleman, but that if he should happen to hear of it there'd be fat in the fire; and no mistake.
He would take it easier from you, George, the responsibility being mine.'

"Lor', how I remember George! He had a way of looking at you as if he couldn't say Boo to a goose; swollen hands and bolting blue eyes, as simple as an infant's. But he wasn't stupid, oh no, and now I reflect, I think he knew that our little plan wouldn't carry very far. But as whatever he might be thinking, he was so awkward with his tongue that he could never find anything to say until it was too late, I left it at that. Besides I had come to know he was with all his faults a young man you could trust for doing what he was told to do. So, as I say, I left it at that.

"What he actually said I never knew. But as for its being of any use, it was more like pouring paraffin on a bonfire. The very afternoon our friend came to the pantry window and stood looking in—swaying he was, on his feet, and I can see the midges behind him, floating in a patch of sunshine as though they were here before my eyes. He was so bad that he had to lay hold of the sill to keep himself from falling. Not thirst this time, but just fury. And then, seeing that mere flaunting of fine feathers wasn't going to inveigle me into a cockfight, he began to talk. No bad language, mind you—*that's* easy to shut your ears to—but cold reasonable abuse, which isn't. At first I took no notice, went on humming and polishing at my leisure, and no hurry. What's the use of arguing with a man, and a Scotchman to boot, that's beside himself with rage? Besides I wanted peace in the house, if only for the old gentleman's sake, who I thought was definitely under the weather and had been coming on very poorly of late.

"'Where's that George of yours,' he said to me at last—with additions. 'Where's that George? Fetch him out, and I'll teach him to come playing holy Moses to my own daughter. Fetch him out, I say, and we'll finish it here and now.' And all pitched high, and half his words no more English than the mewing of a cat.

'But I kept my temper and answered him quite pleasant, as pleasantly as I knew how. 'I don't want to meddle in
anybody's quarrels,' I said. 'So long as George so does his
work in this house as it'll satisfy *my* eye, I am not respon-
sible for his actions in his off-time and out of bounds.'

"How was I to know, may I ask, if it was *not* our Mr.
'Mengus' who had smashed one of my best decanters? What
proof was there? What *reason* had I for thinking else?

"'George is a quiet, unbeseeming young fellow,' I said,
'and if he thinks it's his duty to report any misgoings-on
either to me or to the Reverend, it doesn't concern anybody else.'

"That seemed to sober my fine gentleman. Mind you,
I'm not saying that there was anything unremidibly wrong
with him. He was a first-class gardener, but then he had an
uncommonly good place to match—first-class wages; and
no milk, wood, coals or house rent to worry about. But
making fusses like that, and the Reverend poorly; that's
not what he thought of when he put us all down in his
will. I'll be bound of that. Well, there he stood looking in
at the window, and me behind the table in my green baize
apron as calm as if his wrangling meant no more to me
than the wind in the chimenney. It was the word 'report,'
I fancy, that took the wind out of his sails. It had brought
him up like a station buffer. And he was still looking at
me, and chewing it over, as though he had the taste of
poison on his tongue.

"Then he said very quiet, 'So that's his little game is it?
You are just a pair, then.'

"'If by pair you're meaning me,' I said, 'well, I'm ready
to take on my share of the burden when it's ready to fit my
back. But not before. George may have gone a bit beyond
himself, but he meant well, and you know it.'

"'What I am asking is this,' says our friend, 'have you
ever seen me the worse for liquor? Answer me that!'

"'If I liked your tone better,' I said, 'I wouldn't say as I don't see why it would be necessarily the *worse.'*

"'Eh? You mean, Yes, then?' he said.

"'I meant no more than what I said,' I answered him, looking at him over the cruet as straight as I'm looking at you now. 'I don't want to meddle with your private affairs, and I don't want you to come meddling with mine.' He seemed taken aback by that and I noticed he was looking a bit pinched, and hollow under the eyes.

"But how was *I* to know this grandson of his was out of sorts with a bad throat and that, seeing that he hadn't mentioned it till a minute before? I ask you.

"'The best thing you and George can do,' I went on, 'is to bury the hatchet; and out of hearing of the house, too.'

"With that I turned away and went off into it myself, leaving him there to think things over at his leisure. I am asking you, sir, as a free witness, what else could I have done? . . ."

There was very little light of day left in our waiting-room by this time. Only the dulling glow of the fire and the faint phosphorescence caused by a tiny bead of gas in the incandescent mantles of the great iron bracket over our heads. My realist seemed to be positively in want of an answer to this last question, but as I sat looking back into his intent white face nothing that could be described as of a helpful nature offered itself.

"It may be this anxiety over his grandson had shortened his temper," I said at last. "But I should like to hear what came after."

"What came after, now," the little man repeated, drawing his right hand gingerly out of the depths of his pocket, and smoothing down his face with it as if he were tired. "Well, a good deal came after, but not quite what I expected. And you'd hardly say perhaps that anxiety over his

grandson would excuse him for little short of manslaugh-
ter, and him a good six inches to the good at that? Keeping facts as facts, if you'll excuse me, our friend waylaid
George by the stables that very evening, and a wonderful
peaceful evening it was, shepherd's delight and all that.
But to judge from the looks of the young fellow's face
when he came into the house there hadn't been much of
that in the quarter of an hour they had had together.

"I said, 'Sponge it down, George, sponge it down. And
perhaps the old gentleman won't notice anything wrong.'
It wasn't to reason I could let him off his duties and enter
into long prevarications which in the long run would only
make things worse. And it's that you have to think of. But
as for the Reverend's not noticing it, there, as luck would
have it, I was wrong myself.

"For when him and me were leaving the dining-room
that evening after the table had been cleared and the dessert put on, he looked up from round the candles and told
George to stay behind. Some quarter of an hour after that
George came along to me snuffling as if he'd been crying. But I asked no questions, not me; and, as I say, he
was always pretty slow with his tongue. All that I could
get out of him was that he had decocted a cock-and-bull
story to account for his looks the like of which nobody
in his senses could credit, let alone such a power of ques-
tioning as the old gentleman could bring to bear when
roused and apart from what comes, I suppose, from reading books. So the fat *was* in the fire and no mistake. And
the next thing I heard, after coming back late next evening, was that our Mr. Menzies had been called into the
house and given the sack there and then, with a quarter's
wages in lieu of notice. Which, after all, mind you, was as
good as three-quarters a gift. Not that I'm saying this was
letting him off light, and I agree money isn't necessarily

everything when there's what's called character to take into
account. But if ever there was one of the quality fair and
upright in all his dealings, as the saying goes, then that
was the Reverend Somers. He couldn't abide drink topped
with insolence. That's all.

"Well, our friend came rapping at the back door that
evening, shaken to the marrow if ever man was, and just
livid. I told him, and I meant it too, that I was sorry for
what had occurred. 'It's a bad ending,' I said, 'to a tale
that ought never to have been told.' I said to him the only
thing left now was to let bygones be bygones; that he had
already had his fingers on George, and better go no further. Not he. He said, and he was sober enough then in
all conscience, that, come what come may, he'd be even
with him. Ay, and he made mention of me also, but not so
rabid. A respectable man, too. Never a word against him
till then; and not far short of sixty. And by rabid I don't
mean violent. He spoke as low and quiet as if there was a
judge on the bench there to hear him, sentence said and
everything over. And then . . ."

The old creature paused until a passing train had gone
roaring on its way. "And then he must have gone straight
out—and good-by said to nobody; though he wasn't found
till morning. He must, I say, have gone straight out to the
old barn and hung himself. The mid-most rafter, sir, and a
drop that would have sufficed for a Giant Goliath. And it's
my belief, good-by or no good-by, that it wasn't so much
the *disgrace* of the affair but his daughter—Mrs. Shaw by
name—and his grandson that were preying on his mind.
Yet—why, he never so much as asked me to say a good
word for him. Not one.

"Well, that was the end of that. So far. And it's a very
curious thing to me—though they say the Cartholics aren't
above making use of it—how, going back over the past
clears it all up like; just for the time being. But it's what

you were saying about what's *solid* that set me thinking and keeps repeating itself in my mind. Solid was the word you used. And they seem it, I agree." He deliberately twisted his head and took a prolonged look at the bench on which he was seated. "But it doesn't follow there's much comfort in them because of that. Even if they are solid, they go when all is said to what's little else but gas and ashes once they're fallen to pieces and put on the fire. Which holds good, and even more so, for them that sit on them. Peculiar habit that too! Yes, I've been told, sir, that whittle us down, and all the moisture of us gone up in steam, what's left would scarcely turn the scales by a single hounce!"

If sitting *is* a peculiar habit, it was even more peculiar how etherializing the effect of my new acquaintance's misplaced aspirate had been—his one and only example throughout this interminable monologue.

"They say that we'd amount to no more than what you could squeeze into a walnut. And my point *is*, sir," he was emphasizing, "that if *that's* all the solid there is to you and me, we shouldn't need much of the substantial for what you might call the mere sole look of things, if you follow me, *if* we chose or chanced, I mean, to come back when gone. Just enough, I suppose, to be obnoxious, as the Reverend used to say, to the naked eye.

"But all that being as it may be, the whole thing had tided over, and George pretty nearly himself again, and another gardener advertised for—and I must say the Reverend, though after this horrible affair he was never the same man again, treated the young woman I mentioned very handsomely—I say, the whole thing had tided over, and the house was as silent as a tomb again, ay, as the sepulchre itself, when I began to notice something peculiar.

"At first maybe, little more *than* the silence. What in the contrast, as a matter of fact, I took for peace. But afterward not so. There was a strain, so to speak, as you went about quite naturally. A strain. And especially after dark. It may have been only in one's head. I can't say. But it was there; and I could see without watching that even George had noticed it; and *he'd* hardly notice a black-beetle on a pancake.

"But at last there came something you could put word to, catch in the act, so to speak. I had gone out toward the cool of the evening after a broiling hot day, to get a little air. There was a copse of beeches, which is a very pleasant tree for shade, sir, as perhaps you may know, a little under the mile from the back of the Vicarage. And I sat there quiet a bit, with the birds and all—they were beginning to sing again, I remember. And—you know how memory strays back, though sometimes it's more like a goat tethered to a peg on a common—I was thinking over what a curious thing it is how one man's poison is another man's meat. For the funeral over, and all that, the old gentleman had thanked me for what I had done. You see it had been a hard break in his trust of a man, and he looked up from his bed at me almost with tears in his eyes. He said he wouldn't forget it. I ought to have mentioned pr'aps that he was taken ill the night of the inquest; a sort of stroke, the doctor called it, though he came round remarkably well considering his age.

"Well, I had been thinking over all this in the woods there, and was on my way back again to the house by the field-path, when I looked up sudden-like and saw what I take my oath I never remembered to have noticed there before—a scarecrow; and right in the middle of the corn-field that lay beyond the stream with the bulrushes at the back of the house. Nothing funny in that, you may say. But mark me, this was early September, and the stubble all bleaching in the sun, and it didn't look an *old* scarecrow, neither. It stood up with its arms out, and a hat down over its eyes, bang in the middle of the field, its back to me, and its front to the house. I knew that field like my own face in the looking-glass. Then how could I have missed it? What else then but that I stood still and had a good long stare at it, first because, as I say, I had never seen it before, and next because—but I'll be coming to that later.

"That done, and *not* to my satisfaction, I turned back a little and came along on the other side of the hedge, and so indoors, and went up to the upper storey to have a look at it from the windows. For you never know with these country people what they are up to, though they may seem stupid enough. Looked at from there, it wasn't so much in the middle of the field as I had fancied, seeing it from the other side. But how, thought I to myself, could you have escaped me, my friend, if you had been there all summer? I don't see how it could; that's flat. But if not, then it must have been put up more recent.

"I had all but forgotten about it next morning, but as afternoon came on I went upstairs and had another look. There was less heat-haze or something, and I could see it clearer and nearer, so to speak, but not quite clear enough. So I whipped along to the Reverend's study, him being still, poor gentleman, confined to his bed—in fact he never got up from it—I whipped along, I say, to the study to fetch his glasses, his binoculars, and I fastened them on that scarecrow like a microscope on a fly. Perhaps you will hardly credit me, sir, when I say that what seemed to me most different about it—from what you might expect—was that it didn't look in any ordinary manner of speaking, quite real.

"I could watch it with the glasses as plain as if it had been in touch of my hand, even to the buttons and the hatband. It didn't seem the first time I had set eyes on the *clothes,* either, though I couldn't have laid name to them. Yet there was something in the appearance of the thing, something in the way it bore itself up, so to speak, with its arms thrown up at the sky, and its empty face, which wasn't what you'd expect of mere sticks and rags. Not, I mean, if they were nothing but just real—real like that chair, I mean, you are sitting in now.

"I called George. I said: 'George, lay your eye to these glasses'—and his face was still a bit discolored, though his little affair in the stableyard was now three weeks old. 'Take a squint through these, George,' I said, 'and tell me what you think of *that* over there.'

"George was a slow dawdling mug if ever there was one—clumsy-fingered. But he fixed them at last, and took a good long look. Then he gave them back into my hand. 'Well,' I said, watching his face.

"'Why, Mr. Blake,' he said—meaning me, 'it's a scarecrow.'

"'How would you like it a bit nearer?' I said; just off-hand, like that.

"He looked at me. 'It's near enough in *them*,' he said.

"'Does the air round it strike you as funny at all?' I asked him. 'Out-of-the-way funny—quivering-like?'

"'That's the heat,' he said, but his mouth was trembling.

"'Well, George,' I said, 'heat or no heat, you or me must go and have a look at that thing closer some time. But not this afternoon. It's too late.'

"But we didn't; neither me *nor* him, though I fancy he went on thinking about it on his own account in between. And, lo and behold! when I got up next morning, and slid out of my bedroom, and just as I was, into the corridor to have another look at it—and Lor', as you looked out, the country was all as still as a map—it wasn't there. It wasn't there. It was vanished. Nor could I get a glimpse of it from downstairs through the bushes this side of the stream. And all so still and early you could hear the water moving. Now who, thinks I to myself, is answerable for *this* jiggery-pokery.

"But it's no good in this world, sir, putting reasons to a thing more far-fetched than are necessary to account for it. That you *will* agree. Some farmer's lout, I thought to myself, must have come and moved the thing overnight. But, that being so, what did he ever put it up for; harvest done, mind you, and the crows, one would think, as welcome to what they could pick up in the stubble—if they hadn't picked it up already—as robins to house crumbs?

"I didn't go out next day, not at all; and there being only George and me in the Vicarage, and the Reverend shut off in his room, I never knew such a holy quiet. The heavens like a vault. Eighty-four in the shade by the glass in the verandah, and this the fourth of September. All day long, and I'll vouch for it, the whole twenty acres of that field, but for the peewits and rooks lay empty. And when with the sun going down the harvest moon came up that evening—and that summer it showed up punctual as a clock the whole month round—you could see right across the flat country to the hills. And the nightjars croaking too. You could cut the heat with a knife.

"That time the old gentleman's gruel was gone up and George out of the way, I took yet another squint through the glasses from the upper windows. And I am ready to own that something inside of me gave a sort of a *hump* when, large as life, I saw that the scarecrow was come back again; though this, sir, is where you'll have, if you please, to go careful with me. What I saw the instant before I began to look, and to that I'd lay my affidavit, was something moving, and pretty rapid too, and it was only at the very moment I clapped the glasses on to it that it suddenly fixed itself into what I already *supposed* I should find it to be. I've noticed that—though in little things not mattering much—before. It's your own mind that learns you when what you look for turns out to be what you expect.

"You might be suggesting that both shape and scarecrow too were all my eye and Betty Martin. But we'll see later on about that. And what about George? You don't mean to infer that he could borrow a mere fancy clean out of my head to order, and turn it into a scarecrow in the middle of a field and in broad daylight too? That would be the long bow, and no mistake. Yet, as I say, even when I first cast eyes on it, it looked too real to be real. So there's the two on the one side, and the two on the other, and they don't make four.

"Well, sir, I must say that from that moment on I didn't like the look of things, and never have I shared a meal so mum as when George and me sat to supper that evening. From being a hearty eater his appetite was fallen almost to a cipher. He munched and couldn't swallow. I doubt if his vittles had a taste of them left. And we both of us knew as though it had been printed on the tablecloth what the other was thinking about.

"And it was while we sat there, him and me alone, George on the right and the window opposite, and me on the cupboard side in what was called the servants' hall, that we heard some words said. Not what you could understand, but still, words. I couldn't tell from where, except that it wasn't from the Reverend, and I couldn't tell what, but they dropped upon us and between us as if there had been a parrot in the room, clapping its horny bill, so to say, motionless in the air. At this George stopped munching for good, his face little short of green. But, except for a cockling up inside of me, I didn't make any sign I'd heard. After all, it was nothing that made any difference to *me,* though what was going on was, to say the least of it, not all as it should be. And if you knew the old Vicarage, you'd agree.

"Lock-up time came at last. And George took his candle and went up to bed. Not quite as willing as usual, I fancied; though he had always been a glutton for his full meed of sleep. You could notice by the sound of his feet on the stairs that he was pushing himself on. As for myself, it had always been my way to sit up after him reading a bit with the Reverend's *Times,* but that night I went off early. I gave a last look in on the old gentleman, and I might as well mention a nurse had been sent for, and his sister expected any day from Scotland; then coming back along the corridor I blew out my candle and stood waiting. The candle out, the moon came streaming in, and the outside from the window lay almost as bright as day. I looked this ways and that ways, back and front; but nothing to be seen, nor heard neither. Yet it seemed no more than one deep breath after I had closed my eyes in sleep that I was stark wide awake again, trying to make sense of some sound I'd heard.

"Old houses—I'm used to them. The timbers crinkle like a beehive in the dead of night. But this wasn't timbers, oh no! It might maybe have been wind, you'll say. But what chance of wind with not a hand's-breadth of cloud moving in the sky, and such a blare of moonlight as would keep a field mouse from so much as weeping out of its hole. What's more, not to know whether what you are listening to is in or out of your head isn't much help to a good night's rest. Still I fell off at last, unnoticing.

"Next morning, as George came back from taking up the breakfast tray, I had a good look at him in the sunlight, but you couldn't tell whether the marks round his eyes were natural—from what had gone before with the other, I mean—or from *insommia.* Best not to meddle,

I thought, just wait. So I gave him good morning, and poured out the coffee and we sat to it as usual, the wasps coming in over the marmalade as if nothing had happened.

"All quiet that day, only rather more so, as it always is in a sick-room house. Doctor come and gone, but no nurse yet; and the old gentleman I thought looking very ailing. But he spoke to me quite cheerful. Just like his old self, too, to be sympathizing with me for the double-duty I'd been doing in the house. He asked after the garden, too, though there was as fine a bunch of black grapes on his green plate as any out of Canaan. It was the drought was in his mind. And just as I was leaving the room, my hand on the door, he mentioned one or two nice things about my having stayed on with him so long. 'You can't pay for that out of any bank,' he said to me, smiling at me almost merry-like, his beard over the sheet.

"'I hope and trust, sir,' I said, 'while I am with you, there will be no further fuss.' But I had a surety even as I said the words that he hadn't far to go, so that fusses now didn't really much matter to him. I don't see how you would be likely to notice them when things are coming to a conclusion; though I am thankful to say that what did occur was kept from him to the end.

"That night there came something sounding about the house that wasn't natural, and no mistake. I had scarcely slept a wink, and as soon as I heard it I was on with my tailcoat over my nightshirt in a jiffy, though there was no need for light. I had fetched along my winter coat, too, one the Reverend himself had passed on to me—this very coat on my back—and with that over my arm, I pushed open the door and looked in on George. Maybe he had heard my coming, or the other, I couldn't tell which; but there he was, sitting up in bed—the moon-light flooding in on his long face and tousled hair—and his trousers and braces thrown on the chair beside it.

"I said to him, 'What's wrong, George? Did you hear anything? A voice or anything?'

"He sat looking at me with his mouth open as if he couldn't shut it, and I could see he was shaken to the very roots. Now mind you, here I was, in the same quandary, as they call it, as before. What I'd heard might be real, some animal, fox or the like, prowling round outside, or it might not. If not, and the house being exorcised, as I said, though a long way back, and the Reverend gentleman still in this world himself, I had a kind of trust that what was there, if it was anything, couldn't get in. But naturally I was in something of a fever to make sure.

"'George,' I said, 'you mustn't risk a chill or anything of that sort'—and it had grown a bit cold in the small hours—'but it's up to us, with the Reverend ill and all, to know what's what. So if *you'll* take a look round on the outside, I'll have a search through on the in. What we must be cautious about is that the old gentleman isn't disturbed.'

"George went on looking at me, though he had by this time shuffled out of bed and into the overcoat I had handed him. He stood there, with his boots in his hand, shivering, but more maybe because he felt cold after the warmth of his sheets than because he had quite taken in what I had said.

"'Do you think, Mr. Blake,' he asked me, sitting down again on his bed, 'you don't think he is come back?'

"'Who's, George, come back?' I asked him.

"'Why, what we looked through the glasses at in the field,' he said. 'It had his look.'

"'Why, George,' I said, speaking as quiet as you might to a child, 'we know as how dead men tell no tales. Let alone scarecrows, then. All we've got to do is just to make sure *sure*. You do then as you're bid, lad; you go your way, and I'll go mine. There's never any harm can befall a man if his conscience is easy.'

"But that didn't seem to satisfy him. He gave a gulp and stood up again, still looking at me. Stupid or not, he was always one for doing his duty, was George. And I must say that what I call courage is facing what you're afraid of in your very bones, and not mere crashing into danger, eyes shut.

"'I'd lief as not go down, Mr. Blake,' he said; 'leastways, not alone.'

"'What have you to fear, George, my lad,' I said, 'man or spectre, the fault was none of yours.'

"He buttoned the coat up, same as I am wearing it now, and he gave me just one look more. It's hard to say all that's in a fellow creature's eyes, sir, when they are full of what no tongue in him could tell; but he had shut his mouth at last, and the moon on his face gave him a queer look, far-away-like, as if all that there was of him, this world or the next, had come to keep him company.

"And when the hush that had come down on the house was broken again, and this time it *was* the wind, though away high up over the roof, he didn't look at me any more. It was the last between us. He turned his back on me and went off out into the passage and down the stairs, and I listened until I could hear him in the distance taking down the bar at the back. It was one of those old-fashioned doors, sir, you must understand, loaded with locks and bolts, like in all old places.

"As for myself, I didn't move for a bit—there wasn't any hurry that I could see—except that I sat down on the bed in the place where George had sat; and waited. And you may depend upon it I stayed pretty quick there—with all that responsibility, not knowing what might happen next. And then presently what I heard was as though a voice had said something, very sharp and bitter; then said no more. There was a sort of moan, and then no more again. But by that time I was on my way on my rounds inside the house as I'd promised, and when I got back to my bedroom everything was still and quiet. And I took it of course that George had got back to his . . ."

Though the fire had faded and the day was gone, the fish-like phosphorescence of the gas mantles seemed to have grown brighter, and this elderly man, whose name was Blake I understood, was looking at me out of his white, almost leper-like face in this faint gloom as steadily almost as George must have been looking at him a few minutes before he had descended the back stairs of the Vicarage, never, I gathered, to set foot on them again.

"Did you manage to get any more sleep that night?" I said.

Mr. Blake seemed to be pleasingly surprised at so easy a question.

"That was the mistake of it," he said. "He wasn't found till morning—cold for hours, and precious little to show why."

"So you did manage to get some sleep," I persisted. But this time he made no answer.

"Your share, I suppose, was quite a substantial one?"

"Share?" he said.

"In the will . . . ?"

"Now, didn't I myself tell you," he protested with some warmth, "that that, as it turned out, wasn't so; though why, it would take half a dozen or more of these lawyers to explain. And even at that, I don't know as what I did get has brought me anything much to boast about. I'm a free man; that's true. But for how long? Nobody can stay in this world here for ever, can he?"

With a peculiar rocking movement of his small head he peered round and out of the door. "And though," he went on, "you may have not one *iota* of harm to blame yourself for to yourself, there may be misunderstandings and them that hold them waiting for you in the next. So when it comes to what that captain of the *Hesper* . . ."

But at that moment our prolonged *tête-à-tête* was interrupted by a thick-set vigorous young porter carrying a bucket of coals in one hand and a stumpy torch of smouldering brown paper in the other. He mounted a chair and with a tug of finger and thumb instantly flooded our dingy quarters with an almost intolerable gassy glare. That done, he raked out the ash-gray fire with a lump of iron that may once have been a poker, and flung all but the complete contents of his bucket of coal on to it. Then he glanced round and saw who was sitting there. Me he passed over. I was merely a bird of passage. But he greeted my companion as if he were an old acquaintance.

"Good evening, sir," he said, and in that slightly cosseting voice which suggests past favors. "Let in a little light on the scene! I didn't notice you when I came in, and was beginning to wonder where you had got to."

His patron smirked back at him as if any such trifling little human attention was a peculiar solace. This time the porter deliberately caught my eye, as if—strangers though we were—there were some little privy and amused understanding between us in which this third party was unlikely to share. I ignored it, rose to my feet and clutched my bag. A train had come hooting into the station, its gliding lighted windows patterning the platform planks. Alas, yet again it wasn't mine. Still, such is humanity, I preferred my own company only, just then.

When I reached the door I glanced back at Mr. Blake, sitting there in the overcoat beside the apparently extinguished fire. In a sort of lost-dog fashion he was gazing after me, as though he deplored the withdrawal even of my tepid companionship. But in that dreadful luminosity there was nothing, so far as I could see, that any mortal man could be afraid of, alive or dead. So I left him to the porter, and set out hurriedly for the more comfortable lights and joys and colored bottles of the refreshment room. And as yet we have not met again.

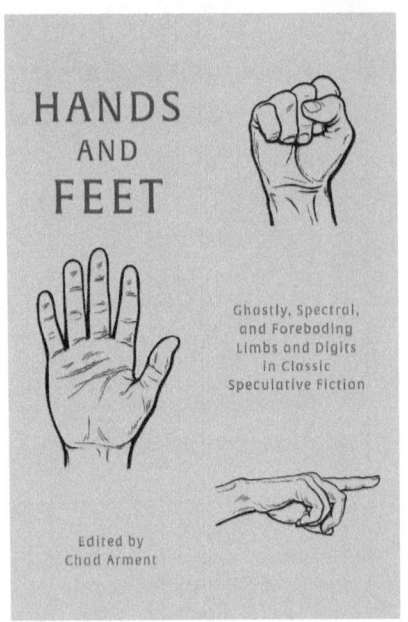

HANDS
AND
FEET

Ghastly, Spectral,
and Foreboding
Limbs and Digits
in Classic
Speculative Fiction

Edited by
Chad Arment

A
HAUNTING
NOTE

Music of the
Uncanny and
Inexplicable
in Classic
Speculative
Fiction

A HOUSE
A-HAUNT

CLASSIC STORIES OF HAUNTED HOUSES,
HORRIFIC ROOMS, AND OTHER GHASTLY ABODES

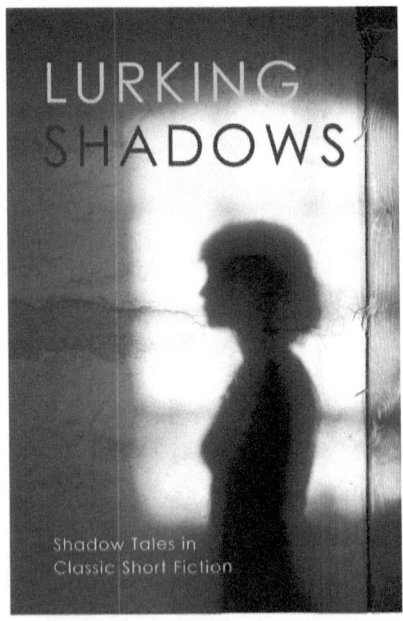

LURKING
SHADOWS

Shadow Tales in
Classic Short Fiction

Coachwhip Publications

CoachwhipBooks.com

Coachwhip Publications

CoachwhipBooks.com

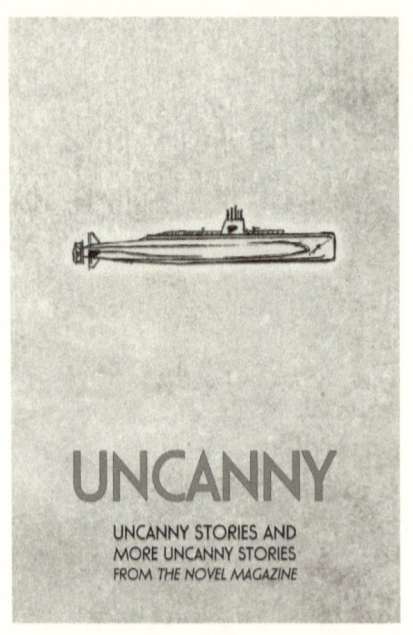

UNCANNY

UNCANNY STORIES AND
MORE UNCANNY STORIES
FROM *THE NOVEL MAGAZINE*

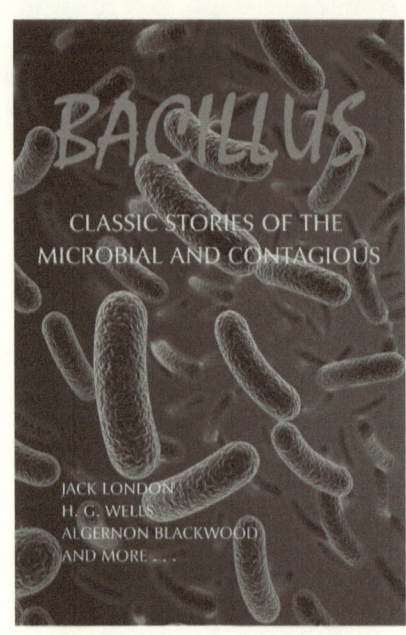

BACILLUS

CLASSIC STORIES OF THE
MICROBIAL AND CONTAGIOUS

JACK LONDON
H. G. WELLS
ALGERNON BLACKWOOD
AND MORE . . .

OTHER LIFE

An Anthology of
Non-Terrestrial Biology

DAYS OF DOOM

APOCALYPTIC VISIONS &
UNEARTHLY NIGHTMARES

OWEN OLIVER

Coachwhip Publications

CoachwhipBooks.com

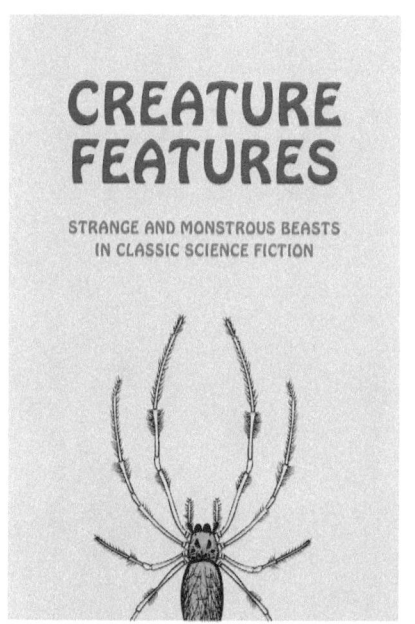

CREATURE FEATURES

STRANGE AND MONSTROUS BEASTS
IN CLASSIC SCIENCE FICTION

ROAMING THE DARK

STORIES BY
RICHARD MIDDLETON
AND
BARRY PAIN

CATS OF SHADOW,
CLAWS OF DARKNESS

Stories of Were-Cats, Ghost Cats,
and Other Supernatural Felines

INTRODUCTION BY TIM PRASIL

ARTHUR MACHEN

THE DYSON
CHRONICLES

THE INMOST LIGHT · THE SHINING PYRAMID
THE RED HAND · THE THREE IMPOSTORS

Coachwhip Publications

CoachwhipBooks.com

GHOST STORIES
AND WEIRD TALES

H. RUSSELL WAKEFIELD

DANCING SHADOWS

TALES OF THE SUPERNATURAL
BY BERNARD CAPES

Bestiarium Cryptozoologicum

Mystery Animals and Unknown Species
in Classic Science Fiction and Fantasy

BESTIA SECRETUM

Further
Explorations into
Classic Cryptozoological Fiction
Edited by Chad Arment

Coachwhip Publications

CoachwhipBooks.com

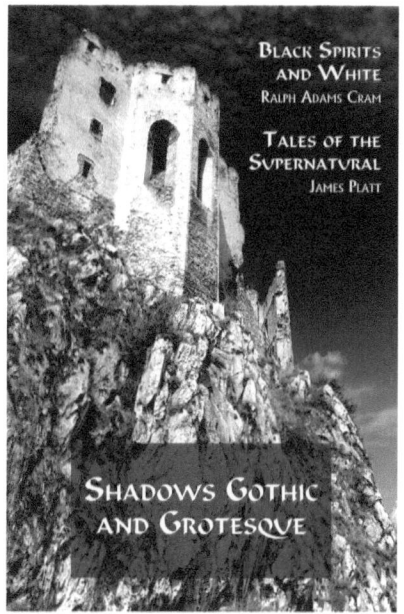

Coachwhip Publications

CoachwhipBooks.com